NEW TOEIC

多益新制黃金團隊

FINAL
終極版

5回全真試題＋詳解

Jade Kim・Sun-hee Kim・NEXUS 多益研究所 / 著

配合最新題型

忠實呈現多益新制題型，新增如三人對話、即時訊息等題型。原有題型也反映新制改版內容，如 Part 2 簡答對話新增間接回應題。

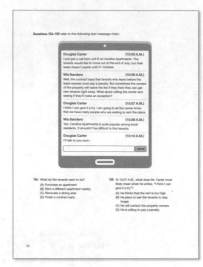

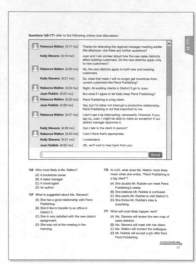

Part 1-7 完整解析

新增聽力詳解，聽力＆閱讀皆附上中英對照、補充單字與詳解說明。

新增〈速解技巧〉
標出〈解題關鍵句〉

解說本針對題型新增〈速解技巧〉與〈換句話說〉，並在題組文章中標出〈解題關鍵句〉，問題點一看就通。

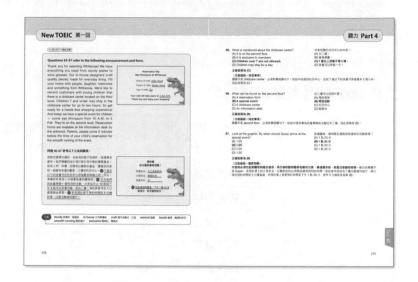

音檔模式最完整

QR Code 音檔附在書中，3 種音檔版本符合各種學習需求：
「標準版」附在題本中，一回一軌，熟悉多益聽力考試。
「白噪音版」附在題本中，加入背景噪音，模擬真實考試。
「單題練習版」附在解說本中，可單題聆聽，節省時間。

♪全書音檔首頁

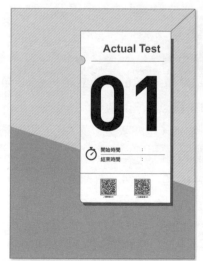

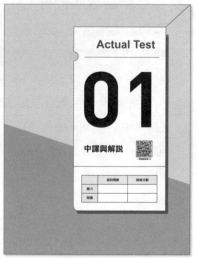

多益新制改制重點

台灣從 2018 年 3 月開始實施多益新制，此考試可反映目前英語使用環境的變化。雖然整體考題數量及考試時間相同，但各部分的考題數量略有差異，且也出現過去較少見的圖形和文字訊息、聊天內容、三人對話等新類型。

🔍 多益新舊制考題結構比較

結構	Part	各 Part 內容	舊制考題數	新制考題數	應答時間	配分
聽力測驗	1	照片描述	10	6	45 分鐘	495 分
	2	應答問題	30	25		
	3	簡短對話	30	39		
	4	簡短獨白	30	30		
閱讀測驗	5	句子填空	40	30	75 分鐘	495 分
	6	段落填空	12	16		
	7	單篇閱讀	28	29		
		雙篇閱讀	20	10		
		三篇閱讀	0	15		
Total	7 Parts		200 題	200 題	120 分鐘	990 分

🔍 多益新制改版分析

❶ Part 1 考題從 10 題減少為 6 題

❷ Part 2 考題從 30 題減少為 25 題

❸ Part 3 考題從 30 題增加為 39 題，增加〈3 人對話〉、〈5 句以上對話〉、〈理解意圖及與視覺資訊相關的問題〉

❹ Part 4 考題同樣為 30 題，增加〈理解意圖問題〉、〈與視覺資訊相關的問題〉

❺ Part 5 考題從 40 題減少為 30 題

❻ Part 6 考題從 12 題增加為 16 題，增加〈插入句〉

❼ Part 7 考題從 48 題增加為 54 題，增加〈文字訊息、線上聊天問題〉、〈理解意圖、插入句〉、〈三篇閱讀〉

多益新制改版重點

Part 3	理解 說話者意圖	2~3 題	詢問對話中說話者話語背後含意的題型
	視覺資訊相關	2~3 題	對話及視覺資訊（圖表、圖形等）間關聯性的題型
	3 人對話	1~2 大題	部分對話中會出現 3 人以上的對話
	5 句以上對話		對話達 5 句以上的對話類型
Part 4	理解 說話者意圖	2~3 題	詢問對話中說話者話語背後含意的題型
	視覺資訊相關	2~3 題	對話及視覺情報（圖表、圖形等）間關聯性的題型
Part 6	插入句子	4 題 （每大題 1 題）	➤ 根據敘述，選擇合適句子填入空格 ➤ 答卷上會提示所有句子，須掌握文章脈絡
Part 7	插入句子	2 題 （每則敘述 1 題）	將提示句插入合適的位置
	文字訊息、 線上聊天	各 1 大題	2 人對話的文字訊息、多人對話的線上聊天
	理解 說話者意圖	2 題 （每大題 1 題）	➤ 詢問說話者話語背後含意的題型 ➤ 從文字訊息、線上聊天當中出題
	三篇閱讀	3 大題	測試對 3 則相關敘述內容的理解程度

高效背誦單字，熟悉考題趨勢
準備多益的不二法門

【整體改制方向】

2018 年初台灣改考新制多益，改制後簡短考題（如圖片題、簡短問答、完成句子）變少，改用長篇的考題（如插入句、三人對話、三篇對話）取代。此改法是為了更符合 TOEIC 中的「C」精神，也就是 Communication（溝通）。畢竟多益是以商務溝通為主要訴求，跟客戶溝通、更改機位、預訂飯店、下訂單，絕非一兩句話就可達成目的。

【原有題型顛覆以往作答習慣】

新制多益除了**增加長篇考題**，原有的題型趨勢也有所改變，如 Part 2 的應答問題，便顛覆了以往教科書所教的問答方式，出現了更多的「**間接回應**」：

題目：How much will it cost to reprint the brochures?（重印手冊要多少錢？）
答案：It depends on the design.（要看設計難易。）

一般聽到 How much 為首的問句，考生直覺會選到金錢或數量的選項，但根據筆者考了多次新制多益的經驗，發現這類非典型的「間接回應」作為正確答案的考題越來越多，而這本書更是忠實呈現此類型考題，實屬難得。

【掌握字首字根，高效累積單字量】

而如先前提到的，多益考題越來越長，考生該如何把英文能力升級到能讀懂或聽懂長篇大論，而非侷限於讀短句聽短語呢？掌握大量單字便是關鍵。

多數考生背單字的方式常流於死背單字而非活記，以至於背了就忘。**若能「先懂再背」，才可能把單字牢牢儲存在長期記憶**。而所謂的「懂」，就要知道造字背後的邏輯，也就是「**字首字根**」。舉例來說，多益常考的動詞 disburse 可視為 dis（away 遠離）+ burse（purse 錢包），離開錢包即為「支出」之意。而 reimburse 視為 re（back 回）+ im（in 裡面）+ burse（purse 錢包），重回錢包即為「補貼」之意。

類似概念還有字根 -ply，指「fold 摺」，衍伸為「方向」，如：

apply = ap（to 往）+ ply（方向），apply for a job 應徵工作
reply = re（back 回）+ ply（方向），reply to letters 回信
comply = com（together 完全）+ ply（方向），comply with policies 遵守規定
supply = sup（under 在底下）+ ply（方向），supply materials 提供原料

發現了嗎？掌握字首字根便能大量累積單字，即使遇到沒看過的單字，也能靠拆解單字的字首字根來掌握意義。

累積大量多益單字只是第一步，離實際應考還有一段距離。因此，做高擬真度的多益試題本是必要的，本書除了忠實呈現最新考題趨勢，許多重要單字（如 remodel、剛剛提到的 reimburse 等）也會在題目中重複出現，寫完 5 回模擬試題後，除了掌握考題方向，許多重要核心多益單字也能順勢記憶起來。

最後，期勉考生勤勞內建單字，大量練習試題，持續往高分前進。

時代國際英日語中心人氣多益講師
黃偉軒 Winston

多益閱讀高分作答策略

許多考生考多益常遇到「閱讀寫不完」，尤其改制後新增的插入句子、三篇閱讀等，更是閱讀測驗的大魔王。本書試題與文章使用的單字準確，詳解也將解題思考流程寫出來，搭配以下以琳分享的閱讀高分策略，你能找出最能發揮實力的作答節奏，大幅提昇閱讀實力。

【妥善分配閱讀作答時間】

閱讀部分首重時間分配，共 75 分鐘的作答時間可做以下分配，最後留 5 分鐘給不確定的題目，並且做最後檢查。

Part 5：30 題，10 分鐘（一題 20 秒以內）

Part 6：16 題，5-8 分鐘（一題 20-30 秒）

Part 7：54 題，45 分鐘（一題 50 秒以內）

【釐清各部分考點，運用策略一一擊破】

Part 5、6 考點是「單字、片語、搭配詞、文法」，建議策略：

1. 看選項找出考點。

2. 抓出關鍵線索，選出答案。

3. 整句速讀一次確認沒有掉入陷阱，換下一題。

如果你重複執行以上步驟但仍卡住，請寫下一題，不要在不會的題目浪費時間，重點是把會的題目寫對。其中文法題最好突破，光看選項就能判斷考點，當你看到選項 (A) reserved；(B) were reserved；(C) reserving；(D) was reserved 就知道考點是動詞或分詞修飾，接著尋找句子的主詞、時態、主被動等線索找出答案。只要掌握多益常出現的關鍵文法，甚至一題 10 秒內就能完成，你就能爭取更多時間給需要看文意的單字、片語、句子選填題。

Part 7 考點是「理解各情境事件及掌握重點的能力」，字數少的單篇閱讀可先看題目再找答案，但字數多的雙篇或三篇閱讀反而不能先看題目。多益改制後**會故意使用文章的單字放在選項中當做誤導選項**，因此先理解文章脈絡，再去細看問題，預測出相關資訊的大概位置，就不會被選項的單字誤導作答，建議：

1. 先掌握每篇文章之間的關聯性。

2. 看每段前二句，掌握大概脈絡。

3. 看題目，由於已理解每篇關係跟大意，大概能預測答案要去哪邊找。

4. 細讀相關段落，找出答案。

【將單字視為閱讀「事件關鍵字」】

多益改制後更著重閱讀理解力，光是會單字不一定能答對題目，重要的是，**透過單字培養對事件（文章）的敏銳度，並將相關單字串連起來。**當你看到 reimbursement「核銷花費」，就要聯想到出差與花費核銷，所以你要把 receipt/invoice「發票收據」與 expense report「支出報告」交給 accounting department「會計部門」，你的 request for reimbursement「核銷要求」會被 approve「批准」。因此若讀到「缺少收據，無法核銷」的段落時，你就能更準確預測到會考的題目。

最後提醒考生，**本書的 5 回試題建議都要做過，並精讀至少 2 回。**檢討時要搞懂整個題目，並思考發生什麼事、目的是什麼、怎麼處理，最後與真實情況做連結。學多益不只是衝分數，而是學習應用一門語言，如此才能從本質提升英文實力。祝福各位考生早日達到理想目標！

考尚樂首席合作多益課程教師

以琳 Yiling

準備時程表

初級考生　具基本英文能力，但無法突破 700 分。

讀過基本多益考試準備書籍，但實戰練習不足。實際考試常有時間不夠用的情況，建議練習時就要像實際在考場一樣進行計時測驗。初級考生的字彙多半不足，請多利用解說本最末的字彙測驗加強。

第 1 天	第 2 天	第 3 天	第 4 天	第 5 天	第 6 天
Test 1 作答 & 確認解答	Test 1 確認聽力解說	Test 1 確認閱讀解說 & 字彙複習	Test 2 作答 & 確認解答	Test 2 確認聽力解說	Test 2 確認閱讀解說 & 字彙複習
第 7 天	第 8 天	第 9 天	第 10 天	第 11 天	第 12 天
Test 3 作答 & 確認解答	Test 3 確認聽力解說	Test 3 確認閱讀解說 & 字彙複習	Test 4 作答 & 確認解答	Test 4 確認聽力解說	Test 4 確認閱讀解說 & 字彙複習
第 13 天	第 14 天	第 15 天			
Test 5 作答 & 確認解答	Test 5 確認聽力解說	Test 5 確認閱讀解說 & 字彙複習			

中級考生　已經鍛鍊出實力，但分數在 800 分上下徘徊。

準備多益一段時間，也考過幾次多益考試，但分數難以提升。針對聽力，若能透過聽寫方式複習，會提升實力。閱讀部分則可配合各部分的解說內容，並配合〈備試技巧分享 2〉內容，加強較不擅長的環節。

第 1 天	第 2 天	第 3 天	第 4 天	第 5 天	第 6 天
Test 1 解題	Test 1 確認答案 & 解說	Test 2 解題	Test 2 確認答案 & 解說	Test 3 解題	Test 3 確認答案 & 解說
第 7 天	第 8 天	第 9 天	第 10 天		
Test 4 解題	Test 4 確認答案 & 解說	Test 5 解題	Test 5 確認答案 & 解說		

高級考生　以 900 分以上為目標，差一點達標。

第 1 天	第 2 天	第 3 天	第 4 天	第 5 天
Test 1 答題 & 解說	Test 2 答題 & 解說	Test 3 答題 & 解說	Test 4 答題 & 解說	Test 5 答題 & 解說

目　錄

TOEIC® 多益分數換算表

得分	Listening Comprehension	得分	Reading Comprehension
96-100	480-495	96-100	460-495
91-95	435-490	91-95	410-475
86-90	395-450	86-90	380-430
81-85	355-415	81-85	355-400
76-80	325-375	76-80	325-375
71-75	295-340	71-75	295-345
66-70	265-315	66-70	265-315
61-65	240-285	61-65	235-285
56-60	215-260	56-60	205-255
51-55	190-235	51-55	175-225
46-50	160-210	46-50	150-195
41-45	135-180	41-45	120-170
36-40	110-155	36-40	100-140
31-35	85-130	31-35	75-120
26-30	70-105	26-30	55-100
21-25	50-90	21-25	40-80
16-20	35-75	16-20	30-65
11-15	20-55	11-15	20-50
6-10	15-40	6-10	15-35
1-5	5-20	1-5	5-20
0	5	0	5

Actual Test

聽力測驗（LISTENING Parts 1-4）

NO.	ANSWER	NO.	ANSWER	NO.	ANSWER	NO.	ANSWER	NO.	ANSWER
	A B C D		A B C D		A B C D		A B C D		A B C D
1	Ⓐ Ⓑ Ⓒ	21	Ⓐ Ⓑ Ⓒ	41	Ⓐ Ⓑ Ⓒ Ⓓ	61	Ⓐ Ⓑ Ⓒ Ⓓ	81	Ⓐ Ⓑ Ⓒ Ⓓ
2	Ⓐ Ⓑ Ⓒ	22	Ⓐ Ⓑ Ⓒ	42	Ⓐ Ⓑ Ⓒ Ⓓ	62	Ⓐ Ⓑ Ⓒ Ⓓ	82	Ⓐ Ⓑ Ⓒ Ⓓ
3	Ⓐ Ⓑ Ⓒ	23	Ⓐ Ⓑ Ⓒ	43	Ⓐ Ⓑ Ⓒ Ⓓ	63	Ⓐ Ⓑ Ⓒ Ⓓ	83	Ⓐ Ⓑ Ⓒ Ⓓ
4	Ⓐ Ⓑ Ⓒ	24	Ⓐ Ⓑ Ⓒ	44	Ⓐ Ⓑ Ⓒ Ⓓ	64	Ⓐ Ⓑ Ⓒ Ⓓ	84	Ⓐ Ⓑ Ⓒ Ⓓ
5	Ⓐ Ⓑ Ⓒ	25	Ⓐ Ⓑ Ⓒ	45	Ⓐ Ⓑ Ⓒ Ⓓ	65	Ⓐ Ⓑ Ⓒ Ⓓ	85	Ⓐ Ⓑ Ⓒ Ⓓ
6	Ⓐ Ⓑ Ⓒ	26	Ⓐ Ⓑ Ⓒ	46	Ⓐ Ⓑ Ⓒ Ⓓ	66	Ⓐ Ⓑ Ⓒ Ⓓ	86	Ⓐ Ⓑ Ⓒ Ⓓ
7		27	Ⓐ Ⓑ Ⓒ	47	Ⓐ Ⓑ Ⓒ Ⓓ	67	Ⓐ Ⓑ Ⓒ Ⓓ	87	Ⓐ Ⓑ Ⓒ Ⓓ
8	Ⓐ Ⓑ Ⓒ	28	Ⓐ Ⓑ Ⓒ	48	Ⓐ Ⓑ Ⓒ Ⓓ	68	Ⓐ Ⓑ Ⓒ Ⓓ	88	Ⓐ Ⓑ Ⓒ Ⓓ
9	Ⓐ Ⓑ Ⓒ	29	Ⓐ Ⓑ Ⓒ	49	Ⓐ Ⓑ Ⓒ Ⓓ	69	Ⓐ Ⓑ Ⓒ Ⓓ	89	Ⓐ Ⓑ Ⓒ Ⓓ
10	Ⓐ Ⓑ Ⓒ	30	Ⓐ Ⓑ Ⓒ	50	Ⓐ Ⓑ Ⓒ Ⓓ	70	Ⓐ Ⓑ Ⓒ Ⓓ	90	Ⓐ Ⓑ Ⓒ Ⓓ
11	Ⓐ Ⓑ Ⓒ	31	Ⓐ Ⓑ Ⓒ	51	Ⓐ Ⓑ Ⓒ Ⓓ	71	Ⓐ Ⓑ Ⓒ Ⓓ	91	Ⓐ Ⓑ Ⓒ Ⓓ
12	Ⓐ Ⓑ Ⓒ	32	Ⓐ Ⓑ Ⓒ	52	Ⓐ Ⓑ Ⓒ Ⓓ	72	Ⓐ Ⓑ Ⓒ Ⓓ	92	Ⓐ Ⓑ Ⓒ Ⓓ
13	Ⓐ Ⓑ Ⓒ	33	Ⓐ Ⓑ Ⓒ	53	Ⓐ Ⓑ Ⓒ Ⓓ	73	Ⓐ Ⓑ Ⓒ Ⓓ	93	Ⓐ Ⓑ Ⓒ Ⓓ
14	Ⓐ Ⓑ Ⓒ	34	Ⓐ Ⓑ Ⓒ	54	Ⓐ Ⓑ Ⓒ Ⓓ	74	Ⓐ Ⓑ Ⓒ Ⓓ	94	Ⓐ Ⓑ Ⓒ Ⓓ
15	Ⓐ Ⓑ Ⓒ	35	Ⓐ Ⓑ Ⓒ	55	Ⓐ Ⓑ Ⓒ Ⓓ	75	Ⓐ Ⓑ Ⓒ Ⓓ	95	Ⓐ Ⓑ Ⓒ Ⓓ
16	Ⓐ Ⓑ Ⓒ	36	Ⓐ Ⓑ Ⓒ	56	Ⓐ Ⓑ Ⓒ Ⓓ	76	Ⓐ Ⓑ Ⓒ Ⓓ	96	Ⓐ Ⓑ Ⓒ Ⓓ
17	Ⓐ Ⓑ Ⓒ	37	Ⓐ Ⓑ Ⓒ	57	Ⓐ Ⓑ Ⓒ Ⓓ	77	Ⓐ Ⓑ Ⓒ Ⓓ	97	Ⓐ Ⓑ Ⓒ Ⓓ
18	Ⓐ Ⓑ Ⓒ	38	Ⓐ Ⓑ Ⓒ	58	Ⓐ Ⓑ Ⓒ Ⓓ	78	Ⓐ Ⓑ Ⓒ Ⓓ	98	Ⓐ Ⓑ Ⓒ Ⓓ
19	Ⓐ Ⓑ Ⓒ	39	Ⓐ Ⓑ Ⓒ	59	Ⓐ Ⓑ Ⓒ Ⓓ	79	Ⓐ Ⓑ Ⓒ Ⓓ	99	Ⓐ Ⓑ Ⓒ Ⓓ
20	Ⓐ Ⓑ Ⓒ	40	Ⓐ Ⓑ Ⓒ	60	Ⓐ Ⓑ Ⓒ Ⓓ	80	Ⓐ Ⓑ Ⓒ Ⓓ	100	Ⓐ Ⓑ Ⓒ Ⓓ

閱讀測驗（READING Parts 5-7）

NO.	ANSWER	NO.	ANSWER	NO.	ANSWER	NO.	ANSWER	NO.	ANSWER
	A B C D		A B C D		A B C D		A B C D		A B C D
101	Ⓐ Ⓑ Ⓒ Ⓓ	121	Ⓐ Ⓑ Ⓒ Ⓓ	141	Ⓐ Ⓑ Ⓒ Ⓓ	161	Ⓐ Ⓑ Ⓒ Ⓓ	181	Ⓐ Ⓑ Ⓒ Ⓓ
102	Ⓐ Ⓑ Ⓒ Ⓓ	122	Ⓐ Ⓑ Ⓒ Ⓓ	142	Ⓐ Ⓑ Ⓒ Ⓓ	162	Ⓐ Ⓑ Ⓒ Ⓓ	182	Ⓐ Ⓑ Ⓒ Ⓓ
103	Ⓐ Ⓑ Ⓒ Ⓓ	123	Ⓐ Ⓑ Ⓒ Ⓓ	143	Ⓐ Ⓑ Ⓒ Ⓓ	163	Ⓐ Ⓑ Ⓒ Ⓓ	183	Ⓐ Ⓑ Ⓒ Ⓓ
104	Ⓐ Ⓑ Ⓒ Ⓓ	124	Ⓐ Ⓑ Ⓒ Ⓓ	144	Ⓐ Ⓑ Ⓒ Ⓓ	164	Ⓐ Ⓑ Ⓒ Ⓓ	184	Ⓐ Ⓑ Ⓒ Ⓓ
105	Ⓐ Ⓑ Ⓒ Ⓓ	125	Ⓐ Ⓑ Ⓒ Ⓓ	145	Ⓐ Ⓑ Ⓒ Ⓓ	165	Ⓐ Ⓑ Ⓒ Ⓓ	185	Ⓐ Ⓑ Ⓒ Ⓓ
106	Ⓐ Ⓑ Ⓒ Ⓓ	126	Ⓐ Ⓑ Ⓒ Ⓓ	146	Ⓐ Ⓑ Ⓒ Ⓓ	166	Ⓐ Ⓑ Ⓒ Ⓓ	186	Ⓐ Ⓑ Ⓒ Ⓓ
107	Ⓐ Ⓑ Ⓒ Ⓓ	127	Ⓐ Ⓑ Ⓒ Ⓓ	147	Ⓐ Ⓑ Ⓒ Ⓓ	167	Ⓐ Ⓑ Ⓒ Ⓓ	187	Ⓐ Ⓑ Ⓒ Ⓓ
108	Ⓐ Ⓑ Ⓒ Ⓓ	128	Ⓐ Ⓑ Ⓒ Ⓓ	148	Ⓐ Ⓑ Ⓒ Ⓓ	168	Ⓐ Ⓑ Ⓒ Ⓓ	188	Ⓐ Ⓑ Ⓒ Ⓓ
109	Ⓐ Ⓑ Ⓒ Ⓓ	129	Ⓐ Ⓑ Ⓒ Ⓓ	149	Ⓐ Ⓑ Ⓒ Ⓓ	169	Ⓐ Ⓑ Ⓒ Ⓓ	189	Ⓐ Ⓑ Ⓒ Ⓓ
110	Ⓐ Ⓑ Ⓒ Ⓓ	130	Ⓐ Ⓑ Ⓒ Ⓓ	150	Ⓐ Ⓑ Ⓒ Ⓓ	170	Ⓐ Ⓑ Ⓒ Ⓓ	190	Ⓐ Ⓑ Ⓒ Ⓓ
111	Ⓐ Ⓑ Ⓒ Ⓓ	131	Ⓐ Ⓑ Ⓒ Ⓓ	151	Ⓐ Ⓑ Ⓒ Ⓓ	171	Ⓐ Ⓑ Ⓒ Ⓓ	191	Ⓐ Ⓑ Ⓒ Ⓓ
112	Ⓐ Ⓑ Ⓒ Ⓓ	132	Ⓐ Ⓑ Ⓒ Ⓓ	152	Ⓐ Ⓑ Ⓒ Ⓓ	172	Ⓐ Ⓑ Ⓒ Ⓓ	192	Ⓐ Ⓑ Ⓒ Ⓓ
113	Ⓐ Ⓑ Ⓒ Ⓓ	133	Ⓐ Ⓑ Ⓒ Ⓓ	153	Ⓐ Ⓑ Ⓒ Ⓓ	173	Ⓐ Ⓑ Ⓒ Ⓓ	193	Ⓐ Ⓑ Ⓒ Ⓓ
114	Ⓐ Ⓑ Ⓒ Ⓓ	134	Ⓐ Ⓑ Ⓒ Ⓓ	154	Ⓐ Ⓑ Ⓒ Ⓓ	174	Ⓐ Ⓑ Ⓒ Ⓓ	194	Ⓐ Ⓑ Ⓒ Ⓓ
115	Ⓐ Ⓑ Ⓒ Ⓓ	135	Ⓐ Ⓑ Ⓒ Ⓓ	155	Ⓐ Ⓑ Ⓒ Ⓓ	175	Ⓐ Ⓑ Ⓒ Ⓓ	195	Ⓐ Ⓑ Ⓒ Ⓓ
116	Ⓐ Ⓑ Ⓒ Ⓓ	136	Ⓐ Ⓑ Ⓒ Ⓓ	156	Ⓐ Ⓑ Ⓒ Ⓓ	176	Ⓐ Ⓑ Ⓒ Ⓓ	196	Ⓐ Ⓑ Ⓒ Ⓓ
117	Ⓐ Ⓑ Ⓒ Ⓓ	137	Ⓐ Ⓑ Ⓒ Ⓓ	157	Ⓐ Ⓑ Ⓒ Ⓓ	177	Ⓐ Ⓑ Ⓒ Ⓓ	197	Ⓐ Ⓑ Ⓒ Ⓓ
118	Ⓐ Ⓑ Ⓒ Ⓓ	138	Ⓐ Ⓑ Ⓒ Ⓓ	158	Ⓐ Ⓑ Ⓒ Ⓓ	178	Ⓐ Ⓑ Ⓒ Ⓓ	198	Ⓐ Ⓑ Ⓒ Ⓓ
119	Ⓐ Ⓑ Ⓒ Ⓓ	139	Ⓐ Ⓑ Ⓒ Ⓓ	159	Ⓐ Ⓑ Ⓒ Ⓓ	179	Ⓐ Ⓑ Ⓒ Ⓓ	199	Ⓐ Ⓑ Ⓒ Ⓓ
120	Ⓐ Ⓑ Ⓒ Ⓓ	140	Ⓐ Ⓑ Ⓒ Ⓓ	160	Ⓐ Ⓑ Ⓒ Ⓓ	180	Ⓐ Ⓑ Ⓒ Ⓓ	200	Ⓐ Ⓑ Ⓒ Ⓓ

等等！開始前務必確認！

- 將書桌整理成和實際測試時一樣，做好心理準備。
- 將手機關機，使用手錶計時。
- 限制時間為 120 分鐘。一定要遵守時間限制。
- 不要因為困難就跳過。盡可能依照順序解題。

Actual Test

01

 開始時間   :

結束時間   :

♪ 標準版-01

♪ 白噪音版-01

LISTENING TEST

In the Listening test, you will be asked to demonstrate how well you understand spoken English. The entire Listening test will last approximately 45 minutes. There are four parts, and directions are given for each part. You must mark your answers on the separate answer sheet. Do not write your answers in your test book.

PART 1

Directions: For each question in this part, you will hear four statements about a picture in your test book. When you hear the statements, you must select the one statement that best describes what you see in the picture. Then find the number of the question on your answer sheet and mark your answer. The statements will not be printed in your test book and will be spoken only one time.

Example

Sample Answer
Ⓐ ● Ⓒ Ⓓ

Statement (B), "The man is working at a desk," is the best description of the picture, so you should select answer (B) and mark it on your answer sheet.

1

2

GO ON TO THE NEXT PAGE

3

4

5

6

PART 2

Directions: You will hear a question or statement and three responses spoken in English. They will not be printed in your test book and will be spoken only one time. Select the best response to the question or statement and mark the letter (A), (B), or (C) on your answer sheet.

7 Mark your answer on your answer sheet.

8 Mark your answer on your answer sheet.

9 Mark your answer on your answer sheet.

10 Mark your answer on your answer sheet.

11 Mark your answer on your answer sheet.

12 Mark your answer on your answer sheet.

13 Mark your answer on your answer sheet.

14 Mark your answer on your answer sheet.

15 Mark your answer on your answer sheet.

16 Mark your answer on your answer sheet.

17 Mark your answer on your answer sheet.

18 Mark your answer on your answer sheet.

19 Mark your answer on your answer sheet.

20 Mark your answer on your answer sheet.

21 Mark your answer on your answer sheet.

22 Mark your answer on your answer sheet.

23 Mark your answer on your answer sheet.

24 Mark your answer on your answer sheet.

25 Mark your answer on your answer sheet.

26 Mark your answer on your answer sheet.

27 Mark your answer on your answer sheet.

28 Mark your answer on your answer sheet.

29 Mark your answer on your answer sheet.

30 Mark your answer on your answer sheet.

31 Mark your answer on your answer sheet.

PART 3

Directions: You will hear some conversations between two or more people. You will be asked to answer three questions about what the speakers say in each conversation. Select the best response to each question and mark the letter (A), (B), (C), or (D) on your answer sheet. The conversations will not be printed in your test book and will be spoken only one time.

32 What most likely is Business Circle?

(A) A trade conference
(B) A Wed site
(C) A magazine
(D) A radio program

33 What is the current status of the trade agreement?

(A) It has gone through.
(B) It is being discussed.
(C) It has been suspended.
(D) It will soon expire.

34 What does the man suggest doing?

(A) Preparing an alternative proposal
(B) Monitoring the situation closely
(C) Advertising job opportunities
(D) Analyzing the negative result

35 What are the speakers mainly talking about?

(A) The advancement of a coworker
(B) The retirement of a manager
(C) A recent business agreement
(D) The relocation of a headquarters

36 What type of company do the speakers most likely work for?

(A) A legal office
(B) A marketing firm
(C) A travel agency
(D) A medical firm

37 What does the man suggest?

(A) Leading a workshop
(B) Holding a farewell event
(C) Checking a report
(D) Asking for more information

38 Why is the woman calling?

(A) To announce a plan
(B) To offer an apology
(C) To request some supplies
(D) To pass along a complaint

39 In which department does Chris probably work?

(A) Housekeeping
(B) Reception
(C) Maintenance
(D) Security

40 What will the woman probably do next?

(A) Make some repairs
(B) Speak to a guest
(C) Call a hardware store
(D) Clean a guest's suite

41 Why does Peter want to go to a restaurant?

(A) To meet some clients
(B) To arrange an event
(C) To pick up an order
(D) To book a place

42 What does the woman mean when she says, "You'll make it"?

(A) She expects a coworker will attend a gathering.
(B) She knows who will prepare a meal.
(C) She thinks a colleague has enough time.
(D) She believes an evaluation will go well.

43 What do the men imply about the neighborhood?

(A) It has some nice restaurants.
(B) It is inconvenient.
(C) It is growing rapidly.
(D) It was featured in a magazine.

GO ON TO THE NEXT PAGE

44 Who most likely are the speakers?

(A) Potential clients
(B) Car dealers
(C) Product designers
(D) Advertising executives

45 What problems are the speakers discussing?

(A) Sales figures are unimpressive.
(B) Advertising is becoming more expensive.
(C) Customer satisfaction is low.
(D) Production is behind schedule.

46 What does the woman suggest?

(A) Reading customer feedback
(B) Reviewing an instruction manual
(C) Reducing prices
(D) Calling a client meeting

47 Who most likely is the man?

(A) A receptionist
(B) A new recruit
(C) A store clerk
(D) A security officer

48 Why does the man visit the woman?

(A) To get a refund
(B) To have an interview
(C) To apply for a card
(D) To pay for items

49 What will the man probably do next?

(A) Send an application form
(B) Have his photo taken
(C) Talk to a colleague
(D) Complete the document

50 What are the speakers mainly discussing?

(A) A research budget
(B) A consumer campaign
(C) A managerial promotion
(D) A marketing survey

51 What do the men suggest?

(A) Emphasizing particular points
(B) Shortening a form
(C) Conducting longer interviews
(D) Extending a deadline

52 What does the woman decide to do?

(A) Make a few revisions to a document
(B) Find a way to satisfy customers
(C) Alter the schedule for a meeting
(D) Relay some feedback

53 What does the woman ask the man to do?

(A) Review her work
(C) Draft a report
(D) Release some records
(D) Update a Web site

54 What kind of organization do the speakers work for?

(A) A marketing company
(B) A banking firm
(C) A newspaper
(D) A software company

55 What does the woman mean when she says, "who can blame them"?

(A) Customers did not cause the problem.
(B) Customers are likely to make some complaints.
(C) Customers' confusion was expected.
(D) Customers' behavior is understandable.

56 What best describes the speakers' jobs?

(A) They are medical staff.
(B) They are cashiers.
(C) They are office employees.
(D) They are restaurant servers.

57 What does Heather ask the other two people to do?

(A) Assign her different hours
(B) Have breakfast with her
(C) Go on a camping trip with her
(D) Fill in for her at work

58 What does Olivia imply?

(A) She cannot accommodate the request.
(B) She'll be off that day.
(C) Heather should return the favor.
(D) Heather should change her appointment.

---

59 Why does the woman ask for advice?

(A) To replace a current service
(B) To purchase a computer
(C) To provide a new device
(D) To design a Web site

60 Why does the woman say, "That's the bottom line"?

(A) She wants the long-term plan.
(B) She wants a cheap price.
(C) She uses Internet frequently.
(D) She wants fast online access.

61 What is the woman advised to do?

(A) Transfer to an overseas branch
(B) Get some feedback
(C) Compare options on the Internet
(D) Read some product instructions

Model	Price ($)
Modern 765 (Black and White)	1,530
Solusi 300 (Color)	1,720
Primark 200 (Black and White)	1,940
Allthatprint 500 (color)	2,250

62 According to the man, what has the advertising department requested?

(A) A client list
(B) A customer code
(C) An office device
(D) An e-mail address

63 Who most likely is Mr. Warren?

(A) A client
(B) A supplier
(C) A manufacturer
(D) A supervisor

64 Look at the graphic. How much will the company most likely pay for the order?

(A) $1,530
(B) $1,720
(C) $1,940
(D) $2,250

GO ON TO THE NEXT PAGE

Jade's Diner

Present this coupon for

30% off Lunch

or

20% off Dinner

Valid for parties of up to 3 | Expires June 18

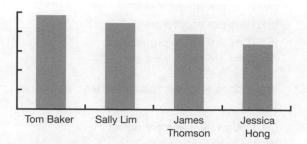

Candidate Test Score

Tom Baker   Sally Lim   James Thomson   Jessica Hong

65 What does the man indicate about the woman?

(A) She ordered a dessert.
(B) She is a regular customer.
(C) She owns a business.
(D) She works near the restaurant.

66 Look at the graphic. How much of a discount will the woman receive?

(A) 5%
(B) 10%
(C) 20%
(D) 30%

67 What does the man say he will do?

(A) Speak to a manager
(B) Accept a credit card
(C) Make a calculation
(D) Fax an invoice

68 How was the job opening probably advertised?

(A) In a trade journal
(B) On some posters
(C) In a newspaper
(D) On a Web site

69 What does the man offer to do?

(A) Reply to an organization
(B) Screen résumés from applicants
(C) Write a job description
(D) Extend a deadline for a project

70 Look at the graphic. Who does the woman say gave the most impressive interview?

(A) Tom Baker
(B) Sally Lim
(C) James Thomson
(D) Jessica Hong

PART 4

Directions: You will hear some talks given by a single speaker. You will be asked to answer three questions about what the speaker says in each talk. Select the best response to each question and mark the letter (A), (B), (C), or (D) on your answer sheet. The talks will not be printed in your test book and will be spoken only one time.

71 What is being advertised?

(A) A tour agency
(B) A hotel chain
(C) A catering service
(D) An airline company

72 According to the advertisement, what advantage does the business offer?

(A) Easy access
(B) Courteous service
(C) Corporate rates
(D) Membership bonuses

73 What will happen in August?

(A) A facility will be expanded.
(B) A discount will be offered.
(C) A Web site will be upgraded.
(D) A selection will be widened.

74 Why has the fight been delayed?

(A) The runway is busy.
(B) The plane has a mechanical problem.
(C) The fog prevented the plane from departing.
(D) Boarding took a long time.

75 What time will the flight depart?

(A) 5:00 P.M.
(B) 5:30 P.M.
(C) 6:00 P.M.
(D) 6:30 P.M.

76 What does the speaker suggest the listeners do?

(A) Relax in the lounge
(B) Take a look at some reading materials
(C) Fill out a form
(D) Revise their schedule

77 Why has the speaker called Mr. Aston?

(A) To ask for some personal information
(B) To solicit his participation
(C) To arrange an interview
(D) To finalize a job offer

78 What did Jennifer Ward do?

(A) She was Mr. Aston's supervisor.
(B) She recommended Mr. Aston.
(C) She is organizing the seminar.
(D) She founded Dantos Incorporated.

79 According to the speaker, what should Mr. Aston do next?

(A) Contact General Consulting
(B) Register for the seminar
(C) Return Ms. Rodriguez's call
(D) Submit the document

80 Who most likely is the speaker?

(A) An author
(B) A food critic
(C) A charity founder
(D) A restaurant manager

81 What has the speaker's organization created?

(A) A documentary film
(B) A complimentary publication
(C) A fundraising competition
(D) A nutrition workshop

82 According to the speaker, what will happen next month?

(A) A new product will be developed.
(B) An event venue will change.
(C) A new branch will open.
(D) A project will be expanded.

GO ON TO THE NEXT PAGE

83 What is true of the weather today?

(A) It is expected to warm up later.
(B) Heavy snowfall is forecast.
(C) It hit a record low temperature.
(D) Heavy rain is expected.

84 What potential hazard does the speaker mention?

(A) Loss of power
(B) Lack of fuel
(C) Shortage of supplies
(D) Health issues

85 What suggestion does the speaker make?

(A) Listeners should stay home.
(B) Listeners should exercise regularly.
(C) People should drive carefully.
(D) People should purchase supplies.

86 Who is the speaker addressing?

(A) University instructors
(B) Newly hired employees
(C) Potential clients
(D) Survey participants

87 According to the speaker, what will Mr. Ambrose do today?

(A) Conduct a series of interviews
(B) Show a video presentation
(C) Introduce the company founder
(D) Distribute guidebooks

88 What does the speaker mean when she says, "make sure to report back to me"?

(A) She is eager to see some results.
(B) She requires feedback from all attendees.
(C) She wants to give further information.
(D) She works as a department supervisor.

89 What is the report mainly about?

(A) The renovation of a town center
(B) The construction of a new facility
(C) The introduction of a new product
(D) The relocation of a stadium

90 What is an advantage of the plan?

(A) It will accommodate more people.
(B) It will reduce expenses.
(C) It will generate more income.
(D) It will improve delivery times.

91 Who is Ian Douglas?

(A) A factory manager
(B) A local land owner
(C) A company spokesperson
(D) A real estate agent

92 Why is the speaker calling?

(A) A change in schedule
(B) An equipment malfunction
(C) A policy proposal
(D) A revision to a manual

93 Why does the speaker say, "That will shut down the system"?

(A) To upgrade a system
(B) To change a suggestion
(C) To explain a process
(D) To make a complaint

94 What does the speaker offer to do?

(A) Email a document
(B) Issue a refund
(C) Install a system
(D) Deliver a new unit

Reservation Slip
See Dinosaurs at Whiterose!

Name of child: <u>Alex Hunt</u>

Parent of child: <u>Susan Hunt</u>

Age of child: <u>Six</u>

Your visit will take place at <u>1:30 P.M.</u>
Thank you and enjoy your shopping!

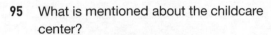

Christchurch Tour – Day One		
Time	Location	Activity
09:00–10:30	Waitomo Caves	Morning walk
11:00–12:00	Central Square	Shopping
12:00–14:00	Victoria Park	Afternoon picnic
14:00–17:00	Bay of Islands	Boat ride

95 What is mentioned about the childcare center?

(A) It is on the second floor.
(B) It is exclusive to members.
(C) Children over 7 are not allowed.
(D) Children may stay for a day.

96 What can be found on the second floor?

(A) A reservation form
(B) A special event
(C) A childcare center
(D) An information desk

97 Look at the graphic. By when should Susan arrive at the special event?

(A) 1:20
(B) 1:25
(C) 1:30
(D) 1:35

98 Who most likely is Phil Goff?

(A) A civil engineer
(B) A famous celebrity
(C) A local politician
(D) A renowned architect

99 According to the speaker, what is the purpose of the trip to Mission Bay?

(A) To ride bicycles
(B) To photograph wildlife
(C) To shop for souvenirs
(D) To visit a castle

100 Look at the graphic. Where will listeners probably go next?

(A) Waitomo Caves
(B) Central Square
(C) Victoria Park
(D) Bay of Islands

This is the end of the Listening test. Turn to Part 5 in your test book.

GO ON TO THE NEXT PAGE

READING TEST

In the Reading test, you will read a variety of texts and answer several different types of reading comprehension questions. The entire Reading test will last 75 minutes. There are three parts, and directions are given for each part. You are encouraged to answer as many questions as possible within the time allowed.

You must mark your answers on the separate answer sheet. Do not write your answers in your test book.

PART 5

Directions: A word or phrase is missing in each of the sentences below. Four answer choices are given below each sentence. Select the best answer to complete the sentence. Then mark the letter (A), (B), (C), or (D) on your answer sheet.

101 Brooks Bookstore can ship an order to your home, business, ------- local post office within 24 hours.

(A) but
(B) that
(C) or
(D) as

102 The use of high-quality yet ------- raw materials led to a cost reduction for Mr. Walton's factory.

(A) inexpensive
(B) unhappy
(C) incomplete
(D) undecided

103 Jason Flowers is always ------- to deliver nice decorations to your special events.

(A) ready
(B) skillful
(C) complete
(D) delicious

104 Kate Vausden was nominated as Best New Artist ------- her elaborate painting now on display at Lindsey Gallery.

(A) about
(B) for
(C) when
(D) since

105 If you want to take advantage of this month's sale, you must do so quickly as ------- ends next week.

(A) it
(B) he
(C) they
(D) your

106 The ------- of video materials to publication can help companies produce promotional merchandise.

(A) content
(B) addition
(C) pictures
(D) advances

107 Opponents of the city's mayor ------- the claim that she has revived the regional economy.

(A) propose
(B) rely
(C) extend
(D) reject

108 We, Sisco Designs, create a ------- of images that express an individual style suitable for your needs.

(A) frequency
(B) length
(C) shortage
(D) series

109 At Isaac Shoe Store, most customized shoes can be made ------- 2 business days.

(A) since
(B) to
(C) at
(D) within

110 Mr. Sanders is not checking his voice mail -------, so you can expect a delay in his response.

(A) scarcely
(B) similarly
(C) frequently
(D) partially

111 To avoid traffic congestion, the ------- of downtown Pleasant Valley requires extensive planning.

(A) restore
(B) restorative
(C) restored
(D) restoration

112 The School Outreach Program honors students ------- volunteer their time to help Twin City.

(A) for
(B) who
(C) those
(D) as

113 The evaluation report will be completed ------- after technicians inspect the lab equipment.

(A) when
(B) only
(C) still
(D) most

114 The construction of the Grunburg Building ------- because of modifications in the original floor plans.

(A) postponed
(B) has been postponed
(C) will postpone
(D) postponing

115 All passengers are advised to check baggage claim tags to verify that retrieved bags are in fact -------.

(A) they
(B) them
(C) theirs
(D) themselves

116 Customers of Charleston Bank can easily transfer funds from one account to -------.

(A) another
(B) either
(C) one
(D) it

117 Henry Bonaducci's proposal was approved in a ------- short time because of its feasibility.

(A) surprised
(B) surprise
(C) surprisingly
(D) surprising

118 Built in 1885, the St. Petersburg Cathedral has been preserved for its historical -------.

(A) signify
(B) significant
(C) significance
(D) significantly

119 After the ------- improvements have been implemented, the production process should run more efficiently.

(A) suggest
(B) suggested
(C) suggesting
(D) suggests

120 Clients should provide both an e-mail address and a telephone number in order to be notified of the most current status of any ------- orders.

(A) dependent
(B) representative
(C) practical
(D) pending

GO ON TO THE NEXT PAGE

121 RT Technology Services will use its training center in Austin ------- preregistered attendees number more than 350.

(A) if
(B) that
(C) either
(D) despite

122 New customers of Ortega Hardware Store ------- receive a 10 percent discount on their first order.

(A) customarily
(B) perfectly
(C) repeatedly
(D) obediently

123 McAfee Manufacturing is known as a company that makes uniquely ------- tools for the construction industry.

(A) precise
(B) precision
(C) precisely
(D) preciseness

124 Ms. Hogan, the director of personnel ------- the company's revised manual for recruiting interns at tomorrow's meeting.

(A) had been addressing
(B) is addressing
(C) will be addressed
(D) should be addressed

125 ------- slow the high-speed printer may be, it is still making copies that are adequate for our purposes.

(A) Rather
(B) Seldom
(C) Thoroughly
(D) However

126 Since the Wisconsin Daily is now available digitally, subscribers can read articles one day ------- the general public.

(A) between
(B) during
(C) ahead of
(D) away from

127 If the lamp had been damaged during shipment, the company ------- to send Mr. Oakley a replacement.

(A) would have offered
(B) has offered
(C) is being offered
(D) would have been offered

128 ------- you have submitted all the required documents for your grant proposal, the decision committee will be convened for evaluation.

(A) Then
(B) Next
(C) Once
(D) Always

129 Store managers will not ------- approve time off for employees during the peak season.

(A) generalization
(B) generalize
(C) generally
(D) general

130 The decision about company relocation will be ------- until the special meeting scheduled for next month.

(A) deferred
(B) resolved
(C) organized
(D) agreed

PART 6

Directions: Read the texts that follow. A word, phrase, or sentence is missing in parts of each text. Four answer choices for each question are given below the text. Select the best answer to complete the text. Then mark the letter (A), (B), (C), or (D) on your answer sheet.

Questions 131-134 refer to the following press release.

For Immediate Release

February 2 — P. H. Manning announces the appointment of Sean Renault as Chief Financial Officer, replacing Sandy Connelly who retired in January.

Prior to ------- P. H. Manning, Mr. Renault worked at KUB Systems. While there, he served in
131.
various accounting and treasury roles, including the role of Chief Financial Officer. He ------- his
132.
career in the audit division of Adams Financial Group.

"Mr. Renault's experience and leadership will be invaluable as we enter our next phase of growth," said Marco Colombo, P. H. Manning's Chief Executive Officer.

Ms. Connelly, the ------- Chief Financial Officer, worked at P. H. Manning for seventeen years.
133.
-------.
134.

131 (A) joining
(B) founding
(C) promoting
(D) completing

132 (A) to begin
(B) begins
(C) began
(D) will begin

133 (A) nearest
(B) former
(C) alternate
(D) potential

134 (A) The accounting team is still hiring new people.
(B) All of our staff members will start work as of tomorrow.
(C) We have made a lot of effort to promote her to CEO.
(D) She will remain as an advisor to the board of directors.

Questions 135-138 refer to the following e-mail.

To: Publishing Department Staff
From: Hans Shuler
Date: February 18
Subject: New Copy Machine

Dear colleagues:

Yesterday a new copy machine was installed in the resource room to replace the one that had

------- broken down. ------- It is an industrial-grade model, so we expect that it will serve us well
  135.   136.

for several years.

To ensure that the copier remains in working order, keep small objects ------- paper clips and
                                                                         137.

staples away from the paper feeder.

You may have questions while learning how to operate the new copier. If so, you can ------- the
                                                                                     138.

manual located in the cabinet next to the copier.

Regards,

Hans

---

135 (A) repeats
    (B) repetition
    (C) repeated
    (D) repeatedly

136 (A) We trust that the new one will be more
        reliable.
    (B) There are several types of copy
        machines available at the store.
    (C) Please let us know what time you would
        like to set up an appointment.
    (D) We can give you an accurate estimate
        later.

137 (A) as well
    (B) such as
    (C) of these
    (D) sort of

138 (A) consult
    (B) discard
    (C) approve
    (D) revise

Questions 139-142 refer to the following article.

February 28 — After two years of construction, the largest hotel in Milwaukee history is almost ready to open. The Mendota Hotel, on the banks of the Cherish River, will have 1,200 rooms for visitors. It will have two conference rooms for groups of up to 300 people. -------. The project is among downtown area hotels currently -------. According to Sanjay Singh, president of Milwaukee Hotel & Lodging Association, these new developments are a -------. "We've had a massive influx of visitors over the past few years," said Mr. Singh. "-------, almost all the hotels in the city are completely full. Clearly, additional hotel rooms are needed."

139 (A) It is unclear whether it will be open to accept reservations or not.
(B) Building renovations will begin next year as originally scheduled.
(C) The first guests will soon arrive as part of a medical technology conference.
(D) There is a speculation that several companies will bid on the project.

140 (A) to construct
(B) are constructing
(C) were constructed
(D) being constructed

141 (A) necessity
(B) nuisance
(C) risk
(D) bargain

142 (A) Likewise
(B) Otherwise
(C) Additionally
(D) Consequently

GO ON TO THE NEXT PAGE

Questions 143-146 refer to the following flyer.

Attention, artists and craftspeople!

------- If so, you are encouraged to apply for a chance to display your artwork at the Bloomberg
143.
County Art Fair on May 17.

Applications are available online at www.bloombergfair.org and will be reviewed by several

professors from the art department of our local college. Together with your completed

application document, please upload ------- of your work. The images will aid the judges in their
144.
review process.

The application deadline is February 15, and the judges' decisions will be made by March 30.

------- applicants will have use of a 5 x 5 meter display booth and will be expected to participate
145.
------- the entire day of the fair.
146.

---

143 (A) If it is possible, we would like to send an invitation to your home to survey the event.
   (B) Are you interested in a unique opportunity to showcase your talent in our area?
   (C) As a loyal customer, you qualify for extended coverage of six years.
   (D) You can see other types of artwork on our Web site.

144 (A) descriptions
   (B) photographs
   (C) requirements
   (D) developments

145 (A) Inviting
   (B) Invites
   (C) Invitation
   (D) Invited

146 (A) in
   (B) to
   (C) through
   (D) toward

PART 7

Directions: In this part you will read a selection of texts, such as magazine and newspaper articles, e-mails, and instant messages. Each text or set of texts is followed by several questions. Select the best answer for each question and mark the letter (A), (B), (C), or (D) on your answer sheet.

Questions 147-148 refer to the following advertisement.

FANCY SKI RESORT
WEEKEND SPECIAL

Fancy Ski Resort is the perfect place for your family or group next weekend vacation.

Spend three nights in a one-bedroom condominium or suite for as low as $240 per person. Our lodgings are conveniently located two miles from scenic Mount Lyon and include an indoor swimming pool, sauna, and ice skating rink. A shuttle service operates between our lodgings and Mount Lyon every half hour from 5 A.M. to 8 P.M.

The Weekend Special price includes two days of skiing on Mount Lyon. This offer is valid from November 11 to February 20, excluding weekdays and holidays. For more information, visit www.skifancy.com.

147 How can customers get to Mount Lyon from their lodgings?

(A) By walking
(B) By driving
(C) By taking a taxi
(D) By taking a shuttle bus

148 What facility is NOT included at the lodgings?

(A) A sauna
(B) A swimming pool
(C) A ski rental service
(D) An ice skating rink

GO ON TO THE NEXT PAGE

ALTON CITY PARKING GARAGE

Please present this ticket with your payment to the attendant when you return to pick up your vehicle.

Date: *7 March*

Time: *9:15 A.M.*

The attendant can accept only cash and credit card payments.

* Monthly rates are available. Save up to 20%!

To obtain details, call 028-555-3421, or visit our Web site at altoncitygarage.co.uk.

149 How do customers pay for parking?
(A) By depositing money in a parking meter
(B) By paying a fee to an attendant
(C) By using a prepaid parking card
(D) By submitting a payment online

150 Why are customers invited to call the telephone number on the ticket?
(A) To request an alternative payment method
(B) To reserve a parking spot for the day
(C) To give feedback about an attendant
(D) To get more information about parking fees

Questions 151-153 refer to the following advertisement.

Attention!

The Capricorn Library Volunteer Association presents its Used Book Sale for four days only from November 3 through 6. You can browse thousands of books, most in excellent condition! There is something of interest for readers of all ages.

Thursday: Preview Sale
6 P.M. – 9 P.M.
$5 admission fee

Friday: General Sale
6 P.M. – 9 P.M.

Saturday: General Sale
9 A.M. – 3 P.M.

Sunday: Clearance Sale
11 A.M. – 2 P.M.
All books 20% off

Proceeds will benefit the building of an addition to the Capricorn Library.

Location: Capricorn Community Center, Main Event Hall, 15 Harper Street

If you have any questions, contact Leslie Ling, president of the Capricorn Library Volunteer Association at 555-0173

Please note that we are no longer accepting donations of books for the sale.

---

151 Where will the event take place?

(A) At a community center
(B) At a local bookstore
(C) At Ms. Ling's residence
(D) At the Capricorn Library

152 What is stated about Thursday's sales?

(A) Profits from the event will go to a charity.
(B) An entrance fee will be charged.
(C) Cash is the only method of payment accepted.
(D) It will run during the whole day.

153 What is NOT suggested about the books being sold?

(A) Some of them are suitable for young children.
(B) Many of them are in good condition.
(C) All of them were donated by library members.
(D) They will be sold at a reduced price on Sunday.

GO ON TO THE NEXT PAGE

Questions 154-155 refer to the following text message chain.

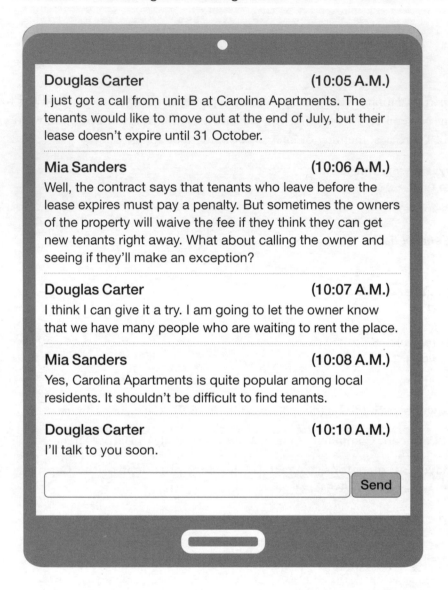

Douglas Carter (10:05 A.M.)

I just got a call from unit B at Carolina Apartments. The tenants would like to move out at the end of July, but their lease doesn't expire until 31 October.

Mia Sanders (10:06 A.M.)

Well, the contract says that tenants who leave before the lease expires must pay a penalty. But sometimes the owners of the property will waive the fee if they think they can get new tenants right away. What about calling the owner and seeing if they'll make an exception?

Douglas Carter (10:07 A.M.)

I think I can give it a try. I am going to let the owner know that we have many people who are waiting to rent the place.

Mia Sanders (10:08 A.M.)

Yes, Carolina Apartments is quite popular among local residents. It shouldn't be difficult to find tenants.

Douglas Carter (10:10 A.M.)

I'll talk to you soon.

Send

154 What do the tenants want to do?

(A) Purchase an apartment
(B) Rent a different apartment nearby
(C) Renovate a dining area
(D) Finish a contract early

155 At 10:07 A.M., what does Mr. Carter most likely mean when he writes, "I think I can give it a try"?

(A) He thinks that the rent is too high.
(B) He plans to ask the tenants to stay longer.
(C) He will contact the property owners.
(D) He is willing to pay a penalty.

Questions 156-157 refer to the following notice.

NOTICE

The ticketing machine in the Garland waiting area near Platform 5 has been removed for repairs. We hope to have a new machine in place by Monday, April 14. Until then, railroad passengers may use the machine in the Midvale waiting area near Platform 7 or see one of the ticketing clerks at the counter in the Main Lobby next to the Information Booth. We apologize for the inconvenience. Passengers are reminded that they can save 10 to 20 percent and avoid lines at ticketing machines by purchasing weekly or monthly passes. Passes are only available online at www.fasttrackservice.com.

156 Where is the notice most likely posted?

(A) In a movie theater
(B) In a rental car agency
(C) In a train station
(D) In an airport

157 What is suggested about the ticketing machines?

(A) They do not sell weekly and monthly passes.
(B) They are for credit card customers only.
(C) They provide tickets that are discounted 10 to 20 percent.
(D) They have not yet been installed in Platform 7.

GO ON TO THE NEXT PAGE

From: Carrie Fenway
To: Harper Randolph
Subject: Keeping on a discussion
Date: December 22

Dear Harper:

It was great to see you at the company's regional managers retreat last week. I wanted to follow up on the discussion we had about your office's upcoming move. The Bristol office's move last year taught me a lot about managing relocation, and I wanted to pass on what I learned to you. –[1]–.

First, I know you are still deciding on whether to close the office for a few days or to keep your office open as usual by moving gradually. I would recommend remaining open if possible. –[2]–. The Bristol office remained open and moved gradually over a period of two weeks, which made the move quite easy. Of course, maintaining the normal work schedule during that time was difficult because some employees had relocated to the new office while their team members remained at the old office. –[3]–. If you choose this approach, I would suggest moving all members of a team at the same time to minimize confusion.

Second, remember that relocation is time-consuming for everyone. Be clear in delivering the message to your employees that you will not be expecting to take on normal workloads during the move. –[4]–. Taking this step ahead of time, as the Bristol office did, greatly improves workflow and reduces stress.

I'll give you a call later this week to talk more about these issues.

Sincerely,

Carrie Fenway
President, Situation Consulting

158 Why is Ms. Fenway writing to Mr. Randolph?

(A) To offer advice
(B) To request a document
(C) To suggest a new project
(D) To appeal a decision

159 What did Ms. Fenway think was the error?

(A) Not closing the office early for a renovation
(B) Not keeping teams of employees together
(C) Not giving employees some time off during the move
(D) Not discussing a new policy with each employee individually

160 In which of the positions marked [1], [2], [3], and [4] does the following sentence best belong?

"Instead, talk in detail with each employee about reducing his or her workload during the relocation period."

(A) [1]
(B) [2]
(C) [3]
(D) [4]

Questions 161-163 refer to the following information on a Web page.

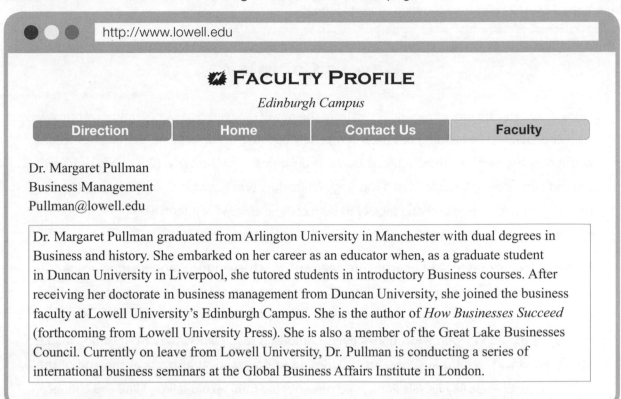

161 What is the purpose of the information?

(A) To announce dates for a business seminar

(B) To publicize facts about an employee

(C) To encourage business owners to buy a book

(D) To provide details about a job applicant

162 Where did Professor Pullman begin her teaching career?

(A) In Liverpool
(B) In Edinburgh
(C) In Manchester
(D) In London

163 What is indicated about Professor Pullman?

(A) She is currently teaching history at a university.

(B) She applied to be a member of a business council.

(C) She is working temporarily in London.

(D) She runs her own business throughout the world.

GO ON TO THE NEXT PAGE

Meyers Complex

Enjoy the scenic beauty of Mendota Bay from the newly renovated Meyers Complex. Formerly a sewing factory, the building has been completely updated to combine modern conveniences and technology with features representative of buildings from the early 1900s. Two years ago Gerund Remodeling Inc., the award-winning architecture firm based in Chicago, undertook the project to convert Fargo's sewing factory to both commercial and residential units. Next month's opening reception will mark the completion of the renovation.

Meyers Complex offers 240 apartments, many of which overlook Fargo Harbor, and 4,500 square meters of commercial space for offices and retail stores. In addition to its sweeping views, it offers beautifully landscaped gardens along the harbor. This appealing, multi-use facility is situated in a prime location. Meyers Complex is just a block away from Fargo's Maple Street, lined with boutique shops, art galleries and restaurants. It also sits at the end of the 23-kilometer Chanda Bay Bicycle Path, which was created from an old railroad line and connects Fargo to Alton City. There are several other well-maintained bicycle trails in the area. To the south, Jacksonville, with all of its attractions, is an easy 30-minute drive away.

To inquire about commercial or residential space, please contact Meyers Complex Property Management at 301-555-3241 or send an e-mail to rentalinfo@meyerscomplex.com. Floor plans for apartments vary. Commercial space can be customized. For more details, visit our Web site, www.meyerscomplex.com.

164 What is the purpose of the advertisement?
(A) To announce a recently approved project
(B) To promote an architectural awards event
(C) To publicize new office and residential space
(D) To explain a reason for the delay of the opening

165 What is mentioned about Gerund Remodeling Inc.?
(A) It is a family-owned business.
(B) It has been recognized for its work.
(C) It specializes in commercial properties.
(D) It is known for its unique sewing techniques.

166 What is NOT stated about Meyers Complex?
(A) It will open next month.
(B) It is right next to a subway station.
(C) It is not far from a shopping district.
(D) It is close to bicycle trails.

167 The word "prime" in paragraph 2, line 4, is closest in meaning to
(A) central
(B) heavy
(C) leading
(D) supreme

Questions 168-171 refer to the following online chat discussion.

Rebecca Walton [4:17 P.M.]	Thanks for attending the regional manager meeting earlier this afternoon. Are there any further questions?
Kelly Stevens [4:18 P.M.]	Juan and I are unclear about how the new sales districts affect existing customers. Do the new districts apply only to new customers?
Rebecca Walton [4:20 P.M.]	No, the new districts apply to both new and existing customers.
Kelly Stevens [4:21 P.M.]	So, does that mean I will no longer get incentives from current customers like Perot Publishing?
Rebecca Walton [4:22 P.M.]	Right. All existing clients in District 5 go to Juan.
Juan Rubble [4:23 P.M.]	But what if I agree to let Kelly keep Perot Publishing?
Rebecca Walton [4:25 P.M.]	Perot Publishing is a big client.
Juan Rubble [4:26 P.M.]	Yes, but I'd rather not interrupt a productive relationship. Perot Publishing is not that important to me.
Rebecca Walton [4:27 P.M.]	I don't see it as interrupting, necessarily. However, if you say so, Juan, I might be able to make an exception if our district manager approves it.
Kelly Stevens [4:28 P.M.]	Can I talk to the client in person?
Rebecca Walton [4:30 P.M.]	I don't think that's appropriate.
Kelly Stevens [4:31 P.M.]	I understand.
Juan Rubble [4:32 P.M.]	OK, we'll wait to hear back from you.

Send

168 Who most likely is Ms. Walton?

(A) A bookstore owner
(B) A sales manager
(C) A travel agent
(D) An author

169 What is suggested about Ms. Stevens?

(A) She has a good relationship with Perot Publishing.
(B) She'd like to transfer to an office in District 5.
(C) She is very satisfied with the new district assignment.
(D) She was not at the meeting in the morning.

170 At 4:25, what does Ms. Walton most likely mean when she writes, "Perot Publishing is a big client"?

(A) She doubts Mr. Rubble can meet Perot Publishing's needs.
(B) She believes Mr. Rubble is confused.
(C) She wants Mr. Rubble to visit District 5.
(D) She thinks Mr. Rubble's idea is surprising.

171 What will most likely happen next?

(A) Ms. Stevens will review the new map of sales districts.
(B) Ms. Stevens will meet with her client.
(C) Ms. Walton will contact the colleague.
(D) Mr. Rubble will accept a job offer from Perot Publishing.

GO ON TO THE NEXT PAGE

The McClellan Theater is one of Dublin's most treasured historic landmarks and needs to be preserved. The building, constructed almost two centuries ago on Dublin's Central Square, features many striking and unique attributes. –[1]–. The ornate plasterwork of its facade is a magnificent example of architecture of the period in which it was constructed. The walls of the lobby are covered by beautiful murals featuring many famous actors who have performed there over the years, including Wendy Ramsey and Madeline Estes. The theater is not only an architectural gem but also a highly valued entertainment venue for area residents, and it supports the local economy by attracting tourists to the area. –[2]–.

Due to the building's deterioration in recent years, it no longer attracts large theater productions and musical acts. Ensuring the theater's continued use would require extensive restoration. –[3]–. Over the next six months, this committee composed of city residents, local business owners and civic leaders will finalize the restoration plans and raise the capital necessary to complete the project. The committee will also be working to locate corporate and community sponsorships throughout Dublin. –[4]–.

For residents interested in following the restoration efforts, the committee will hold public information sessions on the first Tuesday of each month in the community room of the Dublin Public Library. Detailed plans for the project and information about making a donation to the effort are available at www.restoretheMcClellantheater.com.

172 What is the article mainly about?

(A) The award received by a town for its architecture

(B) The results of an election for a committee

(C) Information about an upcoming city project

(D) The dates of a theater's performance schedule

173 What is implied about the McClellan Theater?

(A) It is the largest building in Dublin.

(B) It offers discounted tickets to Dublin residents.

(C) It is no longer open to the public.

(D) It once attracted large crowds.

174 According to the article, how can people learn more about the changes at the McClellan Theater?

(A) By submitting a request to the city government

(B) By attending monthly meetings

(C) By speaking to Ms. Ramsey in person

(D) By singing up for a monthly newsletter

175 In which of the positions marked [1], [2], [3], and [4] does the following sentence best belong?

"For this reason, the McClellan Theater Restoration Committee was formed last month with an ambitious plan for restoring the theater."

(A) [1]

(B) [2]

(C) [3]

(D) [4]

GO ON TO THE NEXT PAGE

April 4

The National Association of Plastic Workers (NAPW) will hold its annual conference in Sydney from June 6 to 8. Once again, it will be held at the Stone Conference Center in Sydney's business district. Stan Keating, NAPW President, says that the organization will return to the venue because of its convenient location and the amenities it offers. Says Stan, "The conference center is state-of-the-art, and the staff members are extremely knowledgeable and helpful."

This year's theme is "Emerging Technologies in Plastic Fabrication and Molding." The keynote address on June will be given by Colleen Allen, CEO of Plastigic Innovators, Inc. In addition to Ms. Allen's speech, during the three-day event there will be twenty presentations and a closing address by Mr. Keating.

To register for the conference, visit the NAPW web site (www.napw.com/conference). The cost of the conference is $85 for NAPW members and $120 for nonmembers. Students, please contact your institution for discount information; the NAPW maintains pricing agreements with a number of universities and technical colleges. Hotel reservations can be made through the Web site as well. Attendees can choose from six area hotels at various price ranges. The NAPW is offering a free shuttle service to and from the participating hotels and conference site.

Mastuki Manufacturing
Expense reimbursement form

Employee name: *Rodney Kruger*
Payroll ID#: *129856*
Manager/supervisor name: *Michelle Robertson*
Purpose: *National Association of Plastic Workers Conference*

Itemized expenses:
Conference fee: $85.00
Bus fare: (round-trip Melbourne/Sydney) $43.34
Accommodation: (1 night at Jefferson Inn on June 6) $126.78

Total: *$255.12*

Attach receipts for all expenses. Allow two to three weeks for processing.

Employee signature: *R. Kruger*
Manager/supervisor signature: *M. Robertson*

Submitted for payment: *June 12*

176 What is stated about the Stone Conference Center?

    (A) It is close to the airport.

    (B) Its staff is very competent.

    (C) It offers a discount on meeting rooms.

    (D) It has recently undergone renovation.

177 Who is Ms. Allen?

    (A) A guest speaker

    (B) A conference organizer

    (C) Mr. Kruger's manager

    (D) The president of the NAPW

178 What does the article suggest about student discounts?

    (A) They are given only to graduate students.

    (B) They are provided to students working as interns.

    (C) They are available through certain schools.

    (D) They are available to international students.

179 What can be found on the NAPW Web site?

    (A) A shuttle schedule

    (B) A list of hotels

    (C) A map of the conference center

    (D) A description of the presentations

180 What can be inferred about Mr. Kruger?

    (A) He did not listen to the closing speech.

    (B) He was reimbursed on June 12 for expenses.

    (C) He drove his car to the NAPW conference.

    (D) He is not a member of the NAPW.

GO ON TO THE NEXT PAGE

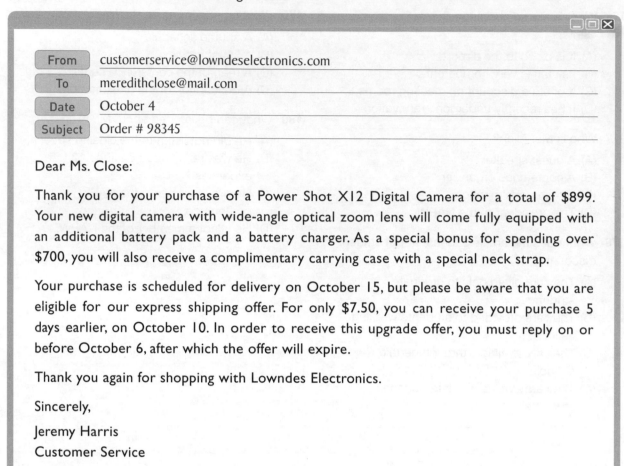

From: customerservice@lowndeselectronics.com
To: meredithclose@mail.com
Date: October 4
Subject: Order # 98345

Dear Ms. Close:

Thank you for your purchase of a Power Shot X12 Digital Camera for a total of $899. Your new digital camera with wide-angle optical zoom lens will come fully equipped with an additional battery pack and a battery charger. As a special bonus for spending over $700, you will also receive a complimentary carrying case with a special neck strap.

Your purchase is scheduled for delivery on October 15, but please be aware that you are eligible for our express shipping offer. For only $7.50, you can receive your purchase 5 days earlier, on October 10. In order to receive this upgrade offer, you must reply on or before October 6, after which the offer will expire.

Thank you again for shopping with Lowndes Electronics.

Sincerely,

Jeremy Harris
Customer Service

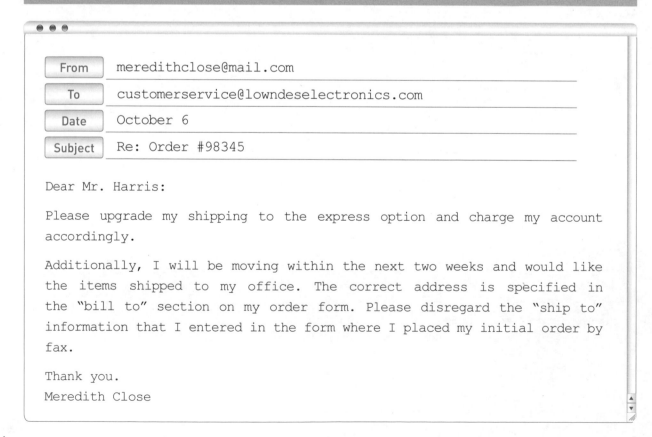

From: meredithclose@mail.com
To: customerservice@lowndeselectronics.com
Date: October 6
Subject: Re: Order #98345

Dear Mr. Harris:

Please upgrade my shipping to the express option and charge my account accordingly.

Additionally, I will be moving within the next two weeks and would like the items shipped to my office. The correct address is specified in the "bill to" section on my order form. Please disregard the "ship to" information that I entered in the form where I placed my initial order by fax.

Thank you.
Meredith Close

181 Why does Mr. Harris write the e-mail?

(A) To inform a customer of an error
(B) To issue an invitation
(C) To apologize for a shipping delay
(D) To present a limited-time offer

182 According to the first e-mail, why will Ms. Close receive a free item?

(A) She opened a business account.
(B) She made a purchase before October 6.
(C) She spent over a stated amount.
(D) She is a returning customer.

183 What can be inferred about Ms. Close?

(A) She would prefer to upgrade the digital camera.
(B) She is moving to an overseas location.
(C) She would like to cancel two items.
(D) She wants the shipment sent to a different address.

184 When will Ms. Close most likely receive her order?

(A) On October 5
(B) On October 6
(C) On October 10
(D) On October 15

185 In the second e-mail, the word "entered" in paragraph 2, line 4, is closest in meaning to

(A) went into
(B) typed
(C) started
(D) thought about

Questions 186-190 refer to the following memo, notice, and letter.

from	Thomas Reilly
To	All students
Date	February 26

Welcome to Stein College Residence.

We would like to welcome freshmen and returning students to our residence. We hope that this year will be as good if not better than the last. We have made some renovations to the building that we think you will really enjoy, including a new lounge with four pool tables, and a brand-new dartboard. This lounge will be open from 10 A.M. until 11 P.M. and will be supported by a café that offers a wide range of beverages and snacks for your pleasure.

For all of us to have a fun and safe year, it is important to set up some ground rules for your behavior. It is very important to note that breaking three rules can result in suspension of privileges, eviction from the residence, and possibly expulsion from school. In addition, you are responsible for the action of any guest that you bring into the residence. This means that upon entry and exit, any guest that you wish to stay with you MUST sign in and out. The maximum number of guests per person is two.

For further details of the residence rules and by-laws of the residence, refer to the notice on the bulletin board in the lobby.

Stein College Residence Rules

1. Drinking in the common spaces — for example, outside of your room — is prohibited.

2. Illegal drugs of any kind are banned.

3. Violence of any kind is prohibited.

4. Damage to the property is not tolerated.

5. Smoking inside the building is not allowed.

6. Noise in the hallways after 10 P.M. is prohibited.

We hope that these main rules will help everyone have a safe and educational year at Stein College.

If you have any questions, please ask the Resident Tutor, Thomas Reilly, in Room 102.

May 1

Dear Mr. Smith:

This letter is being sent to formally notify you that you are being summoned to the residence committee meeting this Friday, May 6. The actions of your guests on the night of April 21 were not in line with our rules, and you, as stated in the memo, are responsible.

Allegedly, your guests were involved in drinking and fighting in the hallway of the 12th floor at 1 o'clock in the morning. Upon arrival of the resident tutor, they were disrespectful and began shoving him around. This is completely unacceptable and requires us to take action. You will have to attend this meeting on the 11th floor of Johnson Hall with the Residence Board of Directors and committee. They will decide your ultimate fate.

Sincerely,

Vanessa Burkowitz
Residence Manager

186 Why was the memo sent?

(A) To ask the students to complete the form
(B) To remind the students to follow the rules
(C) To remind the students to attend the committee meeting
(D) To tell the students how to get into the residence

187 In the memo, the word "suspension" in paragraph 2, line 2, is closest in meaning to

(A) delay
(B) interruption
(C) trial
(D) difficulty

188 What is most likely the purpose of the letter?

(A) To announce the closure of the residence
(B) To suggest moving out of the residence
(C) To invite Mr. Smith to a community event
(D) To call Mr. Smith to a committee meeting

189 What is indicated about Mr. Smith's guests?

(A) They were approached by Thomas Reilly.
(B) They broke ground rules 3 and 5.
(C) They had visited the residence before April 21.
(D) They were supposed to leave the residence before 9.

190 What can be inferred about the meeting on Friday?

(A) Whether Mr. Smith can stay in the residence will be determined.
(B) It is open to all Stein college students.
(C) It is regularly scheduled to be held on Fridays.
(D) Mr. Smith will attend the meeting to select the board members.

http://www.communityboard.com/housing

Name: Donovan Swayze

Date: January 23

I accepted a new position in Kensington and need to relocate near the downtown area before my start date on May 15. I'm seeking a simple, clean, one-bedroom rental or larger, depending on the price. A relaxing location with outdoor seating for entertaining friends or family would be a plus. I do have a car, but I'd appreciate having good access to public transportation. I have a budget of around £1,200 monthly to cover all housing costs, including utilities.

RELAX AT YOUR OWN PLACE IN KENSINGTON

Be the first to rent this two-bedroom apartment upon completion of extensive renovation. This property will be move-in ready on May 1. It will feature a clean modern look, new floors throughout, and all new appliances. It is situated downtown, and students are welcome as it is less than 10 minutes by bus to Trinity University from the City Transportation office. Cats and small dogs are potentially permitted but with conditions, so please inquire. £1,200 also pays for water, sewer, garbage pick-ups, and general upkeep of the property. The electricity and natural gas will be the responsibility of the tenant. A one-time security deposit equal to one month's rent should be paid upon signing the rental agreement.

If you are interested, please email us at nancyphan@kensingtonpalace.com.

To: Nancy Phan
From: Donovan Swayze
Date: January 24
Subject: Apartment

Dear Ms. Phan:

I happened to see your rental advertisement flyer. From the description, it sounds as if it may be just what I've been looking for. I'm eager to look over the apartment, and I am going to be in Kensington all this week for work. My last day in town will be Sunday, January 30. If the place suits me, I'd want to move in the same day that it's expected to be available. The timing would be perfect! I hope to hear from you soon.

Thank you.
Donovan Swayze

191 For what reason is Mr. Swayze relocating?

(A) To launch his own business
(B) To return to his hometown
(C) To work in a new place
(D) To begin his retirement

192 What aspect of the property does NOT match Mr. Swayze's preferences?

(A) The location
(B) The utility costs
(C) The size
(D) The available date

193 Why does Ms. Phan mention that she will need additional information?

(A) For needed changes to the décor
(B) For a tenant who does not pay a security deposit
(C) For remodeling of the apartment
(D) For someone who wants to keep a pet

194 What is the purpose of the e-mail?

(A) To agree to the terms of the contract
(B) To change the details of a residential advertisement
(C) To inquire about the features of the apartment
(D) To make an arrangement to view the property

195 When does Mr. Swayze want to start living in the residence?

(A) January 24
(B) January 30
(C) May 1
(D) May 15

GO ON TO THE NEXT PAGE

Questions 196-200 refer to the following e-mails and newsletter.

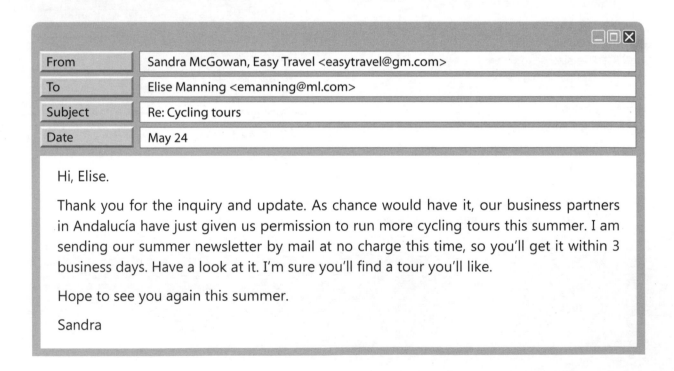

E-Mail Message

From: Elise Manning <emanning@ml.com>
To: Sandra McGowan, Easy Travel <easytravel@gm.com>
Subject: Cycling tours
Date: May 23
Attach: photo (scan #1)

Hi, Sandra.

Well, I'm ready to travel with you again to Andalucía. This time, I want to try one of your cycling tours if you plan on offering them. I'd love to have another look at Almeria Falls from a bike, but I am a beginning cyclist and am not ready for any tough tours. I would also like to take the train rather than the plane back to Valencia this year. Honestly, though, I'm not up to that long journey from Huelva! Would there be any suitable tours for me to join this summer?

I look forward to hearing from you.

Elise

P.S. I've enclosed an updated photo for my Andalucía travel visa, just so you have it on file when I apply for a tour.

From	Sandra McGowan, Easy Travel <easytravel@gm.com>
To	Elise Manning <emanning@ml.com>
Subject	Re: Cycling tours
Date	May 24

Hi, Elise.

Thank you for the inquiry and update. As chance would have it, our business partners in Andalucía have just given us permission to run more cycling tours this summer. I am sending our summer newsletter by mail at no charge this time, so you'll get it within 3 business days. Have a look at it. I'm sure you'll find a tour you'll like.

Hope to see you again this summer.

Sandra

EASY TRAVEL NEWSLETTER new cycling tour opportunities in Andalucía!

After celebrating our 20th anniversary at the Amalia Hotel during last week's National Day tour, EASY TRAVEL secured the rights to once again become the world's only tour company to offer cycling tours in the remote Andalucía area. Our tours are a good value at 1,100 Euros and include all meals, plane/train transport to/from Valencia, and use of mountain bikes. Note that we can now accommodate vegetarian dietary requests.

DATES AND ITINERARIES

TOUR A
July 3-8
Cadiz – Darya – Lenza – Slakotov – Cadiz
Level of difficulty: easy (exit Andalucía by plane only from Cadiz)

TOUR B
July 3-8
Cadiz – Darya – Lenza – Almeria Falls – Cadiz
Level of difficulty: challenging (exit Andalucía by plane or train from Cadiz)

TOUR C
July 3-8
Cadiz – Darya – Almeria Falls – Huelva
Level of difficulty: moderate (exit Andalucía by train from Huelva)

TOUR D
July 3-8
Cadiz – Darya – Almeria Falls – Cadiz
Level of difficulty: easy (exit Andalucía by plane or train from Cadiz)

NOTE: All of our tours rated "easy" and "moderate" offer a combination of light cycling and vehicle transport. If you are a keen cyclist, you should take a tour rated "challenging."

---

196 What is the purpose of the first e-mail?

(A) To schedule a meeting
(B) To request some information
(C) To make hotel reservations
(D) To announce a change in plans

197 Which has Ms. Manning attached with her e-mail?

(A) A project proposal
(B) A photo for visa
(C) A travel itinerary
(D) A tour application form

198 What is NOT mentioned about EASY TRAVEL?

(A) It runs a chain of hotels.
(B) It has been operating for 20 years.
(C) It has exclusive rights to some tours.
(D) It provides riding equipment on some of its tours.

199 Which tour plan is Ms. Manning most likely choose to join?

(A) Tour A
(B) Tour B
(C) Tour C
(D) Tour D

200 What can be implied about Ms. Manning?

(A) She has visited Huelva before.
(B) She likes to travel in winter.
(C) She works as a real estate agent.
(D) She does not subscribe to the Easy Travel newsletter.

Stop! This is the end of the test. If you finish before time is called, you may go back to Parts 5, 6, and 7 and check your work.

等等！開始前務必確認！

- 將書桌整理成和實際測試時一樣，做好心理準備。
- 將手機關機，使用手錶計時。
- 限制時間為 120 分鐘。一定要遵守時間限制。
- 不要因為困難就跳過。盡可能依照順序解題。

Actual Test

02

 開始時間　　　　：

結束時間　　　　：

♪ 標準版-02

♪ 白噪音版-02

LISTENING TEST

In the Listening test, you will be asked to demonstrate how well you understand spoken English. The entire Listening test will last approximately 45 minutes. There are four parts, and directions are given for each part. You must mark your answers on the separate answer sheet. Do not write your answers in your test book.

PART 1

Directions: For each question in this part, you will hear four statements about a picture in your test book. When you hear the statements, you must select the one statement that best describes what you see in the picture. Then find the number of the question on your answer sheet and mark your answer. The statements will not be printed in your test book and will be spoken only one time.

Example

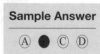

Statement (B), "The man is working at a desk," is the best description of the picture, so you should select answer (B) and mark it on your answer sheet.

1

2

3

4

5

6

GO ON TO THE NEXT PAGE

PART 2

7   Mark your answer on your answer sheet.

8   Mark your answer on your answer sheet.

9   Mark your answer on your answer sheet.

10   Mark your answer on your answer sheet.

11   Mark your answer on your answer sheet.

12   Mark your answer on your answer sheet.

13   Mark your answer on your answer sheet.

14   Mark your answer on your answer sheet.

15   Mark your answer on your answer sheet.

16   Mark your answer on your answer sheet.

17   Mark your answer on your answer sheet.

18   Mark your answer on your answer sheet.

19   Mark your answer on your answer sheet.

20   Mark your answer on your answer sheet.

21   Mark your answer on your answer sheet.

22   Mark your answer on your answer sheet.

23   Mark your answer on your answer sheet.

24   Mark your answer on your answer sheet.

25   Mark your answer on your answer sheet.

26   Mark your answer on your answer sheet.

27   Mark your answer on your answer sheet.

28   Mark your answer on your answer sheet.

29   Mark your answer on your answer sheet.

30   Mark your answer on your answer sheet.

31   Mark your answer on your answer sheet.

PART 3

Directions: You will hear some conversations between two or more people. You will be asked to answer three questions about what the speakers say in each conversation. Select the best response to each question and mark the letter (A), (B), (C), or (D) on your answer sheet. The conversations will not be printed in your test book and will be spoken only one time.

32 Who is the woman talking to?

(A) A graphic designer
(B) A patron
(C) A sales clerk
(D) An interior decorator

33 What does the man expect to happen by the end of this week?

(A) An order will be placed.
(B) A range of new patterns will be designed.
(C) Some supplies will run out.
(D) Additional merchandise will be delivered.

34 What will the woman probably do next?

(A) Visit a different store
(B) Make a purchase
(C) Call a regular customer
(D) Look at color samples

35 Where do the speakers probably work?

(A) At a manufacturing company
(B) At a hockey field
(C) At a department store
(D) At a storage facility

36 According to the man, what did a representative ask to do?

(A) Increase an order
(B) Delay a shipment
(C) Revise a design
(D) Reschedule a visit

37 What does the woman want the man to do?

(A) Draft another design
(B) Arrange a meeting
(C) Send some information
(D) Change a plan

38 Who most likely is Ms. Kammerick?

(A) An actor
(B) A writer
(C) A producer
(D) A critic

39 What does Mr. Simon say about London?

(A) He will meet a publisher there.
(B) He went to university there.
(C) He recently moved there.
(D) He used to work there.

40 What problem does Ms. Kammerick mention?

(A) The cost of living is too high.
(B) Her schedule is full.
(C) The theater is fully booked.
(D) She cannot meet a deadline.

41 What did the man ask the woman to do in his e-mail?

(A) Confirm the length of a presentation
(B) Provide some feedback on his work
(C) Offer some presentation materials
(D) Contact the board of directors

42 What does the woman suggest?

(A) Contacting a coworker
(B) Increasing a budget
(C) Adding a visual aid
(D) Shortening a document

43 What does the woman mean when she says, "I'll leave that to you"?

(A) She plans to give an item to the man.
(B) She does not intend to stay for much longer.
(C) She will not accompany the man.
(D) She will allow the man to make a decision.

GO ON TO THE NEXT PAGE

44 What are the speakers concerned about?

(A) Defective items
(B) Wrong orders
(C) Lack of staff
(D) Rising expenses

45 What does the man suggest?

(A) Changing a supplier
(B) Checking the order form
(C) Reporting to a manager
(D) Discussing a problem

46 What does the woman decide to do?

(A) Cancel orders
(B) Work overtime
(C) Get some price quotes
(D) Help her coworker

47 What is the problem?

(A) The store is under construction.
(B) Only a few items are available.
(C) Some equipment is not working.
(D) A sale has just ended.

48 Why does the man say, "That's probably the case"?

(A) He agrees with the woman.
(B) He is searching in a display case.
(C) He hopes the weather will clear up.
(D) He is offering his idea.

49 Why does the man request the woman's personal information?

(A) To give her details of another location
(B) To tell her about upcoming sale
(C) To offer a membership discount
(D) To notify her when more stock arrives

50 What is the man nervous about?

(A) Making a public speech
(B) Showing his work
(C) Entering a competition
(D) Leading a discussion

51 What does the man say about his work?

(A) It is made from recycled material.
(B) It is being sold at an auction.
(C) It consists mainly of paintings.
(D) It has recently won an award.

52 What does the man suggest the women do?

(A) Collaborate on a design
(B) Support an artist
(C) Attend an exhibition
(D) Cast a vote online

53 What type of business does the man work for?

(A) A tour service
(B) A film production company
(C) A radio station
(D) An airline company

54 What has the man recently done?

(A) Written a book
(B) Attended an international seminar
(C) Returned for a trip abroad
(D) Started his own business

55 Who does the man say he talked with?

(A) Volunteer aid workers
(B) Government officials
(C) Many poor people
(D) Newspaper journalists

56 What activity are the speakers participating in?

(A) Driving to the post office
(B) Operating some office equipment
(C) Placing an order of supplies
(D) Preparing parcels to mail

57 At what time does the conversation most likely take place?

(A) 2:00
(B) 3:00
(C) 4:00
(D) 5:00

58 What does the woman mean when she says, "Let's get on with it, then"?

(A) Everyone should work faster.
(B) The labels are all ready.
(C) There is plenty of time left.
(D) They need to leave right now.

---

59 What is the conversation mainly about?

(A) Preparation for an award ceremony
(B) Plans for an event
(C) The cost of supplies
(D) Directions to a venue

60 What does the man say about the previous year's event?

(A) It had enough space.
(B) It was hard to get to.
(C) It was expensive to rent.
(D) It had free parking.

61 What is indicated about the tickets?

(A) They are quite expensive.
(B) They have already sold out.
(C) The prices are lower than before.
(D) They are selling well.

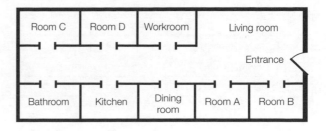

62 Who most likely is the man?

(A) A plumber
(B) An electrician
(C) A real estate agent
(D) A builder

63 Look at the graphic. Where does the woman say she would like to put the bathroom?

(A) Room A
(B) Room B
(C) Room C
(D) Room D

64 What does the man say about the project?

(A) It will take a long time.
(B) It requires a lot of travel.
(C) It will be started next week.
(D) It will be cheap to complete.

GO ON TO THE NEXT PAGE

SCHEDULE	
Tuesday, October 6	Financial Reports Due
Wednesday, October 7	Plant Inspection
Thursday, October 8	Plant Inspection
Friday, October 9	New Item Introduction

65 What is the main topic of the conversation?

(A) A guest speaker
(B) A sporting competition
(C) A welcome event
(D) A local festival

66 Look at the graphic. When most likely will the event be held?

(A) On Tuesday
(B) On Wednesday
(C) On Thursday
(D) On Friday

67 What does the woman say she will do?

(A) Attend a conference
(B) Book a venue
(C) Prepare an inspection
(D) Reserve a hotel room

Name: Joyce Hahn
Patient# 002875

Date:	Wednesday 9/13
Examination	$ 40.00
2x Gum Treatment	$ 200.00
2x Dental Filling	$ 260.00
Toothpaste	$ 10.00
Balance Due	$510.00

68 Look at the graphic. Which charge on the bill is incorrect?

(A) $10
(B) $40
(C) $200
(D) $260

69 What does the man say about the clinic?

(A) It changed its phone number.
(B) It installed a new program.
(C) It hired new staff members.
(D) It purchased new equipment.

70 What does the man say he will do?

(A) Upgrade a system
(B) Issue a refund
(C) Update software
(D) Send another statement

PART 4

Directions: You will hear some talks given by a single speaker. You will be asked to answer three questions about what the speaker says in each talk. Select the best response to each question and mark the letter (A), (B), (C), or (D) on your answer sheet. The talks will not be printed in your test book and will be spoken only one time.

71 Where does the announcement take place?

(A) In a train station
(B) At an airport
(C) On an express train
(D) At an express bus terminal

72 Why is the announcement being made?

(A) To provide information on destinations
(B) To explain a schedule change
(C) To ask passengers to start boarding
(D) To apologize for a delay

73 What are listeners asked to do?

(A) Proceed to a different platform
(B) Present their documents
(C) Wait for more instructions
(D) Confirm they are in the correct place

74 What is being celebrated?

(A) An opening of a new branch
(B) A business anniversary
(C) A retirement ceremony
(D) A special award

75 What is the restaurant planning to do on Friday?

(A) Extend its hours of operation
(B) Offer musical entertainment
(C) Provide complimentary meals
(D) Discount certain items

76 What does the speaker say about the restaurant?

(A) It uses local produce.
(B) It hired a renowned chef.
(C) It has multiple locations.
(D) It is under new ownership.

77 Where is the talk probably taking place?

(A) At an electronics store
(B) In a research center
(C) In a conference room
(D) At a construction site

78 Who most likely are the listeners?

(A) New employees
(B) Company investors
(C) Store patrons
(D) Factory workers

79 What does the speaker mean when he says, "let's get started"?

(A) A tour is about to begin.
(B) Some delivery is ready to be shipped.
(C) Listeners should go back to work immediately.
(D) Listeners should fill out some forms.

80 What type of organization recorded this message?

(A) A radio station
(B) A transportation service
(C) The National Weather Service
(D) A local school

81 What does the speaker say about Florence?

(A) Its roads have been repaved.
(B) It will experience a snowstorm.
(C) Its schools will all be closed.
(D) It is the largest city in the region.

82 What are listeners asked to do?

(A) Attend the afternoon classes
(B) Check for updated information
(C) Design a new Web site
(D) Listen to an upcoming broadcast

GO ON TO THE NEXT PAGE

83 What is the purpose of the talk?

(A) To introduce a new employee
(B) To reschedule a farewell party
(C) To explain about new policy
(D) To announce the resignation of an employee

84 What has Mr. Lansing recently done?

(A) Accepted a promotion
(B) Created an advertisement
(C) Submitted a report
(D) Attended a seminar

85 What will the speaker probably do next?

(A) Join a conference
(B) Talk to a supervisor
(C) Receive an electronic mail
(D) Send detailed information

86 What is mentioned about the property?

(A) It's newly renovated.
(B) It is for up to 15 persons.
(C) It offers on-site parking.
(D) It is close to the station.

87 According to the message, what feature is Mr. Gupta looking for?

(A) A fully furnished office
(B) A convenient location
(C) Modern equipment
(D) Adequate parking

88 Why does the speaker recommend viewing the building as soon as possible?

(A) It will rent out quickly.
(B) Its price will go up soon.
(C) It will be renovated shortly.
(D) It will be advertised on TV.

89 Who is the intended audience for this talk?

(A) Golfers
(B) Caddies
(C) Teachers
(D) Volunteers

90 What is mentioned about the tournament?

(A) It is a national competition.
(B) It will last three days.
(C) It is an annual event.
(D) It will be rescheduled.

91 What is one instruction given to the listeners?

(A) Speak loudly during play
(B) Stay off the greens
(C) Ask questions to the athletes
(D) Check out the schedule

92 What is the report mainly about?

(A) A planned closure of a facility
(B) An acquisition of two companies
(C) A new line of product
(D) A company's expanded operation

93 Who is Jack Wentworth?

(A) A company spokesperson
(B) A corporate executive
(C) A broadcast reporter
(D) A news reader

94 What does the speaker mean when he says, "That would make perfect sense"?

(A) United Textiles is an international company.
(B) Any local government would favor such a plan.
(C) Textile sales are strong in the local area.
(D) United Textiles is famous in the region.

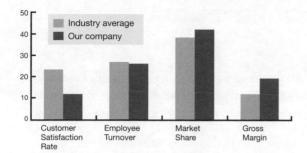

Alice Spring Regional Weather Report		
Day	Skies	Temperature
Tuesday	Sunny	Hot
Wednesday	Sunny	Warm
Thursday	Sunny	Warm
Friday	Cloudy	Cool

95 Why does the speaker thank the listeners?

(A) They formed a committee.
(B) They finished a quarterly report.
(C) They distributed a notice.
(D) They gathered quickly.

96 Look at the graphic. What area does the board of directors most want to improve?

(A) Customer satisfaction rate
(B) Employee turnover
(C) Market share
(D) Gross margin

97 What will Ms. Gallagher have to do?

(A) Use a different facility
(B) Create a document
(C) Report a current issue
(D) Contact a manager

98 According to the speaker, what is the park known for?

(A) Impressive rock formations
(B) Native species
(C) Exotic flowers
(D) High numbers of visitors

99 Look at the graphic. When does the talk probably take place?

(A) On Tuesday
(B) On Wednesday
(C) On Thursday
(D) On Friday

100 What does the speaker advise listeners to do?

(A) Take a lot of photographs
(B) Draw some pictures
(C) Wear sunglasses
(D) Stay on the hiking trail

This is the end of the Listening test. Turn to Part 5 in your test book.

GO ON TO THE NEXT PAGE

READING TEST

In the Reading test, you will read a variety of texts and answer several different types of reading comprehension questions. The entire Reading test will last 75 minutes. There are three parts, and directions are given for each part. You are encouraged to answer as many questions as possible within the time allowed.

You must mark your answers on the separate answer sheet. Do not write your answers in your test book.

PART 5

Directions: A word or phrase is missing in each of the sentences below. Four answer choices are given below each sentence. Select the best answer to complete the sentence. Then mark the letter (A), (B), (C), or (D) on your answer sheet.

101 Bergeson's began as a small retail store, but ------- transitioned into a large wholesaler.

(A) quickly
(B) well
(C) quite
(D) highly

102 The open-access database can be used to search ------- job opportunities at Jefferson Electronics.

(A) for
(B) up
(C) as
(D) to

103 It is ------- that managers be made aware of a shortage of supplies when it occurs.

(A) sudden
(B) actual
(C) eventful
(D) critical

104 Most of the employees at the company have work experience, but only a handful of ------- can see the future importance of current trends.

(A) we
(B) us
(C) our
(D) ourselves

105 Please read through ------- page of the contract carefully before signing on the final page.

(A) all
(B) each
(C) whole
(D) complete

106 A ------- shopping bag is a necessary item for someone who does not like the ordinary plastic bags from the grocery store.

(A) rigorous
(B) comparable
(C) durable
(D) vigorous

107 The judges for this year's debate competition include ------- from a broadcasting station.

(A) represents
(B) representatives
(C) represented
(D) represent

108 The filters of your Total Water Purifier must ------- at least once a month to keep the appliance functioning properly.

(A) be cleaned
(B) cleaning
(C) have cleaned
(D) clean

109 Mr. O'Neil ------- his speech when he realized that he hadn't printed out the draft.

(A) achieved
(B) improvised
(C) commanded
(D) officiated

110 Varner Bank works ------- with customers to establish long-term partnerships.

(A) nearly
(B) recently
(C) closely
(D) newly

111 The updated safety analysis report is limited to site supervisors ------- the Russell Software System.

(A) within
(B) until
(C) during
(D) since

112 ------- needs to be highlighted is the area of agriculture and natural resources.

(A) What
(B) Which
(C) Whichever
(D) Whose

113 San Remo Lemonade maintained ------- sales all year around though promoted as a summertime drink.

(A) final
(B) correct
(C) steady
(D) seasoned

114 Morrison Electronics is acquiring Yearwood Tech. for ------- $35 million in stocks and cash.

(A) approximates
(B) approximation
(C) approximately
(D) approximate

115 The building may be accessed only by personnel ------- have attended the employee orientation.

(A) must
(B) since
(C) who
(D) some

116 New technologies have ------- Poland Cell Tech. to expand its network and explore sales opportunities.

(A) emerged
(B) improved
(C) introduced
(D) enabled

117 Mr. Long repaired the fax machine ------- last Friday because the maintenance department was short on staff.

(A) his
(B) his own
(C) himself
(D) him

118 You can have fun at our indoor waterpark all through the year, ------- of the season.

(A) regardless
(B) regarded
(C) regarding
(D) regard

119 A panel may begin to review the entries ------- the deadline for submitting designs has passed.

(A) how
(B) nor
(C) whether
(D) now that

120 For results to be convincing, the temperature and humidity in the laboratory must remain ------- the same throughout the experiment.

(A) exacted
(B) exactness
(C) exact
(D) exactly

GO ON TO THE NEXT PAGE

121 ------- Ms. Motohashi missed her train, she was fortunately still on time for the awards ceremony.

(A) Though
(B) Despite
(C) As if
(D) Just as

122 Karl Byquist at Gordon Architecture, a British Company, is the ------- of this year's Master Architects Award.

(A) receiving
(B) received
(C) recipient
(D) receipt

123 Results of the two audit findings report ------- the director's expectations.

(A) surpassed
(B) surpassing
(C) to surpass
(D) having surpassed

124 If you have not visited the Valley Restaurant recently, you may be ------- to see how the interior has changed.

(A) pleasing
(B) pleased
(C) please
(D) pleaser

125 A nine-mile ------- of Fosberg Road between Norview Road and Harriot Avenue will be resurfaced in September.

(A) journey
(B) duration
(C) stretch
(D) instance

126 Article submissions to Journal Explore Nature must not exceed 2,000 words, ------- references.

(A) exclude
(B) excluding
(C) exclusive
(D) exclusion

127 Registration for the community programs will start with residents, ------- are students.

(A) inasmuch as
(B) the reason being
(C) because of them
(D) most of whom

128 The board meeting ended so ------- that few members had an opportunity to comment on the proposed road construction project.

(A) abruptly
(B) broadly
(C) practically
(D) obviously

129 Because of her lack of experience, Ms. Abraham was ------- to volunteer for the astronaut training.

(A) reluctance
(B) more reluctantly
(C) reluctance
(D) reluctant

130 In order to make an official purchase agreement, a manager must submit ------- from at least three qualified experts.

(A) combinations
(B) appointments
(C) estimates
(D) comprises

PART 6

Directions: Read the texts that follow. A word, phrase, or sentence is missing in parts of each text. Four answer choices for each question are given below the text. Select the best answer to complete the text. Then mark the letter (A), (B), (C), or (D) on your answer sheet.

Questions 131-134 refer to the following memo.

To: All staff

The Light Cloud Airlines' board of directors is pleased to announce that board chair Mathew Mavens has been appointed the new interim president of the foundation ------- the departure of **131.** Roberto Rinaldi. -------. We also wish him the best in his future endeavors. In the meantime, the **132.** committee for the new permanent president has been formed. Mr. Mavens will resume his duty as board chair ------- the new president of the organization is chosen. **133.**
If you have any questions or concerns, please feel free to contact me while we ------- the **134.** transition in leadership.

Thank you.
Rajiv Shrestha
Communication Director

---

131 (A) following
    (B) follow
    (C) follows
    (D) followed

132 (A) I am happy to inform you that we have found the product he is looking for and have placed an order.
    (B) I forgot to tell you that I would not be able to make it to the meeting because I have to meet some board members.
    (C) Let me know if there's anything I can do for you to make the hiring process run smoothly.
    (D) The board and staff greatly appreciate Mr. Rinaldi's commitment to our mission over the past seven years.

133 (A) so
    (B) when
    (C) because
    (D) although

134 (A) question
    (B) reconsider
    (C) undergo
    (D) avoid

Questions 135-138 refer to the following announcement.

Qualified candidates are now being considered for the position of lead web designer at Gibson Ltd.

A well-known advertising firm, Gibson Ltd. provides businesses with the innovative technical resources that are ------- of dramatically increasing a company's presence on the Internet. As
135.
demand for this unique service continues to grow, so does the number of Gibson Ltd.'s -------. In
136.
fact, new offices have recently opened as far away as Berlin, Tokyo, and Abu Dhabi.

As a member of Gibson Ltd.'s production division, the new lead Web designer ------- the efforts
137.
of a team responsible for developing and maintaining client Web sites. -------.
138.

135 (A) capably
(B) capabilities
(C) capability
(D) capable

136 (A) locations
(B) instructions
(C) reports
(D) schedules

137 (A) had overseen
(B) will oversee
(C) was overseen
(D) has been overseeing

138 (A) Thank you for your e-mail and for sharing the positive feedback from your clients.
(B) A full job description and other information for applicants are available at www.gibson.com/jobs.
(C) It has been a great pleasure working with you and the entire Gibson staff.
(D) If our work doesn't meet your standards, we will honor our guarantee.

Questions 139-142 refer to the following article.

November 29 — Jake's Restaurant on Sheboygan Street recently submitted an application

for an entertainment permit. If -------, the permit will enable the restaurant to host live musical
139.

performances nightly.

The restaurant is located in what is primarily a residential area, and some neighbors are

concerned that they will be exposed to loud music ------- a regular basis. Others don't think that
140.

it will be a major -------, "We won't have a problem," said resident Beth Martinez.
141.

-------. However, the decision ultimately lies with the staff in the city licensing office.
142.

---

139 (A) approved
(B) approving
(C) approves
(D) approval

140 (A) at
(B) on
(C) from
(D) among

141 (A) investment
(B) issue
(C) deadline
(D) act

142 (A) Residents may still contact the town council to voice their concerns.
(B) We are looking for some volunteers to help perform at the restaurant.
(C) To make the transition go faster, please remove your personal items.
(D) This is one of the changes the management plans to implement.

Questions 143-146 refer to the following e-mail.

To: Fred Jaspers <fjaspers@westfordmarketing.com>
From: Winnie Price <WPrice@lapimaelectronics.com>
Date: April 8
Subject: New Marketing Campaign
Attachment: Electronics

Hello, Fred.

Lapima Electronic Store will receive its summer inventory shortly. -------, I would like to begin
                                                              143.
another print and online advertisement campaign to promote our new products.

I would like to feature Mason's new home appliance line, which is made from 100 percent

recycled materials. Lapima Electronic Store is ------- of only two local retailers to offer this line,
                                                144.
so we want it ------- in our ads. -------. You may use these images at will.
            145.   **146.**

Thank you.

Winnie Price
Vice President of Sales, Lapima Electronic Store

143 (A) Accordingly
    (B) Likewise
    (C) Moreover
    (D) Nevertheless

144 (A) some
    (B) both
    (C) one
    (D) other

145 (A) emphasis
    (B) emphasizes
    (C) emphasized
    (D) emphasizing

146 (A) I would like to know what is going on
        with the order.
    (B) I just wanted to remind you that we're
        meeting before the ceremony.
    (C) I ordered a heater from your online store
        last Friday.
    (D) I have attached some photos of the
        electronics for you.

PART 7

Directions: In this part you will read a selection of texts, such as magazine and newspaper articles, e-mails, and instant messages. Each text or set of texts is followed by several questions. Select the best answer for each question and mark the letter (A), (B), (C), or (D) on your answer sheet.

Questions 147-148 refer to the following text message.

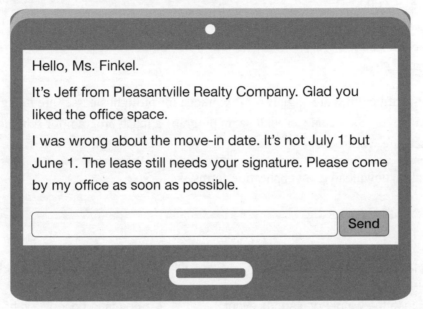

Hello, Ms. Finkel.

It's Jeff from Pleasantville Realty Company. Glad you liked the office space.

I was wrong about the move-in date. It's not July 1 but June 1. The lease still needs your signature. Please come by my office as soon as possible.

Send

147 What is the purpose of the message?

(A) To purchase an apartment
(B) To introduce a moving company
(C) To give directions to an office
(D) To correct some information

148 What is Ms. Finkel asked to do?

(A) Sign a document
(B) Mail a package
(C) Make a donation
(D) Pay some fees

Questions 149-150 refer to the following Web page.

 http://www.sanremowellbeingfoundation.com

San Remo Well-being Foundation is pleased to announce that we are now accepting applicants for our annual grants. Each year, we provide four grants to projects throughout the world that are committed to improving the health and well-being of a community.

The award amounts are detailed below.

◇ First place £2,000
◇ Second place £1,500
◇ Third place £1,000
◇ Fourth place £500

Only not-for-profit entities are eligible for our grants; for-profit businesses are ineligible. Previous years' winners include an adult swim program, a lunch program for schoolchildren, and a series of pet care workshops.

Click this link to download grant application forms.

149 What is the purpose of the Web page?

(A) To solicit a government grant
(B) To announce the winner of a sports event
(C) To encourage participation in an event
(D) To remind people that a new school has opened

150 What have San Remo Well-being grants been used for in the past?

(A) Educating people on how to take care of pets
(B) Organizing singing contests for children
(C) Purchasing medical equipment for community hospitals
(D) Holding an international conference on health

Questions 151-152 refer to the following text message chain.

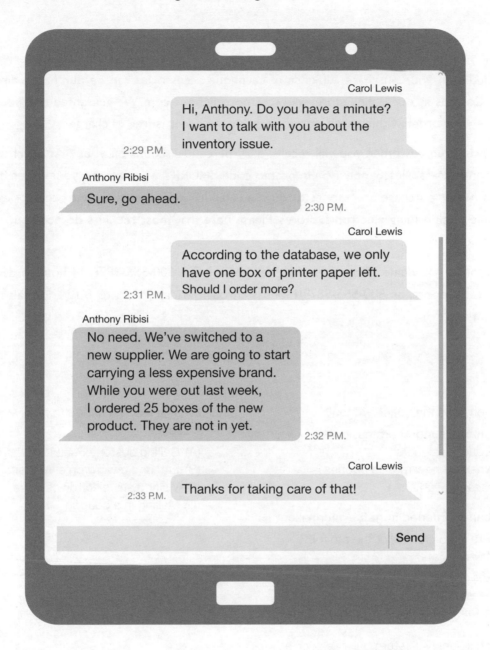

Carol Lewis

Hi, Anthony. Do you have a minute? I want to talk with you about the inventory issue.

2:29 P.M.

Anthony Ribisi

Sure, go ahead.

2:30 P.M.

Carol Lewis

According to the database, we only have one box of printer paper left. Should I order more?

2:31 P.M.

Anthony Ribisi

No need. We've switched to a new supplier. We are going to start carrying a less expensive brand. While you were out last week, I ordered 25 boxes of the new product. They are not in yet.

2:32 P.M.

Carol Lewis

2:33 P.M. Thanks for taking care of that!

Send

151 At 2:30 P.M., what does Mr. Ribisi most likely mean when he writes, "go ahead"?

(A) He has time to answer Ms. Lewis' questions.
(B) He did what Ms. Lewis requested.
(C) He agrees to meet with Ms. Lewis.
(D) He gave Ms. Lewis permission to work on a project.

152 What is mentioned about Ms. Lewis?

(A) She created a new database.
(B) She received a delivery today.
(C) She placed an order last week.
(D) She recently took some time off.

GO ON TO THE NEXT PAGE

Questions 153-155 refer to the following information

Thank you for purchasing a brand-new Cosmos 7 cell phone. An additional battery pack is included in your purchase. All kinds of cellphone accessories can be purchased directly from Cosmos at our online store, www.cosmoscellphone.com. We guarantee that you will receive your order within seven working days or the order is free of charge.

As a preferred customer, you will receive a 20 percent discount off your first purchase of cellphone accessories. Simply type in promo code BHURRY when placing your order. If you would rather purchase accessories through a retail location, our cellphone accessories are available at all leading electronics stores. Please note that most retailers do not honor our corporate discount.

Questions or feedback about your new cell phone? Call 800-555-9876 24 hours a day for technical support, or 800-555-9878 Monday through Friday 7 A.M to 8 P.M. for sales and accounts.

153 For whom was the notice written?

(A) Technical support professionals
(B) Product designers
(C) Owners of new mobile phones
(D) Research workers

154 What can be inferred from the information?

(A) There is no charge for the order if delivery is late.
(B) Sales representatives are available at all times.
(C) The product is under warranty for a full year.
(D) Technicians will return calls as soon as possible.

155 What is recommended to receive a discount?

(A) Calling customer service
(B) Entering a word on a Web site
(C) Visiting any electronics store
(D) Mailing in a coupon

Questions 156-157 refer to the following notice.

Easton's Books is pleased to host a public reading by writer Annette Lyons on Wednesday, August 12, from 3 P.M. to 5 P.M. A two-time winner of the prestigious Reily Award for best science fiction, Ms. Lyons will read excerpts from *Behind the Doors*. This fiction book, the fifth and final installment in her *Kingdoms of the Unknown* series, has topped the best-selling lists and earned enthusiastic praise from book reviewers. Don't miss an opportunity to hear one of the most popular SF authors of the last decade read from her latest work.

Tickets are $5 and can be purchased at Easton's Books, 27 Grey Lane, Memphis, or by calling the store's customer service line at 080-555-4834.

---

156 Who is Ms. Lyons?

(A) A librarian at a famous university
(B) The owner of Easton's Books
(C) A literary critic from a publishing company
(D) The author of a popular book

157 What is mentioned about *Behind the Doors*?

(A) It was written over a ten-year period.
(B) It received an important award.
(C) It is the last book in a series.
(D) It sold more than half a million copies.

GO ON TO THE NEXT PAGE

New Take Off for Edgerton

Vernon City, September 2 – Revised plans for the Edgerton International Airport were presented to the Vernon City Transportation Board by Nina Grant, the project's chief engineer, on August 30. –[1]–.

Plans for the new airport, to be located just west of Vernon City, were first approved three years ago. However, a study commissioned by the Transportation Board last year concluded that the number of passengers traveling by air to the region is expected to increase substantially within the next few years. –[2]–. This is largely a result of the decision by Marcus Hotel Ltd. to open a large beach resort about twenty kilometers north of Vernon City. –[3]–.

Proposed changes include lengthening the runways to accommodate the large-capacity planes, expanding the passenger waiting areas, and adding shopping areas to the passenger terminal. –[4]–.

Board chairperson Jenny Mason noted that the board is likely to approve the revised plans within the month, which will allow the first of four construction phases for the airport to begin in January as originally scheduled.

---

158 What is the reason for the meeting of Ms. Grant and board members?

(A) To request that research be conducted
(B) To announce an appointment of her company's new president
(C) To keep them updated about design plans
(D) To explain why construction work will start later than expected

159 What is suggested about the Edgerton International Airport?

(A) It will be able to accommodate large-capacity planes.
(B) It will be located to the north of Vernon City.
(C) It will have three passenger terminals.
(D) It will have the largest shipping area of any airport in the region.

160 In which of the positions marked [1], [2], [3], and [4] does the following sentence best belong?

"Plans for the design of the airport cargo terminal, already on track to be the largest in the region, remain unchanged."

(A) [1]
(B) [2]
(C) [3]
(D) [4]

Questions 161-164 refer to the following letter.

Whitfield Grocery

July 1

Dear Customer:

Exciting changes are happening at Whitfield Grocery! We hope you will visit us later this month and see the improvements we are making in order to enhance your shopping experience.

As you may know, we have been undergoing a significant renovation that is adding about 8,000 square meters to our store. Beginning on July 10, our produce section will be nearly twice as big, which will allow us to offer a variety of fruits and vegetables and allow you to move around the store with ease. We are also expanding our bakery section to provide you with freshly baked bread.

We will be celebrating the renovations on Saturday, July 20. There will be cooking demonstrations and free food tastings. In addition, we will start opening on Saturdays at 6 A.M. instead of 7 A.M.

To encourage you to visit the new Whitfield Grocery, we have enclosed discount coupons. The coupons are good until July 31. You will also find a calendar indicating special sale days.

Sincerely,

Ann O'Connor
Store manager

161 What is the purpose of the letter?

(A) To publicize the completion of a store renovation
(B) To advertise custom-made baking goods
(C) To announce a change in a store's ownership
(D) To promote a new store location

162 What is NOT mentioned in this letter?

(A) A wider selection of products
(B) Increased floor space
(C) Extended hours of operation
(D) Additional cashiers

163 What is included in the letter?

(A) A questionnaire
(B) A schedule of events
(C) A list of products
(D) A product sample

164 In the letter, the word "good" in paragraph 4, line 2, is closest in meaning to

(A) enough
(B) valid
(C) kind
(D) efficient

MEMO

To: Clarion Market Project Team Members
From: Marijus Fitzgerald
Date: September 4
Subject: Project Results

First, I would like to thank everyone for their hard work with the Clarion Outdoor Market held over the weekend at Jefferson Park. The event was a success overall, raising a large amount of proceeds for the medical center like we had hoped, and will definitely be continued. Nevertheless, we will need to improve a few areas before conducting the second installment of the event the month after next.

The main concern is inclement weather. As many of you noticed, despite the rain on Sunday, we still had a large turnout of guests, which was fantastic. Sadly, we had not prepared for this, and received a number of complaints from both merchants and customers about not having protective coverings on the booths. I have discussed this with staff at the park, and they are willing to provide us with several large tents for future markets.

On another note, we may also want to consider eliminating the registration fee, since some of the merchants complained about a lack of sales. Instead, we could consider collecting a percentage of what they earn in transactions. I would like for everyone to propose another suggestion to alleviate this problem, or perhaps methods that could be used to implement this idea without making the process unnecessarily difficult. If you have any ideas, please send them to Adam Mosley, the outdoor market coordinator.

Marijus Fitzgerald
Director, Clarion Market Project

165 What can be inferred about the Market Project?

(A) It has only been held one time.
(B) It takes place once a month.
(C) It was canceled due to weather.
(D) It will be changing locations.

166 What did the customers complain about?

(A) The expensive registration fee
(B) The lack of protection from rain
(C) The small number of merchants
(D) The low amount of product variety

167 What does Mr. Fitzgerald ask the members of the project to do?

(A) Organize a new event
(B) Contact park officials
(C) Submit some suggestions
(D) Speak with the merchants

Questions 168-171 refer to the following article.

THIS MONTH'S HIGHLIGHT

Susie Murray, who plans to step down as chief accountant in May, has served Harrison Accounting Firm in many capacities for 32 years. –[1]–. The president of the firm, Mario Vinchenso, said, "It's rare to find anyone who has the range of experience at Harrison that Susie has."

Ms. Murray began her career in accounting as a temporary receptionist at Miller Creek Accounting in Milwaukee. –[2]–. She was then hired as a full-time receptionist at Harrison's Norfolk branch. After two years of answering telephones and directing customers' calls, Ms. Murray was hired as a manager at Harrison Accounting's Richmond branch, and in less than a year was promoted to head manager.

–[3]–. Ms. Murray's promotions did not end there, however. She recounted, "I enjoyed working with numbers and wanted to move into the accounting department. My manager at the Richmond branch, Galen Broadbent, gave me advice on how I could achieve my goal. On Galen's recommendation, I decided to pursue an accounting degree at Whitney College in Norfolk, just as Galen had done some years before. –[4]–. By applying for a student loan and continuing to work as a part-time employer, I was able to complete the accounting program in five years."

Once she had received her degree from Whitney College, Ms. Murray joined the accounting department at Harrison Accounting's headquarters. Three years later, she was appointed assistant to Chief Accountant Jeanne Archer, and when Ms. Archer transferred to the commercial accounting division, Ms. Murray was chosen to fill the position. "Just think about that," Ms. Murray said, "I started out handling telephone calls, and I ended up as chief accountant at the firm's headquarters."

168 What is the article mainly about?
(A) An announcement of a result from a customer survey
(B) A variety of open positions at a bank
(C) A reason for holding special training programs
(D) A profile of an employee at an accounting firm

169 What is indicated about Mr. Broadbent?
(A) He is a part-time worker at Harrison.
(B) He was interviewed for the article.
(C) He studied accounting.
(D) He has experience as a professor.

170 What is suggested about Harrison Accounting?
(A) Its headquarters are in Richmond.
(B) It has a commercial accounting division.
(C) Its employees can receive a discount on college tuition.
(D) It recently merged with Miller Creek Accounting.

171 In which of the positions marked [1], [2], [3], and [4] does the following sentence best belong?

"She found the work to be very rewarding and, when her contract ended, began searching for a permanent position in the industry."

(A) [1]
(B) [2]
(C) [3]
(D) [4]

GO ON TO THE NEXT PAGE

Questions 172-175 refer to the following online chat discussion.

Sheila Paxton   — X

Sheila Paxton [10:13 A.M.]   I invited Rob Housewell as one of the guest speakers for our workshop on Friday.

Emily Miller [10:14 A.M.]   That's great! He even won a prestigious Paddington Award for his book, *Attractions and Consumers*. I admire the depth of his insight into our field.

Martin Richards [10:15 A.M.]   Yeah, I know. I heard he is also a great speaker.

Sheila Paxton [10:25 A.M.]   I believe he can inspire our employees to make more creative and appealing advertisements. By the way, I think it would be nice for all of us to take him out to someplace fun while he is in town.

Emily Miller [10:26 A.M.]   If the weather stays nice, maybe we can do something outdoors.

Martin Richards [10:28 A.M.]   What time do you have in mind?

Sheila Paxton [10:29 A.M.]   Well, Professor Housewell told me he has plans for Friday afternoon. He is going to meet with a publisher about the book he is working on.

Emily Miller [10:30 A.M.]   Then we should plan something we can do in the evening.

Martin Richards [10:32 A.M.]   How about dinner at the Thai Restaurant right next to Mendota Lake?

Emily Miller [10:33 A.M.]   Yes! They have great live music on weekend nights.

Martin Richards [10:34 A.M.]   They also have good quality food, and this place also has a great view of the city. Mr. Housewell definitely will love that restaurant.

Sheila Paxton [10:35 A.M.]   I bet! Thank you, guys. When specific schedules come out, I'll let you know.

[   ]   Send

172 At what kind of company do the writers most likely work?

(A) An advertising firm
(B) An accounting office
(C) A publishing company
(D) A catering service

173 What can be inferred about Mr. Housewell?

(A) He teaches management at a local university.
(B) He has written several award-winning books.
(C) He has a meeting and a speech on the same day.
(D) He has met with all of the writers before.

174 What is suggested about the Thai Restaurant?

(A) It is located on the top floor of a building.
(B) It is a waterfront restaurant.
(C) It has music performances every night.
(D) It is open for dinner by reservation only.

175 At 10:35 A.M., what does Ms. Paxton mean when she writes, "I bet"?

(A) She thinks the restaurant is fully booked on Friday.
(B) She is confident that Mr. Housewell will like the place.
(C) She will contact Mr. Housewell in person.
(D) She needs to be in a hurry to organize a workshop.

GO ON TO THE NEXT PAGE

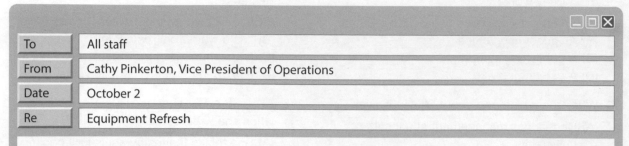

To	All staff
From	Cathy Pinkerton, Vice President of Operations
Date	October 2
Re	Equipment Refresh

Please be reminded that it is again time to place orders for office equipment. Company policy states that standard equipment, such as computers, telephones and fax machines, is eligible for replacement after five years. To replace an item that is any newer, it must be determined that the cost of repair exceeds the cost of replacement. The staff in Purchasing Department will be happy to assist you in researching these costs.

Please use the attached form to list equipment requests. Photocopies of this form may be made as needed. All requests must have the signature of your department manager indicating his or her approval. Note that the Purchasing Department will return the form to its sender if any information is omitted. Make sure that a serial number or ID number appears for the items listed. Forward the completed form to Frank Wong, Purchasing Department, Building C, by October 14. Requests received after that date will be considered in the following quarter.

Thank you for your consideration.

CONNOR CHEMICALS
OFFICE EQUIPMENT ORDER FORM

Employee Name: Martin Jacobs

Title and Department: Quality Control Inspector, Production Department

Equipment Description	Serial Number	Age (years)
Photo Jet Printer	8 HDQ5	5
Computer Monitor		7
Power Cable	PH-3 AL	4

Approved by Daniel Donaldson

Date October 15

176 Why is the memo being sent?

(A) To notify staff about a budget reduction for office equipment

(B) To describe how the cost of office equipment is calculated

(C) To explain the process of new office equipment requests

(D) To revise the manual for the office equipment setup

177 What is mentioned about the forms?

(A) They are reviewed by the operation department once every five years.

(B) They should include the signature of department managers for submission.

(C) They must be submitted to the purchasing office by October 15.

(D) They have been issued in a variety of formats.

178 What is suggested about the power cable?

(A) Its purchase price is less than the repair costs.

(B) Its production was discontinued last year.

(C) It comes with an extended warranty.

(D) It is not compatible with the company's computers.

179 What staff position does Mr. Donaldson most likely hold?

(A) Purchasing director

(B) Repair technician

(C) Production manager

(D) Administrative assistant

180 Why would Mr. Jacobs most likely have the form returned to him?

(A) Because he submitted a photocopy of the form

(B) Because he left out some necessary information

(C) Because he listed equipment for his personal use

(D) Because he needed to obtain Ms. Pinkerton's signature

GO ON TO THE NEXT PAGE

www.tartanairlines.com

| Tartan Airlines | New Services and Special Offers | **Reservations** | Tartan Airlines Plus Program |

Tartan Airlines is proud to offer new services from the Nashik Airport to the following destinations.

Kolkata - September 5
Agra - September 20
Chennai - September 15
Mumbai - September 25

Book a flight now and save money! Members of the Tartan Airlines frequent-flyers program, Tartan Airlines Plus, who book a flight for one of the above inaugural flights, will receive a 25% discount.

Click on Reservations to book a flight now.

Restrictions and other Reminders

** This offer is valid for one-way or round-way travel for flights originating from the Nashik Airport only on the dates specified above.

** Frequent Flyers can receive a 25% discount by using the Tartan Airlines Plus Membership number when reserving their flights.

** Tartan Airlines is no longer issuing paper tickets. Upon purchasing their tickets, passengers receive e-mails confirming their reservations. This includes an 8-digit confirmation number. Please, keep this number handy to speed your check-in process; passengers are asked to enter it at one of the self-check-in stations.

** In order to offer the lowest possible airfares, Tartan Airlines no longer offers free newspapers, magazines, or headsets and no food or snacks are served during flights. Each passenger is entitled to one complimentary beverage; beverage choices include fruit juice, coffee, tea or water.

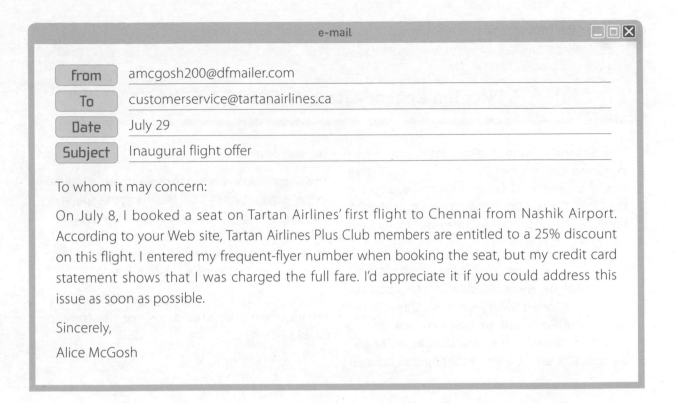

e-mail

from	amcgosh200@dfmailer.com
To	customerservice@tartanairlines.ca
Date	July 29
Subject	Inaugural flight offer

To whom it may concern:

On July 8, I booked a seat on Tartan Airlines' first flight to Chennai from Nashik Airport. According to your Web site, Tartan Airlines Plus Club members are entitled to a 25% discount on this flight. I entered my frequent-flyer number when booking the seat, but my credit card statement shows that I was charged the full fare. I'd appreciate it if you could address this issue as soon as possible.

Sincerely,

Alice McGosh

181 What is NOT mentioned about Tartan Airlines?

(A) It is offering service to four new destinations.
(B) It charges customers a penalty of $25 to change itinerary.
(C) It has stopped providing customers with paper tickets.
(D) It currently provides one soft drink at no charge during flights.

182 According to the information, what must customers do to receive the advertised discount?

(A) Supply their frequent-flyer program number
(B) Make a reservation at least two weeks in advance
(C) Apply for membership in the frequent-flyer program
(D) Purchase tickets to any two of the featured destinations

183 Why did Ms. McGosh send the e-mail?

(A) To complain about delays she experienced on a recent trip
(B) To make a change to her departure date
(C) To ask for a replacement confirmation number
(D) To report a billing mistake with her reservation

184 When is Ms. McGosh scheduled to depart?

(A) On September 5
(B) On September 15
(C) On September 20
(D) On September 25

185 In the e-mail, the word "address" in paragraph 1, line 4, is closest in meaning to

(A) speak
(B) remark
(C) deal with
(D) write

GO ON TO THE NEXT PAGE

Vancouver (March 10)

❈ Regina Regency Resorts Get Bigger ❈

The Seattle-based Regina Hotel Group has acquired Orchid Inc., a small but exclusive locally owned hotel chain. With the addition of the Orchid properties, Regina now operates 11 hotels in the Vancouver area with more than 800 guest rooms.

Prior to the acquisition, Regina had been best known for its Regina Travel Suites, smaller hotels designed with business travelers in mind. Orchid's four properties include the luxurious Grand Hall Hotel, built in 1924, and the Hotel Olivia, a high-end hotel that opened just last year.

The Orchid Hotels are a very welcome addition to the Regina Brand, said Regina spokesperson Douglas Wong. Orchid has a solid reputation in Vancouver, and with accommodations that appeal especially to tourists, they are a perfect complement to Regina's existing hotels.

Regina loyalty-club members can now earn points when they stay at any of the former Orchid Hotels.

Your Home in Vancouver City Center

Visiting Vancouver? Want to be in the heart of the city? Choose Regina Hotel. Our hotel family now includes the popular Orchid Hotels. Below are a few of our most popular hotels in the downtown area.

■Moon Hotel
From complimentary wireless Internet service to deluxe bed, large-screen TVs and an indoor swimming pool. This hotel has something for everyone. Great for families!

■Hotel Fantastic Plaza
"Fantastic" does not begin to describe this hotel! Enjoy our newly refurbished luxurious guest rooms, fine dining at our recently remodeled restaurant, and convenient access to theaters, shopping and sightseeing.

■Hotel South
With free transportation to the airport and a fully equipped business center, this is the perfect hotel for business travelers. It features conference rooms and complimentary wireless Internet service. This hotel makes it easy to work while traveling.

■Cozy Inn
An old-fashioned inn with modern conveniences such as microwaves and hair dryers in every room. With its charming decor, tasty complimentary breakfast, and proximity to public transportation, this is a wonderful place to stay during your Vancouver holiday.

Or choose one of our many other hotels in the Vancouver region. When you choose Regina, you choose the best!

http://vancouverdays.com/review

| RESTAURANTS | HOTELS | ATTRACTIONS | TRANSPORTATION |

I really enjoyed my recent stay at the Hotel Fantastic Plaza. My room was comfortable and well furnished, and all my meals at the hotel restaurant were expertly prepared. The hotel staff provided outstanding service as well. I only wish there had been a shuttle service. I had a difficult time getting a taxi to the airport, and it was expensive. Aside from that minor inconvenience, I enjoyed my stay very much.

Shirley Rogers
London

186 What is the article mainly about?

(A) New trends in the hotel industry
(B) The results of a committee election
(C) The merger of two businesses
(D) Announcement of a new construction site

187 What can be inferred about Regina Regency Resorts?

(A) It is relocating its headquarters.
(B) It has discontinued its membership program.
(C) It specializes in luxury hotels.
(D) It attempts to draw a wider variety of customers.

188 What is indicated about the hotels in the advertisement?

(A) They all have swimming pools.
(B) They were first built in 1920.
(C) They are centrally located in downtown.
(D) They offer discounts to business travelers.

189 In the advertisement, the word "proximity" in paragraph 5, line 2, is closest in meaning to

(A) subsequence
(B) approximation
(C) nearness
(D) possibility

190 What is mentioned about the hotel in which Ms. Rogers has stayed?

(A) It is not far from the shopping place.
(B) Its restaurant recently hired a new chef.
(C) It is wheelchair-accessible.
(D) It offers free admission to the hotel facilities.

GO ON TO THE NEXT PAGE

International Auto Trade Fair

This year's International Auto Trade Fair will be held at the MXFM Convention Center in Detroit from August 6th through 13th, and we will have some of the hottest cars and trucks you've ever seen – all under one roof! More sneak peeks, more new production models, and more concept vehicles than ever before. This year only, Cervi Automotive will be showcasing all of its vehicles from director Meredith Grazinski's blockbuster movie *Before the Sun Goes Down*. Stars of that movie, Peter Wiseman and Alicia Michel, will be on hand on August 11th and 12th to demonstrate some of the vehicles' super effects.

La Siesta

NINTH INTERNATIONAL AUTO TRADE FAIR IN DETROIT

• **Public Show Dates**
Friday, August 6th through Friday, August 13th
11:00 A.M. – 10:30 P.M. (Sunday: 10:00 A.M. – 7:30 P.M.)

• **Special Public Sneak Preview**
Friday, August 6th: 11:00 A.M. – 10:30 P.M.

• **Official Opening Day**
Saturday, August 7th
Festivities begin at 9:00 A.M.
The showroom floor opens at 11:00 A.M.

• **Press Preview**
Wednesday, August 11th & Thursday, August 12th
Media credentials required

• **Dealer Preview**
Thursday, August 12th from 4:00 P.M. – 10:00 P.M. (by invitation only)
Credentials required

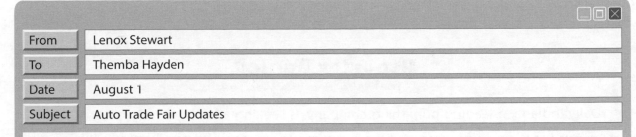

From | Lenox Stewart
To | Themba Hayden
Date | August 1
Subject | Auto Trade Fair Updates

Dear Themba,

I am sorry I couldn't meet with you yesterday. I was busy meeting representatives from the various automakers that will be participating in this year's show. Today, I am meeting with the publicist from Zen Motors at one of its dealerships in the area.

There are a few things I need to talk to you about. The first is that Ms. Michel will not be able to attend the show because of scheduling conflicts with another film she's making. Her agent, Charles Levingston, called yesterday to inform me.

Another problem, and one that could potentially have a more damaging effect, is something that Ms. Woodward in admissions brought to my attention. Apparently all orders for advance tickets were supposed to be accompanied by a certificate that would be good for discounts at area hotels. Unfortunately, only about a third of the people who bought advance tickets received these certificates in time. Ms. Woodward wants to know if we can work out a system where we give the certificates to the people when they arrive for the show, to be retroactively applied to their hotel bills. I like this idea, but let me know what you think.

Sincerely,

Lenox Stewart
Public Relations Manager

191 What is the purpose of the notice?

(A) To explain the details of a new policy
(B) To promote an upcoming event
(C) To advertise a new line of products
(D) To raise money for an organization

192 What is mentioned about the event?

(A) Registration is required to attend.
(B) People can attend before the official opening.
(C) Invitations have been sent to only the media.
(D) A local industry will be hosting it.

193 Who is allowed to attend the Dealer Preview?

(A) All certified dealers
(B) All press officials
(C) Anyone who has paid for advance tickets
(D) People who are invited to come

194 What does Ms. Woodward suggest doing?

(A) Issuing certificates at the convention center
(B) Mailing out letters of apology
(C) Contacting each customer as soon as possible
(D) Waiting to see if there are any complaints

195 Who will probably attend the event on August 12?

(A) Mr. Granzinski
(B) Mr. Wiseman
(C) Ms. Michel
(D) Mr. Levingston

GO ON TO THE NEXT PAGE

Questions 196-200 refer to the following advertisement and e-mails.

Reporter Wanted

Daily Indiana, a leading publishing company, is seeking a reporter to join our team at our location in downtown Bloomington. The successful candidate will have previous experience as a reporter, preferably in a high-profile publishing company. Responsibilities include reading opinions from subscribers, contacting correspondents, processing mail, and other clerical work. This part-time position is 20 hours a week including evening and Saturday hours, which are paid at our overtime rate. Interested individuals should send résumés to hr@dailyindiana.ca.

E–Mail Message

To: hr@dailyindiana.ca
From: lstein@gmail.com
Date: August 8
Subject: Reporter position
Attachment: Stein_résumé; Stein_samples

Dear Human Resources,

I'm writing to express my interest in the reporter position. Though I'm a professional photographer, I have four years of experience working in office settings. While in art school, I worked for three years as an editor at a university newspaper. I also worked in a mailroom of a large corporation. In addition, I'm proficient at several software programs that can be used in editing articles.

Currently, I work as a reporter and photographer at a magazine. Since I only work three mornings a week, I want additional work to fill out my schedule. Though this would be my first job in a newspaper company, I'm willing to learn new skills, and the skills I have would be an asset to you. I'm sending my résumé and my sample work when I worked as an editor in a university newspaper. They demonstrate my writing and interview skills. I look forward to hearing from you and appreciate your consideration.

Sincerely,

Lucy Stein

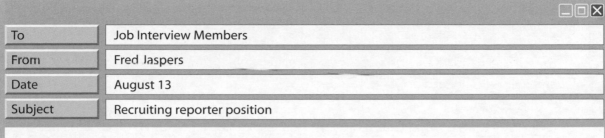

To	Job Interview Members
From	Fred Jaspers
Date	August 13
Subject	Recruiting reporter position

Hello, everyone.

Our final interview will take place tomorrow at 9:30 A.M. We will be interviewing Ms. Stein. Please read the materials that she submitted so that the information is fresh in your mind during the interview. I know that some of you are concerned about her qualifications, but she could be easily trained to do routine office tasks. In my opinion, she offers much more. In fact, the materials she submitted demonstrate a creativity that could really spice up our marketing materials. If you would like to discuss anything before the interview, please contact me.

Fred

---

196 According to the advertisement, what is a duty of the reporter position?

(A) Reviewing feedback
(B) Scheduling board meetings
(C) Writing editorials
(D) Calling subscribers

197 What aspect of the position is likely the most appealing to Ms. Stein?

(A) The newspaper's reputation
(B) The downtown location
(C) The job responsibilities
(D) The work schedule

198 What is indicated about Ms. Stein?

(A) She is currently writing for a newspaper company.
(B) She will enroll as an art student.
(C) She has never worked for a newspaper before.
(D) She will relocate to Bloomington.

199 What is the purpose of the second e-mail?

(A) To encourage more interviewers to participate in the board
(B) To ask the job interview members to review some materials
(C) To remind staff members that an interview has been canceled
(D) To inform new employers about an orientation session

200 What does Mr. Jaspers think makes Ms. Stein a good candidate for the position?

(A) Her experience as an editor
(B) Her availability for extended work hours
(C) Her expertise in dealing with clients
(D) Her skills as a computer programmer

Stop! This is the end of the test. If you finish before time is called, you may go back to Parts 5, 6, and 7 and check your work.

等等！開始前務必確認！

- 將書桌整理成和實際測試時一樣，做好心理準備。
- 將手機關機，使用手錶計時。
- 限制時間為 120 分鐘。一定要遵守時間限制。
- 不要因為困難就跳過。盡可能依照順序解題。

Actual Test

03

 開始時間 ：

結束時間 ：

 ♪ 標準版-03

 ♪ 白噪音版-03

LISTENING TEST

In the Listening test, you will be asked to demonstrate how well you understand spoken English. The entire Listening test will last approximately 45 minutes. There are four parts, and directions are given for each part. You must mark your answers on the separate answer sheet. Do not write your answers in your test book.

PART 1

Directions: For each question in this part, you will hear four statements about a picture in your test book. When you hear the statements, you must select the one statement that best describes what you see in the picture. Then find the number of the question on your answer sheet and mark your answer. The statements will not be printed in your test book and will be spoken only one time.

Example

Sample Answer

Statement (B), "The man is working at a desk," is the best description of the picture, so you should select answer (B) and mark it on your answer sheet.

1

2

GO ON TO THE NEXT PAGE

3

4

5

6

GO ON TO THE NEXT PAGE

PART 2

Directions: You will hear a question or statement and three responses spoken in English. They will not be printed in your test book and will be spoken only one time. Select the best response to the question or statement and mark the letter (A), (B), or (C) on your answer sheet.

7 Mark your answer on your answer sheet.

8 Mark your answer on your answer sheet.

9 Mark your answer on your answer sheet.

10 Mark your answer on your answer sheet.

11 Mark your answer on your answer sheet.

12 Mark your answer on your answer sheet.

13 Mark your answer on your answer sheet.

14 Mark your answer on your answer sheet.

15 Mark your answer on your answer sheet.

16 Mark your answer on your answer sheet.

17 Mark your answer on your answer sheet.

18 Mark your answer on your answer sheet.

19 Mark your answer on your answer sheet.

20 Mark your answer on your answer sheet.

21 Mark your answer on your answer sheet.

22 Mark your answer on your answer sheet.

23 Mark your answer on your answer sheet.

24 Mark your answer on your answer sheet.

25 Mark your answer on your answer sheet.

26 Mark your answer on your answer sheet.

27 Mark your answer on your answer sheet.

28 Mark your answer on your answer sheet.

29 Mark your answer on your answer sheet.

30 Mark your answer on your answer sheet.

31 Mark your answer on your answer sheet.

PART 3

Directions: You will hear some conversations between two or more people. You will be asked to answer three questions about what the speakers say in each conversation. Select the best response to each question and mark the letter (A), (B), (C), or (D) on your answer sheet. The conversations will not be printed in your test book and will be spoken only one time.

32 What item does the man ask about?

(A) A color printer
(B) A copy machine
(C) A laptop
(D) A scanner

33 What does the woman say will happen next month?

(A) New equipment will be purchased.
(B) She will resign from her company.
(C) A new model will be released.
(D) Her work location will change.

34 What does the woman offer to do for the man?

(A) Remain after work
(B) Discount a price
(C) Speak with a seller
(D) Arrange a delivery

35 What is the purpose of the man's call?

(A) To request a discount
(B) To make a payment
(C) To inquire about a bill
(D) To open an account

36 What type of business is the man calling?

(A) A bank
(B) An Internet service provider
(C) An electric company
(D) An insurance company

37 What does the woman offer to do?

(A) Give a discount
(B) Fix some device
(C) Provide new service
(D) Return a payment

38 What does the woman say about the employee from Mitchell Cleaning?

(A) He was late for the meeting.
(B) He offered a persuasive deal.
(C) He left a product pamphlet.
(D) He will stop by the next day.

39 What does Oscar say about the company's current cleaning service?

(A) It is highly dependable.
(B) It charges less money.
(C) It has an international reputation.
(D) It offers a discount.

40 What does the woman suggest?

(A) Keeping the current service
(B) Negotiating better service
(C) Postponing a decision
(D) Searching for a different service

41 Who most likely is the man talking to?

(A) A tour conductor
(B) A secretary
(C) A manager
(D) A taxi driver

42 What will the man do next Monday?

(A) Tour the city
(B) Attend a convention
(C) Meet his friend
(D) See a client

43 How long will the man be away?

(A) About three days
(B) About a week
(C) More than two weeks
(D) More than a month

GO ON TO THE NEXT PAGE

44 What most likely did the man do last week?

(A) He emailed a document.
(B) He sent a floor plan.
(C) He changed the schedule.
(D) He analyzed the sales data.

45 What does the woman mean when she says, "There is just one thing that worries me"?

(A) The budget may not be sufficient.
(B) Information could have been missing.
(C) The layout might need adjusting.
(D) There may be a shortage of staff.

46 What does the man say he will do?

(A) Send the woman the modified document
(B) Call the woman later in the day
(C) Give the woman his feedback
(D) Visit the woman's office

47 Who most likely are the speakers?

(A) Company executives
(B) Business consultants
(C) New interns
(D) Seminar organizers

48 What does the man want to know about the workshops?

(A) The dates
(B) The registration fees
(C) The levels
(D) The attendees

49 What does the woman tell the man to do?

(A) Apply for the position
(B) Organize the event
(C) Speak to a manager
(D) Contact the person in charge

50 What will the speakers' company do in Europe during the fall?

(A) Conclude a research study
(B) Launch a product line
(C) Construct a new facility
(D) Open a new branch

51 Why does the woman say, "That's great. Congratulations"?

(A) The man was promoted to an executive position.
(B) The man finished a project ahead of schedule.
(C) The man enrolled in a well-known university.
(D) The man was given an important assignment.

52 According to the man, what will a former coworker help him do?

(A) Locate a residence
(B) Arrange transportation
(C) Prepare for a course
(D) Make professional contacts

53 Where does the conversation most likely take place?

(A) At a bus stop
(B) On a plane
(C) At an airport
(D) At a city center

54 What will the woman probably do next?

(A) Take a shuttle bus
(B) Purchase a ticket
(C) Exchange money
(D) Take a taxi

55 How many shuttle buses run per hour?

(A) One
(B) Two
(C) Three
(D) Four

56 What does Angela suggest doing?

(A) Remodeling the office
(B) Repainting a sign
(C) Selecting colors
(D) Buying more paint

57 What will most likely happen tomorrow?

(A) Angela will use the paint.
(B) Nathan will throw away the materials.
(C) Ms. Morris will install the shelves.
(D) They will go to the head office.

58 What does the man say he will do?

(A) Consult with his colleague
(B) Hire a professional
(C) Attend a workshop
(D) Renovate a staff lounge

---

59 What are the speakers mainly talking about?

(A) A missing flight
(B) A lost item
(C) A delayed flight
(D) A rude passenger

60 What does the woman mean when she says, "I'll start looking into it"?

(A) She will start an investigation.
(B) She will check out some information.
(C) She will book a flight.
(D) She will contact a colleague.

61 What does the woman ask the man to give her?

(A) Some traveler's checks
(B) His boarding pass
(C) His passport
(D) Some documents

The Triumph Building Directory

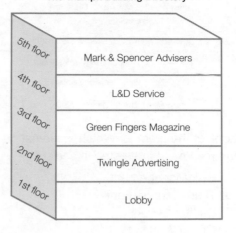

5th floor	Mark & Spencer Advisers
4th floor	L&D Service
3rd floor	Green Fingers Magazine
2nd floor	Twingle Advertising
1st floor	Lobby

62 What kind of company has moved out of the building?

(A) An accounting company
(B) A legal office
(C) An advertising agency
(D) A publishing company

63 Look at the graphic. At what company do the speakers most likely work?

(A) Mark & Spencer Advisers
(B) L&D Service
(C) Green Fingers Magazine
(D) Tingle Advertising

64 What does the man suggest?

(A) Reviewing a document
(B) Planning an event
(C) Visiting a friend
(D) Hiring a lawyer

GO ON TO THE NEXT PAGE

Management & Marketing Conference Presentations in July
Dr. Edward Williamson, Risk Management
Dr. Raymond Gomez, Time Management
Dr. Hillary Palin, Decision Making
Dr. Jina Hong, Group Working

65 Look at the graphic. Which presentation is the man most interested in seeing?

(A) Risk Management
(B) Time Management
(C) Decision Making
(D) Group Working

66 What does the woman advise the man to do?

(A) Arrive at the venue early
(B) Make a reservation
(C) Contact a presenter
(D) Create a credit card

67 According to the woman, what can the man do at the Web site?

(A) Sign up for the conference
(B) Access research data
(C) Check out the schedule
(D) Confirm the credit card number

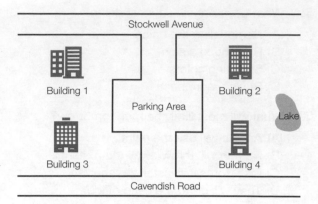

68 What does the man say is a near-term goal of the company?

(A) Reducing expenses
(B) Producing more energy
(C) Opening a new branch
(D) Completing a project

69 What does the woman say is ideal?

(A) The amount of sunlight
(B) Weather condition
(C) The worksite
(D) The work hours

70 Look at the graphic. Where will the installation be done?

(A) On building 1
(B) On building 2
(C) On building 3
(D) On building 4

PART 4

Directions: You will hear some talks given by a single speaker. You will be asked to answer three questions about what the speaker says in each talk. Select the best response to each question and mark the letter (A), (B), (C), or (D) on your answer sheet. The talks will not be printed in your test book and will be spoken only one time.

71 What is the purpose of the talk?

(A) To prepare for a meeting
(B) To vote on a proposal
(C) To change a presenter
(D) To appoint a project manager

72 What does the speaker suggest?

(A) Arriving ahead of time
(B) Postponing a meeting date
(C) Making a presentation
(D) Cutting a budget

73 Where are listeners asked to meet tomorrow morning?

(A) At a café
(B) In a parking lot
(C) At the park
(D) In a seminar room

74 Who most likely are the listeners?

(A) Office workers
(B) Computer technicians
(C) Packaging designers
(D) Factory workers

75 What is an advantage of the new machine?

(A) It uses less power.
(B) It requires fewer operators.
(C) It performs more quickly.
(D) It is easier to maintain.

76 According to the speaker, what will Ms. Miller do next?

(A) Distribute some documents
(B) Contact another department
(C) Give a demonstration
(D) Install some equipment

77 What kind of business is Ms. Holton calling?

(A) An architectural firm
(B) An art gallery
(C) An event agency
(D) A real estate agency

78 What does the speaker mean when she says, "that'll be all"?

(A) She thinks the event will finish soon.
(B) She has completed preparations.
(C) She bought new equipment.
(D) She has found what she was looking for.

79 What does Ms. Holton say she will do next week?

(A) Sign a contract
(B) Contact a manager
(C) Visit a client
(D) Revise an estimate

80 What is main topic of this report?

(A) The results of a sports match
(B) The completion of roadwork
(C) The expansion of a stadium
(D) The construction of a tennis court

81 According to the report, what caused the delay?

(A) Insufficient funding
(B) A legal dispute
(C) A supply shortage
(D) Inclement weather

82 What does the speaker say about the Wimbledon Tennis Tournament?

(A) It will attract many people to the area.
(B) It will not start on schedule.
(C) It is causing some traffic detours.
(D) It is held on a regular basis.

GO ON TO THE NEXT PAGE

83 What will the listener most likely do on Friday morning?

(A) View product samples
(B) Reserve a place
(C) Make a phone call
(D) Create a window display

84 Why is the speaker calling?

(A) To report an error
(B) To reschedule an appointment
(C) To give a reminder
(D) To make a sale

85 What does the speaker mean when he says, "I've really got to hand it to you"?

(A) He wants to give an item to the listener.
(B) He needs to rearrange the window display.
(C) He wants to offer the listener help.
(D) He thinks the listener deserves praise.

86 What type of information does Developing Yourself probably focus on?

(A) Developing new products
(B) Fashion trends
(C) Technological innovations
(D) Career advice

87 According to the broadcast, what has Sarah Parker done?

(A) She published a book.
(B) She ran a school.
(C) She took an online course.
(D) She owned a company.

88 What will Ms. Parker do at the end of the show?

(A) Take calls from listeners
(B) Introduce another guest
(C) Attend the educational training
(D) Make a questionnaire

89 What is the purpose of the talk?

(A) To announce a new policy
(B) To introduce a new employee
(C) To plan a company event
(D) To inform about a business hour

90 What does the speaker mean when she says, "So, we're lucky"?

(A) The company has received the media attention.
(B) Brian Price has accepted the job offer.
(C) Glen Keys will join the company.
(D) The company has been highly ranked in the industry.

91 What will most likely happen next?

(A) The employees will introduce themselves.
(B) There will be a discussion session.
(C) The staff will submit the forms.
(D) Mr. Price will speak about the company's future.

92 Why is the speaker calling?

(A) To congratulate on the success
(B) To complete the sales report
(C) To decline an invitation
(D) To confirm a meeting agenda

93 What does the speaker mean when he says, "A lot has to be done over and over again"?

(A) He bought several computers.
(B) He lost some of his work.
(C) He attended a variety of workshops.
(D) He needed to call a manager repeatedly.

94 According to the speaker, what did a department manager ask for?

(A) A deadline extension
(B) A personal visit
(C) Modification of information
(D) Completion of a questionnaire

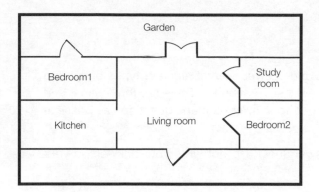

95 What type of business do the listeners probably work for?

(A) A furniture dealer
(B) An interior design agency
(C) A cleaning service
(D) A moving company

96 Look at the graphic. Where should the green boxes be placed?

(A) Bedroom 1
(B) Bedroom 2
(C) The study room
(D) The living room

97 What does the speaker say Ms. Clarkson will do?

(A) Leave the entrance open
(B) Unpack some boxes
(C) Clean up the new home
(D) Lock up some valuable items

98 What kind of event is going to be held?

(A) A product launch
(B) A business gathering
(C) A sales workshop
(D) A special dinner

99 Look at the graphic. Which venue does the speaker recommend?

(A) Lloyds Building
(B) Wallace Center
(C) Mansion House
(D) Duke Hall

100 How can the listeners contact the speaker?

(A) By text message
(B) By electronic mail
(C) By fax
(D) By extension phone

This is the end of the Listening test. Turn to Part 5 in your test book.

GO ON TO THE NEXT PAGE

READING TEST

In the Reading test, you will read a variety of texts and answer several different types of reading comprehension questions. The entire Reading test will last 75 minutes. There are three parts, and directions are given for each part. You are encouraged to answer as many questions as possible within the time allowed.

You must mark your answers on the separate answer sheet. Do not write your answers in your test book.

PART 5

Directions: A word or phrase is missing in each of the sentences below. Four answer choices are given below each sentence. Select the best answer to complete the sentence. Then mark the letter (A), (B), (C), or (D) on your answer sheet.

101 ------- new dental office will occupy the third floor of the new building on Mason Street.

(A) We
(B) Our
(C) Ours
(D) Us

102 Bus passengers ------- bicycles are responsible for securing them appropriately.

(A) with
(B) over
(C) of
(D) from

103 The advance deposit is ------- refundable as long as the rental car is returned without damage.

(A) full
(B) fully
(C) fuller
(D) fullest

104 ------ has worked harder than Lisa Stanley to market New Skin's new line of hair treatment products.

(A) Whoever
(B) Nothing
(C) Nobody
(D) Any

105 The ------- of the construction project was covered by a generous donation from some local entrepreneurs.

(A) currency
(B) benefit
(C) account
(D) cost

106 Please remember to double-check the spelling of Mr. Prichard's name when ------- the document.

(A) revising
(B) revises
(C) revised
(D) revise

107 Recruiting interns is a ------- solution to filling entry-level positions eventually at Cypher Bank.

(A) talented
(B) various
(C) willing
(D) sensible

108 Delegates visited the mayor to ask ------- developers will preserve the work of ancient artisans.

(A) although
(B) since
(C) whether
(D) both

109 Workers now send in travel requests electronically ------- submitting a paper form.

(A) instead of
(B) because of
(C) through
(D) which

110 Tenants who are ------- in renewing their lease should follow the process outlined on the Lakeview Apartments Web site.

(A) interest
(B) interests
(C) interested
(D) interesting

111 Juan Reyes, the newest employee of the Manheim Film Production, ------- worked in London for eight years.

(A) consequently
(B) always
(C) still
(D) previously

112 ------- Ms. Jenkins wrote her thesis on housing markets, she knew how to make profitable property investments.

(A) Either
(B) Rather
(C) Unless
(D) Because

113 At the Board meeting, it was mentioned that there is a slight ------- that the Carmichael Arts Center will be closed.

(A) possible
(B) possibility
(C) possibly
(D) possibilities

114 ------ receiving the prestigious Evangeline Award, Ms. Mehta made a point of thanking her long-time colleagues.

(A) Onto
(B) Unlike
(C) About
(D) Upon

115 Because the rates for the Wellington Hotel were very high, Logisoft Inc. will hold a workshop ------- this year.

(A) seldom
(B) recently
(C) somewhat
(D) elsewhere

116 Dr. Di Scala indicates that important shopping trends become ------- with the use of data analysis.

(A) predict
(B) prediction
(C) predictable
(D) predictably

117 ------- to Braxton Drive will be limited to one side of the street after the road work begins next month.

(A) Access
(B) Accesses
(C) Accessible
(D) Accessing

118 Professor Hillsman's ------- for teaching at Malkin College remains still strong at the age of 65.

(A) enthusiasm
(B) assortment
(C) likeness
(D) inclusion

119 To be eligible for the Jessie's Electronics discount, you must submit the coupon ------- in the mail.

(A) has sent
(B) have to send
(C) that was sent
(D) for sending

120 With the rainy season, Faye's Bicycle Rentals will most likely have ------- customers this month.

(A) neither
(B) every
(C) fewer
(D) higher

GO ON TO THE NEXT PAGE

121 ------- all interview processes have been completed, the top three candidates for the advertising director position will be contacted.

(A) Compared to
(B) As soon as
(C) So that
(D) Not only

122 ------- the assigned speaking time not work for you, please let Ms. Everett know, so she can rearrange the presentation schedule.

(A) Whenever
(B) Anywhere
(C) As well as
(D) Should

123 The hiring committee will ------- an offer of employment to Dwan Willis next Monday.

(A) extend
(B) assign
(C) displace
(D) commit

124 If you lose your identification card, the security manager will deactivate it and issue -------.

(A) other
(B) other one
(C) one another
(D) another

125 City inspectors will evaluate every office on 5th floor next week ------- determine how to best reduce energy usage.

(A) even if
(B) in order to
(C) after all
(D) given that

126 To select its Audit Committee members, Blake Techline Ltd. ------- employees who are ready for a challenge.

(A) seeking
(B) is seeking
(C) are sought
(D) have been sought

127 Ms. Perone provided an explanation of recent changes to keep the funding arrangement process as ------- as possible.

(A) interested
(B) forceful
(C) transparent
(D) remarkable

128 The workplace safety at Glaxton-Jenner Company is something ------- will never be compromised.

(A) where
(B) that
(C) when
(D) then

129 Relevant documents are ------- delivered to the lawyer's office by our secretary from the Legal Department.

(A) timely
(B) identifiably
(C) highly
(D) typically

130 Technicians will inspect the historic Karen Marx Building next week to ------- the building is still architecturally sound.

(A) ensure
(B) measure
(C) modify
(D) accept

PART 6

Directions: Read the texts that follow. A word, phrase, or sentence is missing in parts of each text. Four answer choices for each question are given below the text. Select the best answer to complete the text. Then mark the letter (A), (B), (C), or (D) on your answer sheet.

Questions 131-134 refer to the following memo.

From: Jin Li Zhang
To: All staff
Date: April 10
Subject: Natalie Albright

As some of you know, Natalie Albright, our head landscaper, will soon be leaving our company.

She has ------- a position in residential construction industry. Natalie has been interested in that
         131.

field for some time. -------. Even so, we are ------- sorry to see her go.
                    132.   133.

Natalie's last day with us is Friday, 25, April. At 2:30 P.M., on that day, we have a farewell

gathering in company cafeteria ------- her ten year service with us. We look forward to seeing you
                               134.

all.

Marry Rogers
Facilities Director

131 (A) advertised
(B) supported
(C) accepted
(D) indicated

132 (A) Her new job is more in line with her ultimate goal of becoming construction engineer.
(B) Managers meetings will move from 10 A.M. to 2 P.M. starting next Monday.
(C) The human resources director will explain health insurance offered by the company.
(D) Employees are required to arrive at work at least five minutes before 9 A.M. every day.

133 (A) very
(B) rather
(C) too
(D) such

134 (A) has recognized
(B) is recognizing
(C) would recognize
(D) to recognize

GO ON TO THE NEXT PAGE

Questions 135-138 refer to the following brochure excerpt.

-------. Sponsored by the Bronxville Visitor Bureau, each tour is led ------- a knowledgeable guide
    135.   **136.**
and features a unique area of town.

The most popular focuses on Cyrus Square are the town's theater -------.
                                                     137.

In addition to three playhouses and two music halls, Cyrus Square includes an opera house and several historic hotels that represent a range of architectural styles. The tour lasts approximately two hours and ------- with a delicious meal at the Waterfront Café, one of Bronxville's best known
                         138.
dining establishments.

To register for the Cyrus Square tour or learn about the other tours, call the Bronxville Visitor Bureau at 555-0114.

135 (A) Customers waited in line for six hours to purchase new guide books and city maps.
    (B) Explore the town of Bronxville through one of our four regularly scheduled walking tours.
    (C) The city gallery will feature relics about the Tang Dynasty in its spring exhibit.
    (D) We think it's a great idea that will generate more revenue from the sale of food and beverages.

136 (A) for
    (B) by
    (C) during
    (D) behind

137 (A) actors
    (B) programs
    (C) district
    (D) school

138 (A) exits
    (B) orders
    (C) reserves
    (D) concludes

Questions 139-142 refer to the following memo.

From: Gabrielle Rothschild, Building Manager
To: All employees
Date: Thursday, August 9
Re: Construction work

As you are -------, renovations to our office building will begin on Monday, August 13, and
       139.
continue until the end of the day on Friday, August 17. As a result, you may experience some

-------.
140.

-------. Employees who regularly use this elevator should take the stairs or use the elevator on
141.
the south side of the building.

-------, the entrance on the northwest side of the building facing Ali Avenue will be closed on
142.
Tuesday through Thursday. All other entrances to the building will be open as usual during this

time.

139 (A) helpful
(B) aware
(C) informing
(D) famous

140 (A) inconvenience
(B) assignment
(C) addition
(D) interference

141 (A) Noise levels must be kept at a minimum
at all times.
(B) Please dispose of garbage in the proper
receptacles.
(C) The north-side elevator will be out of
service for the entire week.
(D) Employees are forbidden from entering
private area designated for CEO.

142 (A) However
(B) Instead
(C) Previously
(D) Also

Questions 143-146 refer to the following news article.

July 1 – Beginning in September, the South Central School District will rely ------- on Chester
                                                                               143.
Educational Publishing Group for health-related learning and teaching materials. -------.
                                                                                  144.

As of July 30, the school board ------- its contracts with the other two vendors. This decision
                                 145.
was based on a survey of teachers and school nurses, who attested to the superior quality

of Chester's products. ------- the cost of Chester's textbooks is high, its workbooks, models,
                        146.
and teacher's guides are less expensive than those of its competitors, helping to keep overall

expenditures within budget.

143 (A) formally
(B) periodically
(C) initially
(D) solely

144 (A) Thank you for your cooperation in
abiding by all the teaching rules.
(B) Users of the Web site will be able to
download the files for teaching.
(C) Chester also work closely with teachers
to provide bilingual assistance if
necessary.
(D) Historically, Chester was one of three
preferred vendors for such content.

145 (A) was discontinuing
(B) is discontinued
(C) will discontinue
(D) would have discontinued

146 (A) Even though
(B) Unless
(C) Because
(D) As soon as

PART 7

Directions: In this part you will read a selection of texts, such as magazine and newspaper articles, e-mails, and instant messages. Each text or set of texts is followed by several questions. Select the best answer for each question and mark the letter (A), (B), (C), or (D) on your answer sheet.

Questions 147-148 refer to the following tag.

JUNG & JO APPAREL
MEDIUM

100% wool

Wash by hand or by machine on gentle cycle with similar colors.
Wash in cold water only.
Machine dry on coolest setting.

Please note that variations in color are an intended feature of this fabric.
With repeated washing, texture also may alter further.

Made in Italy

---

147 According to the tag, how should the item be care for?

(A) By washing it at a low temperature
(B) By drying it for a specific time
(C) By soaking it in warm water
(D) By wiping it with a damp cloth

148 What is stated about the item?

(A) It was made by hand.
(B) It will shrink after washing.
(C) It may change in texture.
(D) It was produced in France.

GO ON TO THE NEXT PAGE

Questions 149-150 refer to the following advertisement.

Major Technical Institute

Are you considering returning to school? Education can be an important part of your career path, and Major Tech. is pleased to offer a variety of continuing-education courses for the busy professional. In addition to our regular daytime course offerings, we now offer classes online that conveniently fit into anyone's schedules.

Choose from many training programs, including computer networking, food preparation, and medical technology. Consult our Web site www.majortech.edu for a complete list of courses available.

For detailed information regarding our certification programs, please contact admission at 090-555-7890 or send an e-mail to info@majortech.edu.

149 According to the advertisement, what is a recent development at Major Tech.?

(A) Courses over Internet
(B) Free consultation for graduates
(C) A revised admission policy
(D) Brand-new computers and monitors

150 What is NOT stated as a way to learn more about Major Tech.?

(A) Making a phone call
(B) Sending an e-mail
(C) Visiting the Web site
(D) Going to the campus

Questions 151-153 refer to the following Web page.

http://fantasticspain.com

Fantastic Spain Travels

| HOME | DESTINATIONS | REVIEW | CONTACT |

Recently, a colleague and I were on business in Madrid and had a free day for sightseeing. On advice from the clerk at the front desk of our hotel, we booked a tour of the royal palace through Fantastic Spain Travels (FST). It was my colleague's first chance to see this attraction and my second. The first time I visited, though, I was with a large group. I felt very rushed and was not able to really appreciate the palace or take as many photos as I would have liked. This time, I was happy to book a pricier private excursion, led by guide Juan Dominguez.

In contrast to my last tour, which did not include transportation, Mr. Dominguez took us to the palace by car. We could tell that Mr. Dominguez's historical knowledge was extensive. Since my colleague and I were his only clients, we were able to ask a lot of questions and took our time.

I was pleased that the entrance fees were covered by the excursion price, and that FST obtained our tickets in advance, so that we would not have to wait in line when we arrived. Lunch at a delicious local restaurant was provided, so we didn't even have to spend time looking for a good place to eat.

This tour is a great value and much more worth the price.

Jane Weatherly (Calcutta, Australia)

151 Who introduced FST to Ms. Weatherly?

(A) A travel agent
(B) A business associate
(C) A hotel employee
(D) A local friend

152 What was NOT covered in the price of tour?

(A) A souvenir photograph
(B) A meal
(C) Transportation
(D) Admission charges

153 What is suggested about Ms. Weatherly?

(A) She travels often for business.
(B) She is Mr. Dominguez's colleague.
(C) She has visited Madrid before.
(D) She is interested in Spanish history.

Questions 154-155 refer to the following text message chain.

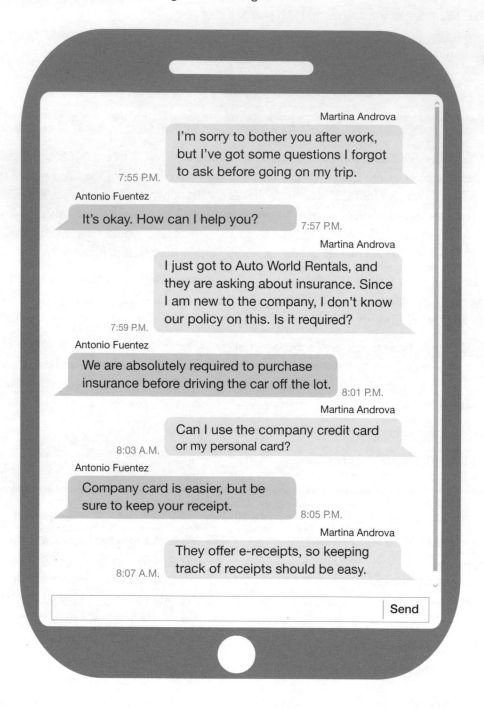

Martina Androva

I'm sorry to bother you after work, but I've got some questions I forgot to ask before going on my trip.

7:55 P.M.

Antonio Fuentez

It's okay. How can I help you?

7:57 P.M.

Martina Androva

I just got to Auto World Rentals, and they are asking about insurance. Since I am new to the company, I don't know our policy on this. Is it required?

7:59 P.M.

Antonio Fuentez

We are absolutely required to purchase insurance before driving the car off the lot.

8:01 P.M.

Martina Androva

Can I use the company credit card or my personal card?

8:03 A.M.

Antonio Fuentez

Company card is easier, but be sure to keep your receipt.

8:05 P.M.

Martina Androva

They offer e-receipts, so keeping track of receipts should be easy.

8:07 A.M.

Send

---

154 At 7:57 P.M., what does Mr. Fuentez mean when he writes, "It's okay"?

(A) Ms. Androva can submit proof of purchase electronically.

(B) Information on company travel is easy for Ms. Androva to obtain.

(C) He suggests that Ms. Androva not purchase insurance.

(D) He is willing to answer Ms. Androva's questions.

155 What is indicated about Ms. Androva?

(A) She has applied for a credit card.

(B) She is recently hired at the company.

(C) She would like a refund for travel expenses.

(D) She needs transportation to an airport.

Questions 156-157 refer to the following notice.

Ranger Carpet Store

2389 Market Street

Laramie, WY 39877

902-555-0145 www.rangercarpet.ca

Don't miss out our special event on October 2!

As one of our best customers, you are invited to a special event marketing the introduction of Comfortzone, a new line of carpets featuring a revolutionary new carpet fiber. Factory tests show that Comfortzone carpets trap up to 25 percent less dirt and last longer than comparably priced carpets. And if you purchase a Comfortzone carpet at our store on October 2, you can save up to 40 percent off the regular price. Simply bring this notice to our store on October 2 and show it to a store employee to gain admission to the Comfortzone show room. We look forward to seeing you!

156 What is indicated about Comfortzone carpets?

(A) They come in a variety of colors.
(B) They are produced with a special new material.
(C) They last 40% longer than more expensive carpets.
(D) They can be delivered complimentarily.

157 How can a customer quality for a discount on a Comfortzone carpet?

(A) By ordering the carpet online
(B) By participating in a store event
(C) By presenting a document
(D) By completing a customer survey

GO ON TO THE NEXT PAGE

May 10 – Media Tree, the company that contributed to artwork for the popular Look at Others billboard campaign, has been nominated for the prestigious Malta Award, which has been recognizing innovation in published artwork and illustration for 40 years. Selected from almost 2,000 entrants, Media Tree is the first Taipei-based illustration studio to be nominated for the artwork. –[1]–. All of this year's Malta Award winners will be announced on June 15 during a ceremony in London.

 "We are very excited about this nomination, which is a testament to the high level of skill, expertise, and creativity of our staff," said Melinda Bonner, founder and CEO of the company.

–[2]–. The Malta Award judges, a group of twelve leading art executives from museums and galleries across the globe, noted that Media Tree was nominated based on the diversity, quality, and sophistication of its portfolio of art. "We illustrate everything from magazines and children's literature to cosmetics and food packaging," noted Ms. Bonner, "and we work closely with our clients to ensure the end product exceeds their expectations."

–[3]–. Since the names of the nominees were released, the studio has seen a large increase in the number of requests for its services. "There is no way we can meet the growing demand unless we hire more illustrators and project managers. Of course, that's exactly what we are going to do now," said Ms. Bonner.

More information about Media Tree can be found at www.mediatree.co.in. Details about the Malta Award are at www.maltaaward.org. –[4]–.

158 What is suggested about the Malta Award?

(A) It was established by a single individual.
(B) It has been awarded to advertising companies before.
(C) It gives cash prizes to its recipients.
(D) It was first awarded forty years ago.

159 According to the article, what does Ms. Bonner plan to do?

(A) Recruit new employees
(B) Open a second branch
(C) Decrease the publicity budget
(D) Attend a ceremony in Taipei

160 In which of the positions marked [1], [2], [3], and [4] does the following sentence best belong?

"Apart from the honor, the nomination has produced publicity and increased business for Media Tree."

(A) [1]
(B) [2]
(C) [3]
(D) [4]

PERFECT HEALTH AND FITNESS CENTER
Notes from the Board Meeting

■**Financial**

Last year ended with a surplus of £3,100. This year's budget is estimated to have a surplus of £6,291.

■**Membership/Retention**

This year is starting off strong in terms of membership numbers. January's New Year's Bash brought in 176 new members.

Not including the New Year's Bash, Fitness Center memberships were up 8% in January. In an effort to continue increasing membership, we are implementing a free one-week trial period.

Total membership is up from January last year, reflecting new membership sales as well as an increased percentage of renewing members. Membership usage has increased, which has caused some concern especially in the facilities located near office parks. We will need to address parking and locker availability in the near future.

Test 03

161 What is stated about the coming year's budget?

(A) It is estimated to have a surplus.
(B) Several programs will need to be cut.
(C) Membership sales account for 60% of the budget.
(D) It is balanced for the first time in five years.

162 What is Perfect Health and Fitness Center offering?

(A) Free fitness tests
(B) A week-long trial period
(C) Three free training sessions
(D) One-time payment for individual classes

163 What will Perfect Health and Fitness Center need to address in the future?

(A) Extending the center's operating hours
(B) Adding more fitness classes and equipment
(C) Opening new centers closer to downtown
(D) Making more storage space available at centers

164 The word "reflecting" in paragraph 4, line 1, is closest in meaning to

(A) showing
(B) concerning
(C) returning
(D) wondering

Questions 165-167 refer to the following memo.

A Memo from the Editor

This November issue of *Cuisine in New Orleans* marks the magazine's first anniversary. Just one year ago, we distributed our first issue, and since then we have become one of the area's most widely read magazines on regional cooking. Our circulation recently reached 50,000, and the number continues to climb. Local food enthusiasts have praised our publication, and at last month's New Orleans Food Fest we became the proud recipient of an award for best new culinary magazine. As editor-in-chief, I would like to share my appreciation for our hardworking staff, our contributors, our advertisers, and our expanding community of readers, all of whom have played an important part in our success.

Colin Green

165 What is the purpose of the memo?

(A) To express gratitude
(B) To extend an offer
(C) To introduce a contributor
(D) To send an invitation

166 What is mentioned about *Cuisine in New Orleans*?

(A) It is seeking additional writers.
(B) It will soon be distributed internationally.
(C) It is growing in popularity.
(D) It has increased its advertising rates.

167 Why does Mr. Green mention the New Orleans Food Fest?

(A) To give a cooking demonstration there
(B) To recruit staff members to volunteer there
(C) To indicate that the magazine sponsored the event
(D) To note that the magazine was honored at the event

Questions 168-171 refer to the following online chat discussion.

Lydia Johnson [11:30 A.M.]		Marie and I are grabbing a bite to eat for lunch around 12:30. Anyone wants to join us?
Joanie Lockhart [11:31 A.M.]		Maybe. I still have some work to do on the mid-year report. Where are you planning to go?
Lydia Johnson [11:32 A.M.]		We're thinking of trying the new Thai restaurant on Rexington Road. It's called Erawan Hit.
John Randolph [11:33 A.M.]		You're out of luck. That place closed a few days ago.
Lydia Johnson [11:34 A.M.]		Sorry to hear about that. People said great things about it.
John Randolph [11:36 A.M.]		How about Kaosan Road around the corner? They always have a special menu on Fridays.
Lydia Johnson [11:37 A.M.]		That would be great. Do you guys want to go Kaosan Road?
Joanie Lockhart [11:38 A.M.]		OK. But I won't be able to get there until about one.
Marie Cantanzaro [11:39 A.M.]		Sounds good to me. Joanie, I just sent you the updated figures for the report.

Send

168 What are the people discussing?

(A) The place to hold an award ceremony
(B) The best restaurant in the area
(C) Today's special at Erawan Hit
(D) The place for lunch

169 What information does Mr. Randolph provide about Erawan Hit?

(A) It has a good reputation for seafood.
(B) It usually closes on Sundays.
(C) It offers food at a low price.
(D) It does not operate any more.

170 At 11:34 A.M., why most likely does Ms. Johnson write, "Sorry to hear about that"?

(A) She wanted to try a new place.
(B) Mr. Randolph cannot complete a project.
(C) A restaurant is too small for everyone.
(D) She has a scheduling conflict.

171 What does Ms. Lockhart decide to do?

(A) Browse nearby restaurants
(B) Change her work shift tomorrow
(C) Have lunch with her colleagues
(D) Ask Ms. Johnson to get some sandwiches

GO ON TO THE NEXT PAGE

IOFF

International Office Furnishing Foundation
40 Block Road
Bloomington, IN 01398

May 4

Risa Daniels
Taylor Office Furniture
14 Pine Street
Belleville, IL 80214

Dear Ms. Daniels,

On behalf of the IOFF board, I thank you for your early registration for the IOFF trade show in Bloomington this summer. We are confident that this year's event will be our best ever. Not only are we moving to a more spacious venue but the keynote speaker for the convention will be renowned furniture designer Lisa DeNoble.

As always, IOFF wishes to provide an enjoyable atmosphere where the top furniture designers can exhibit their works and develop professional relationships with high-end retailers throughout Bloomington. –[1]–. To accommodate a growing number of exhibitors, this year's event will be held at the Lafayette Convention Center. The center has over 70,000 square meters for exhibition and meeting spaces, and is located only minutes from Bloomington's central commercial area with easy access to restaurants, shops, and theatres. –[2]–. To help you prepare for participation in the convention, please read carefully the enclosed brochure.

One of our goals is to facilitate your installation in the exhibition hall. –[3]–. Please note the time and dates for exhibitor check in, set up, teardown for the trade show. IOFF volunteers will process on-site registration, check in registered exhibitors and hand out name badges at the registration desk outside Hall A, starting at noon, Sunday, August 24. Hall A and Hall B will be open on that day for installation from noon to 7 P.M. Teardown will be on Thursday, August 28 from 1 P.M. to 6 P.M. IOFF volunteers will be available to assist you on both days for set up and teardown.

The convention brochure has a complete event calendar and a map of the Convention Center including designated unloading areas. –[4]–. If you have questions beyond the scope of this letter and brochure, our special support staff are on site to help you with any matters. Just call us at 033-555-0011.

We are really honored to be having you at our convention and wish the event to be the most successful one.

Sincerely,

John Ellsworth
Senior Event Manager

172 According to the letter, what is a new feature of the IOFF convention?

(A) It will include entertainment performances.
(B) It will start at an earlier time.
(C) It will provide a wider range of events.
(D) It will take place at a bigger venue.

173 What is indicated about the Convention Center?

(A) The building was recently renovated.
(B) It is near Bloomington's business district.
(C) It has the latest technological equipment.
(D) The building includes restaurants and shops.

174 What is NOT mentioned as one of the ways IOFF volunteers will help at the convention?

(A) Registering participants
(B) Handing out badges
(C) Assisting with exhibits
(D) Answering phones

175 In which of the positions marked [1], [2], [3], and [4] does the following sentence best belong?

"A list of frequently asked questions with responses are also included."

(A) [1]
(B) [2]
(C) [3]
(D) [4]

GO ON TO THE NEXT PAGE

May 1st

Aberman Books Announces New Young Authors Titles

Don't Look Back in Anger by Gabr Alfarsi

With a storm brewing off the coast and a newcomer in town, this gripping mystery set in a lighthouse is full of surprising twists. This is also the first of the enchanting series.

The Visigoths the Western Goths by Kenneth Ling

In this anthology of essays, world traveler Kenneth Ling recounts his expeditions to the Iberian Peninsula in a way that reads like delightful fiction. Includes a classroom discussion guide.

All the Way Up by Ricardo Gomez

No one knows what to expect when the queen of Geizan disappears and her young daughter inherits the throne. This humorous look at royal life is comedy writing at its best.

Sit Next to Me by Joseph Gustaferro

A group of acquaintances vacationing in a quiet, seaside town learn about each other's past. This tale, from the winner of the Lennox Fiction Prize, deftly analyzes the power of friendship.

For immediate release contact:

Grover Misra at (212) 555-0130

Upcoming Events in Woodward Bookstore

Saturday, July 12

Woodward Bookstore (455 Mason Avenue) will host a panel discussion moderated by Sanjay Dellegrio, associate editor of Writing & Publishing Magazine. Authors Gabr Alfarsi, Kenneth Ling, Ricardo Gomez whose first books were released by Aberman Books earlier this year, will speak about how they became published authors. They'll answer questions and give advice to those hoping to do the same. A book signing will take place after the event. Call (212) 555-0187 for more information.

176 What do all of the books in the announcement have in common?

(A) They are all mystery books.
(B) They are being published at the same time.
(C) They are intended for young adults.
(D) They are written by young writers.

177 In the announcement, the word "recounts" in paragraph 3, line 1, is closest in meaning to

(A) describes
(B) calculates
(C) estimates
(D) returns

178 What is the topic of the July 12 event?

(A) How bookstores can attract customers
(B) How aspiring writers can get published
(C) How to become a magazine editor
(D) How to write lesson plans for a class

179 What will Mr. Dellegrio do at the event?

(A) Sign a book for fans
(B) Give teaching advice
(C) Lead a group discussion
(D) Serve refreshments

180 What book will NOT be signed by its author at the event?

(A) *Don't Look Back in Anger*
(B) *The Visigoths the Western Goths*
(C) *All the Way Up*
(D) *Sit Next to Me*

GO ON TO THE NEXT PAGE

Questions 181-185 refer to following e-mails.

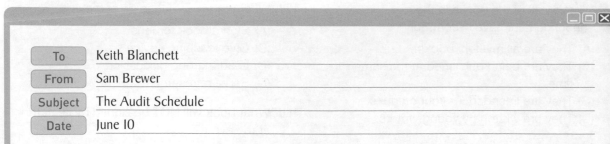

To	Keith Blanchett
From	Sam Brewer
Subject	The Audit Schedule
Date	June 10

Dear Mr. Blanchett:

Thank you for contracting with Environment Safe. We are proud to be your choice for corporate environmental standards certification of your company and look forward to working with you.

As we discussed, the audit will determine whether your company is in compliance with government regulations regarding clean air, clean water, and waste disposal. It will cover four main categories: general practices, the quality of discharged air, the quality of discharged water, and waste removal and recycling. Ratings for each category will be included in the report along with an overall rating of your business. We will perform separate audits and ratings for your manufacturing facility, warehouse and shipping center.

As you know, the audit period lasts two weeks and must occur when all operations are running normally. On your enrollment application, you requested that the audit occur during the last two weeks of August. This time frame works well for us. Unless I hear from you otherwise, I will assume that this is the best time to schedule environmental assessment of your company. Please contact me at your convenience to go over the details of how to prepare for the audit.

Thank you,

Sam Brewer
Public Relations Manager
Environment Safe

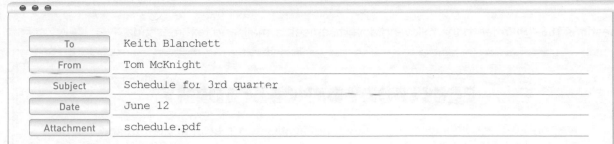

To	Keith Blanchett
From	Tom McKnight
Subject	Schedule for 3rd quarter
Date	June 12
Attachment	schedule.pdf

Dear Keith,

I have attached the current draft of the company schedule for July, August and September. Please note that the warehouse staff will most likely need to work additional hours during these months depending on the Roberts Plumbing orders. We expect the orders to come in by the end of this week, at which point we should be able to finalize the schedule. All other existing orders have been finalized and entered into the schedule.

At our last meeting, you mentioned that we might add to the schedule. I have entered the July safety training sessions on it already, but could you let me know what else I should add? I'd like to send the schedule to the regional managers by the beginning of next week.

Tom

---

181 According to the first e-mail, what service does Environment Safe provide?

(A) Hiring of manufacturing and warehousing staff
(B) Preparing financial reports for companies
(C) Recycling of paper and other materials
(D) Rating companies' compliance with government rules

182 According to the second e-mail, what will likely happen next month in the warehouse?

(A) Some employees will be working extra hours.
(B) Some advanced equipment will be serviced.
(C) Waste materials will be collected for reprocessing.
(D) The revised company policy will be posted.

183 What does Mr. McKnight hope to do by the end of this week?

(A) Evaluate Environment Safe's offer
(B) Complete the company's calendar
(C) Begin an environmental standards assessment
(D) Order supplies from Roberts Plumbing

184 In the second e-mail, the word "note" in paragraph 1, line 2 is closest in meaning to

(A) write down
(B) pick up
(C) take out
(D) bear in mind

185 What will Mr. Blanchett probably say in his response to the second e-mail?

(A) Manufacturing facilities must prepare for increased business.
(B) An audit of the company must be added to the calendar.
(C) A safety training session must be arranged for September.
(D) The method for updating the calendar must be revised.

GO ON TO THE NEXT PAGE

CRESTPORT DANCE ACADEMY

Crestport Dance Academy is pleased to announce its next season of performances. From modern dance and hip-hop to classical ballet — come and see all that we have to offer! You can purchase tickets for the entire season or for single performances. Season ticket subscribers also receive 50 percent off same-day ticket purchases.

January 18 - 22
• The Shelburne Group comes with hip-hop music.

February 7
• Catelynn Martin performs her award-winning dance.

February 15-21
• The Strauss Trio puts on an amazing ballet performance.

February 22-27
• Zachary Keaton dances while accompanied by live piano.

To: Tara Craft
From: Jeanne Harris
Cc: Ben Springer
Subject: Your Visit to Belle Systems
Date: December 29

Dear Ms. Craft:

On behalf of Belle Systems, I would like to let you know how much we are looking forward to adopting the document maintaining project you will teach us about on February 21 and 22. I reserved a room, laptop, projector, and microphone as you requested. Please let me know if you need further assistance with your presentation.

Our department head, Ben Springer, has made a special plan to express our gratitude and make your visit more enjoyable. He has planned dinner with you at an acclaimed local restaurant on the first evening of your visit, followed by an outing to a dance performance offered by Crestport Dance Academy.

Sincerely,

Jeanne Harris
Marketing Manager
Belle Systems

To: Jeanne Harris
From: Ben Springer
Received: 8:33 A.M.

I just heard from Ms. Craft. Her connecting flight has been delayed. She has confirmed her new arrival time and we will still be able to hold the meetings today. Ms. Craft requested that the entertainment be moved to tomorrow, so we aren't rushed. If I order the tickets myself tomorrow rather than today we can receive a substantial discount. Would you reschedule the taxi service to and from the airport? I will postpone the dinner reservation.

Send

186 What is suggested about Crestport Dance Academy?

(A) It has been in operation over the past 20 years.
(B) It is now recruiting dance instructors.
(C) It showcases different styles of dance.
(D) It offers dance lessons to the public.

187 What is the purpose of the e-mail?

(A) To provide details about the schedule
(B) To explain improvements in equipment
(C) To give information to a potential client
(D) To suggest a new date for a meeting

188 What performance was Ms. Craft originally scheduled to attend?

(A) The Shelburne Group
(B) Catelynn Martin
(C) The Strauss Trio
(D) Zachary Keaton

189 According to the text message, what does Mr. Springer ask Ms. Harris to do?

(A) Reserve a meeting room
(B) Prepare dinner
(C) Rearrange transportation
(D) Cancel a performance

190 What can be inferred about Mr. Springer?

(A) He has not confirmed Ms. Craft's schedule yet.
(B) He is not sure whether Ms. Craft will like the performance.
(C) He will soon be able to get a credit for the old tickets.
(D) He has a subscription to Crestport Dance Academy.

Zentron Systems Inc.

At Zentron Systems Inc., our product testers' opinions are a key part of our market research work. We are one of the best-known research centers in the city, and we are now expanding our staff and product testers to meet higher demand. We help companies develop new and innovative products — from food to toys to electronics. We also follow rigorous quality standards. By becoming a product tester for Zentron Systems Inc., you can earn cash and even great prizes. Just click www.zentronsystems.org/tester and refer to our "Rewards program."

 http://www.zentronsystems.org/tester/register

HOW TO BECOME A PRODUCT TESTER

THE FIRST STAGE

Complete our "new tester" registration form (click here), and then create a password that you will use every time you log on from this Web site. This registration places you on a list of available product testers.

THE SECOND STAGE

As product tests arise, you will be informed via phone or e-mail. Some people get called more than others; it all depends. However, we do not call any of our registered testers more than once a month.

THE THIRD STAGE

When you have expressed interest in a product test, our recruitment specialist will ask you some questions about your product preferences to see if you are a good match for the research study.

THE FOURTH STAGE

When chosen for a product test, the recruitment specialist will inform you how much it pays. Most tests take about 1 hour and pay $30 to $40 cash.

REWARDS PROGRAM

All product testers who register with us for the first time will automatically be entered into a random drawing to win $100 or a brand-new digital camera. No entry form is required. Current product testers who refer a friend to Zentron Systems Inc. will receive $25 when that person completes his/her first study. For more information on the program, click here.

http://www.zentronsystems.org/tester/register

Date: October 29th
Sandra Stable

Being a tester at Zentron Systems Inc.

I joined Zentron Systems Inc. as a product tester last year, and since then I've gotten paid to try beverages, soda, and much more. Registering is easy — you simply complete an online application and make a password — and the tests are fun and interesting. I usually get paid $40 cash for just one hour of testing each time I visit, but they call a lot! I received 5 to 6 calls a week during a month when I was out of the country, and my voicemail was full. It's a good way to earn money, but they do ask a number of questions about what products you like. That's part of the qualifying process for tests.

To participate as a product tester, just sign up here: www.zentronsystems.org.

I recommend joining! The testing facility, in Napa Valley, is near a city bus stop and there is also plenty of free parking in the lot in front of the building.

191 How most likely would a new registrant win $100 from Zentron Systems Inc.?

(A) By conducting a customer survey
(B) By doing two product tests
(C) By completing an entry form
(D) By being selected randomly

192 The word "refer" in paragraph 5, in line 3 of the Web page, is closest in meaning to

(A) address
(B) guide
(C) promise
(D) transport

193 What can be inferred about Ms. Stable?

(A) She used to be a recruiter for Zentron Systems Inc.
(B) She heard about Zentron Systems Inc. from a friend.
(C) She has tested various drinks in the past.
(D) She does not usually qualify for product tests.

194 Based on the review, which part of the Web page is most likely not accurate?

(A) The first stage
(B) The second stage
(C) The third stage
(D) The fourth stage

195 What is NOT mentioned about Zentron Systems Inc.?

(A) They are conveniently located in a city.
(B) They have free parking available.
(C) They give cash payments to product testers.
(D) They visit you in person with the product.

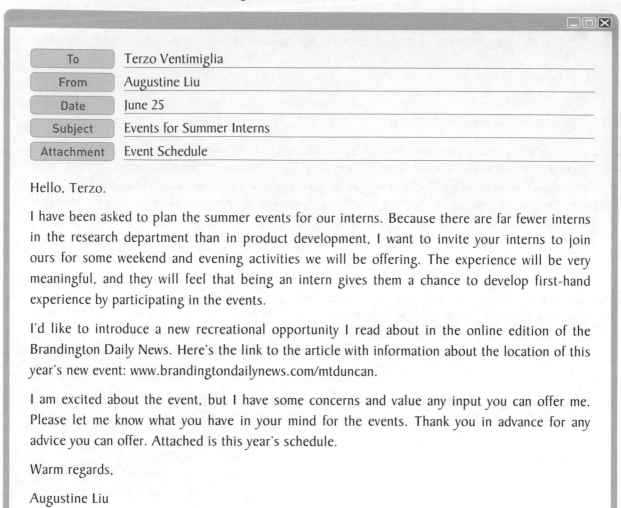

To	Terzo Ventimiglia
From	Augustine Liu
Date	June 25
Subject	Events for Summer Interns
Attachment	Event Schedule

Hello, Terzo.

I have been asked to plan the summer events for our interns. Because there are far fewer interns in the research department than in product development, I want to invite your interns to join ours for some weekend and evening activities we will be offering. The experience will be very meaningful, and they will feel that being an intern gives them a chance to develop first-hand experience by participating in the events.

I'd like to introduce a new recreational opportunity I read about in the online edition of the Brandington Daily News. Here's the link to the article with information about the location of this year's new event: www.brandingtondailynews.com/mtduncan.

I am excited about the event, but I have some concerns and value any input you can offer me. Please let me know what you have in your mind for the events. Thank you in advance for any advice you can offer. Attached is this year's schedule.

Warm regards,

Augustine Liu
Product Development Manager

SUMMER CAMP SCHEDULE

July 6	Agricultural Fair at the Corners Farms in East Pleasantville
July 28	Day at the Topenski Amusement Park
August 14	Movie Night featuring Great Skies
September 10	Outdoor Hiking Day Trip

Please note that this year's schedule of activities is slightly different from that of previous years.

Brandington Daily News

Improved Trails on Mount Duncan to Open Next Week

June 23 – Park officials announced on Friday that three new hiking trails will be open to the public on July 1. Construction began on the trails last autumn. Work on the trails, which had been suspended from December through March due to winter weather, has been ongoing throughout April and May. The new trails are designed for beginners and will not require participants to have any experience and expertise.

Park and Recreation Director Nancy Phan said she is "thrilled" by the new opportunities the trails offer for recreation in the area. "Mount Duncan has always been a beloved local landmark," Ms. Phan said, "but it was previously accessible only to experienced hikers. Now, everyone in our community will be able to enjoy it." Ms. Phan added that she hopes the trails will increase tourism and create future business opportunities by providing a desirable location for corporate excursions and families on vacation.

196 What is the main purpose of the e-mail?

(A) To request feedback from a coworker
(B) To inquire about organizing a workshop
(C) To correct an event schedule
(D) To cancel a product demonstration

197 What does Ms. Liu suggest in the e-mail?

(A) Increasing the number of interns hired in the Research Department
(B) Planning a joint summer camp between two departments
(C) Decreasing the number of social gatherings to save money
(D) Appointing one of the interns to organize the event

198 What date does Ms. Liu suggest for this year's new activity?

(A) July 6
(B) July 28
(C) August 14
(D) September 10

199 What was the reason for construction being halted?

(A) Weather conditions
(B) Budgetary considerations
(C) A delay in obtaining city permits
(D) A lack of experienced workers

200 What can be suggested about Mount Duncan?

(A) Several sports competitions are scheduled to take place.
(B) Experienced hikers now enjoy the challenge to climb there.
(C) It becomes easily accessible to the general public.
(D) Its construction has been completed ahead of schedule.

Stop! This is the end of the test. If you finish before time is called, you may go back to Parts 5, 6, and 7 and check your work.

等等！開始前務必確認！

- 將書桌整理成和實際測試時一樣，做好心理準備。
- 將手機關機，使用手錶計時。
- 限制時間為 120 分鐘。一定要遵守時間限制。
- 不要因為困難就跳過。盡可能依照順序解題。

Actual Test

04

 開始時間   :

結束時間   :

♪ 標準版-04

♪ 白噪音版-04

LISTENING TEST

In the Listening test, you will be asked to demonstrate how well you understand spoken English. The entire Listening test will last approximately 45 minutes. There are four parts, and directions are given for each part. You must mark your answers on the separate answer sheet. Do not write your answers in your test book.

PART 1

Directions: For each question in this part, you will hear four statements about a picture in your test book. When you hear the statements, you must select the one statement that best describes what you see in the picture. Then find the number of the question on your answer sheet and mark your answer. The statements will not be printed in your test book and will be spoken only one time.

Example

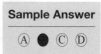

Sample Answer
Ⓐ ● Ⓒ Ⓓ

Statement (B), "The man is working at a desk," is the best description of the picture, so you should select answer (B) and mark it on your answer sheet.

1

2

GO ON TO THE NEXT PAGE

3

4

5

6

PART 2

Directions: You will hear a question or statement and three responses spoken in English. They will not be printed in your test book and will be spoken only one time. Select the best response to the question or statement and mark the letter (A), (B), or (C) on your answer sheet.

7   Mark your answer on your answer sheet.

8   Mark your answer on your answer sheet.

9   Mark your answer on your answer sheet.

10   Mark your answer on your answer sheet.

11   Mark your answer on your answer sheet.

12   Mark your answer on your answer sheet.

13   Mark your answer on your answer sheet.

14   Mark your answer on your answer sheet.

15   Mark your answer on your answer sheet.

16   Mark your answer on your answer sheet.

17   Mark your answer on your answer sheet.

18   Mark your answer on your answer sheet.

19   Mark your answer on your answer sheet.

20   Mark your answer on your answer sheet.

21   Mark your answer on your answer sheet.

22   Mark your answer on your answer sheet.

23   Mark your answer on your answer sheet.

24   Mark your answer on your answer sheet.

25   Mark your answer on your answer sheet.

26   Mark your answer on your answer sheet.

27   Mark your answer on your answer sheet.

28   Mark your answer on your answer sheet.

29   Mark your answer on your answer sheet.

30   Mark your answer on your answer sheet.

31   Mark your answer on your answer sheet.

PART 3

Directions: You will hear some conversations between two or more people. You will be asked to answer three questions about what the speakers say in each conversation. Select the best response to each question and mark the letter (A), (B), (C), or (D) on your answer sheet. The conversations will not be printed in your test book and will be spoken only one time.

32 Who most likely is the woman?

(A) An instructor
(B) A customer
(C) A personal assistant
(D) A delivery person

33 According to the man, what is the problem?

(A) A manager is not available.
(B) A list of customers is incomplete.
(C) A document has been misplaced.
(D) A meeting was postponed.

34 What will the woman do next?

(A) Contact the relevant person
(B) Check the customer list
(C) Search the Internet
(D) Provide an e-mail address

---

35 What does the woman complain about?

(A) A water leakage
(B) A broken electrical wire
(C) A cracked bathtub
(D) A locked door

36 What floor is the woman staying on?

(A) The second floor
(B) The fourth floor
(C) The sixth floor
(D) The eighth floor

37 What does the woman ask the man to do?

(A) Give her a wake-up call
(B) Bring her some refreshments
(C) Assist her with the luggage
(D) Pick up her laundry

38 What is the woman calling to discuss?

(A) An open position
(B) A university program
(C) A marketing proposal
(D) A fashion magazine

39 What does the man tell the woman?

(A) He is out of town.
(B) He is on another line.
(C) He has a flexible plan.
(D) He is in a hurry.

40 What does the woman want the man to review?

(A) A detailed résumé
(B) A job description
(C) A business report
(D) A magazine article

---

41 Why is the man impressed with the library?

(A) The membership fee is free.
(B) The library is open all year round.
(C) The library's selection is broad.
(D) The library is open until late.

42 How many books can the man borrow if he has a regular card?

(A) 5 books
(B) 10 books
(C) 15 books
(D) 20 books

43 What does the woman say is special about the library card?

(A) It requires no payment.
(B) It can be used indefinitely.
(C) It expires every 10 months.
(D) It can be replaced with an ID card.

GO ON TO THE NEXT PAGE

44 What are the speakers discussing?

(A) The number of participants
(B) A registration fee
(C) Enrollment in a course
(D) The process of a survey

45 What information does the woman give the man?

(A) A location of a brasserie
(B) Details of the delivery
(C) An updated number of guests
(D) A name of managing director

46 What does the man ask the woman about?

(A) If the woman has spoken with the managing director
(B) Whether food will be delivered
(C) Whether the woman has gotten any messages
(D) If the woman contacted a guest

47 What are the speakers concerned about?

(A) The size of the workforce
(B) New regulations
(C) The newspaper subscription
(D) The store location

48 What does the woman offer to do?

(A) Contact an executive
(B) Place an order
(C) Speak with a customer
(D) Give a raise

49 Why will Frank contact Steve?

(A) To correct an error
(B) To set up a meeting
(C) To create an advertisement
(D) To conduct an interview

50 What is the man asked to do?

(A) Provide a new password
(B) Help writing an e-mail
(C) Assist with getting online
(D) Analyze some data

51 What was the issue?

(A) The computer was broken.
(B) The password had been changed.
(C) The e-mail address was wrong.
(D) The connection was wrong.

52 Why does the woman say, "So that's all!"?

(A) She found an e-mail address.
(B) She understood the problem.
(C) She fixed the laptop.
(D) She had to restart the computer.

53 What work will be finished by Wednesday?

(A) Wall painting
(B) A floor plan
(C) Electrical construction
(D) A promotional campaign

54 What does the man say about the painting?

(A) The cost is reasonable.
(B) The work takes a long time.
(C) The painters delayed the schedule.
(D) The work will commence next Tuesday.

55 How does the woman say she will find more tenants?

(A) By passing out leaflets
(B) By designing a new Web site
(C) By advertising in a newspaper
(D) By talking to other tenants

56 Which city does the man probably work in?

(A) Bangkok
(B) Boston
(C) San Diego
(D) Los Angeles

57 Why can't the man leave on Thursday?

(A) He has other plans.
(B) He can't afford the price.
(C) He doesn't like a layover.
(D) He would arrive too late.

58 What decision does the man make?

(A) To postpone his workshop
(B) To pay for first class
(C) To depart on Tuesday
(D) To arrive on Friday

---

59 What is the purpose of the man's call?

(A) To reschedule a visit
(B) To change his physician
(C) To get a prescription
(D) To make an appointment

60 What does the woman mean when she says, "the next day is Saturday"?

(A) Dr. Leon usually works on weekends.
(B) The office is closed on weekends.
(C) Saturday is available for a reservation.
(D) Mr. Johnson is fully booked on Saturday.

61 On what day will the man visit the office?

(A) Tuesday
(B) Thursday
(C) Friday
(D) Saturday

Harvey Nichols Department Store
Clothing Department
€10.00 OFF
Any piece of clothing priced over €50
Expires Oct 19

62 What does the woman ask the man about?

(A) The hours of operation
(B) The price of a certain item
(C) The duration of a sale
(D) The location of a section

63 Where does the man suggest the woman go?

(A) To a staff lounge
(B) To a fitting room
(C) To a service desk
(D) To the main entrance

64 Look at the graphic. How much would the woman have to pay for the skirt?

(A) €50
(B) €60
(C) €70
(D) €80

GO ON TO THE NEXT PAGE

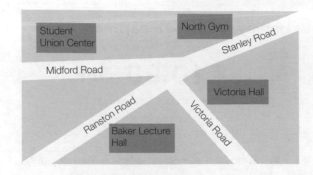

Items for repair		
Item	Quantity	Time
Fax machines	2	1:00 P.M.
Photocopiers	2	2:00 P.M.
Scanners	3	3:00 P.M.
Color printers	4	4:30 P.M.

65 What does the man ask the woman to do?

(A) Take a map
(B) Make an appointment
(C) Arrange a tour
(D) Apply for a position

66 What most likely is the problem?

(A) An interview has been postponed.
(B) Some people do not like a tour.
(C) A guide is not available.
(D) There will not be another meeting.

67 Look at the graphic. Which building is under construction today?

(A) North Gym
(B) Student Union Center
(C) Baker Lecture Hall
(D) Victoria Hall

68 Who most likely is Mr. Rodriguez?

(A) A client
(B) An accountant
(C) An assistant
(D) A supervisor

69 What does the man say he has already done?

(A) Sent some tools
(B) Brought items for repair
(C) Purchased new equipment
(D) Contacted a manager

70 Look at the graphic. What items will be repaired first?

(A) Fax machines
(B) Photocopiers
(C) Scanners
(D) Color printers

PART 4

Directions: You will hear some talks given by a single speaker. You will be asked to answer three questions about what the speaker says in each talk. Select the best response to each question and mark the letter (A), (B), (C), or (D) on your answer sheet. The talks will not be printed in your test book and will be spoken only one time.

71 What is the purpose of today's session?

(A) To evaluate staff performance
(B) To conduct an interview
(C) To gather opinions
(D) To explain a company regulation

72 According to the speaker, how has the new device been improved?

(A) It performs more easily.
(B) It is light-weight.
(C) It is faster to use.
(D) It is a cost-effective product.

73 What will the listeners probably do next?

(A) Ask questions
(B) View package designs
(C) Create the advertisement
(D) Call a client's office

74 What is the purpose of the speech?

(A) To request funding
(B) To report research findings
(C) To accept an award
(D) To welcome guests

75 Where is the speech probably taking place?

(A) At a university
(B) At a firm's auditorium
(C) At a city's arena
(D) At a town center

76 What does the speaker mean when she says, "They are certainly in a class of their own"?

(A) Some of the researchers are excluded.
(B) Several of the colleagues are exceptional.
(C) Some of the instructors teach only one class.
(D) Several students contributed their ideas.

77 What type of business is being advertised?

(A) A beauty clinic
(B) A cosmetic company
(C) A stationery store
(D) A fitness center

78 What will happen tomorrow?

(A) A new product will be launched.
(B) A special offer will end.
(C) A consultation will begin.
(D) New premises will open.

79 What is offered at a 30 percent discount?

(A) A consultation
(B) Any treatment
(C) A training session
(D) All products

80 What is being reported?

(A) A stock offering
(B) A retirement event
(C) A construction project
(D) A business take-over

81 What did Glen Lunar do three months ago?

(A) He founded a new company.
(B) He opened a new store.
(C) He retired from his career.
(D) He launched a new line of products.

82 What does the speaker mean when he says, "Mr. Lunar supported the move"?

(A) Mr. Lunar approved of a decision.
(B) Mr. Lunar wanted to relocate the headquarters.
(C) Mr. Lunar provided financial assistance.
(D) Mr. Lunar rejected the offer.

GO ON TO THE NEXT PAGE

83 Who most likely are the listeners?

(A) Department heads
(B) Fitness instructors
(C) Marketing representatives
(D) Factory workers

84 What will happen next week?

(A) The company will move to a new building.
(B) Some employees will be recruited.
(C) The budget will be shortened.
(D) New tasks will be assigned.

85 What are some listeners requested to do?

(A) Contact their supervisors
(B) Put in extra hours
(C) Submit their report
(D) Assign a task

86 Who is the announcement intended for?

(A) Restaurant servers
(B) Hotel employees
(A) Married couples
(D) Overseas tourists

87 According to the speaker, what is contained in the folder?

(A) An employee ID card
(B) A floor plan
(C) An employee manual
(D) A wage slip

88 What does the speaker ask listeners to do next?

(A) Evaluate staff members
(B) Take a short break
(C) Work in groups
(D) Complete a questionnaire

89 What type of company does the speaker probably work for?

(A) A moving company
(B) A real estate agency
(C) An appliance dealer
(D) A cleaning service

90 What does the speaker offer to do tomorrow?

(A) Dispose of old equipment
(B) Repair a product
(C) Give a brochure
(D) Call before his arrival

91 What does the speaker imply when he says, "Don't worry about it"?

(A) His staff will not damage anything.
(B) His team will take care of a task.
(C) He will be able to sell the furniture.
(D) He will get an estimate.

92 What is the problem?

(A) Some cereal cartons have wrong information.
(B) Some products have been mislabeled.
(C) Some cereal cartons are not full.
(D) Some products are of poor quality.

93 What is mentioned about the packing equipment?

(A) It is no longer malfunctioning.
(B) It will be replaced next month.
(C) It had been repaired before the incident.
(D) It will be inspected regularly.

94 What will customers who return cartons receive?

(A) A new box of cereal
(B) A refund
(C) A complimentary gift
(D) A discount coupon

Customer Rating by Flavor

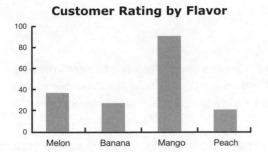

Hall Name	Event	Time

The Future Conference Center
Friday, June 18

Hall Name	Event	Time
Apollo Hall	Employee Workshop	6:00 P.M. – 9:00 P.M.
Dominion Hall	Product Launching event	7:30 P.M. – 10:00 P.M.
Empire Hall	Retirement Party	6:30 P.M. – 9:30 P.M.
Warner Hall	Award Ceremony	8:00 P.M. – 11:00 P.M.

95 What does the speaker's company produce?

(A) Canned fruit
(B) Milk
(C) Bottled drinks
(D) Ice cream

96 According to the speaker, what did the company do last week?

(A) Conducted product trials
(B) Added a new facility
(C) Reduced a product price
(D) Launched an advertising campaign

97 Look at the graphic. Where most likely is the result of this graph relevant?

(A) California
(B) Florida
(C) Texas
(D) Colorado

98 Why is the speaker delivering this speech?

(A) To introduce a celebrity
(B) To celebrate a company's anniversary
(C) To introduce a new employee
(D) To recognize an employee's service

99 What kind of services does M&T provide?

(A) Landscaping
(B) Product development
(C) Accounting
(D) Retail management

100 Look at the graphic. Where is the event taking place?

(A) Apollo Hal
(B) Dominion Hall
(C) Empire Hall
(D) Warner Hal

This is the end of the Listening test. Turn to Part 5 in your test book.

GO ON TO THE NEXT PAGE

READING TEST

In the Reading test, you will read a variety of texts and answer several different types of reading comprehension questions. The entire Reading test will last 75 minutes. There are three parts, and directions are given for each part. You are encouraged to answer as many questions as possible within the time allowed.

You must mark your answers on the separate answer sheet. Do not write your answers in your test book.

PART 5

Directions: A word or phrase is missing in each of the sentences below. Four answer choices are given below each sentence. Select the best answer to complete the sentence. Then mark the letter (A), (B), (C), or (D) on your answer sheet.

101 The owner of Casper Airline announced that ------- is negotiating a deal with Super Jet to buy new airplanes.

(A) him
(B) he
(C) his
(D) himself

102 ------- the last ten years, Madison City's population has grown by about 30 percent.

(A) As
(B) Again
(C) During
(D) Below

103 ------- to all the facilities is included with your stay at the Grand Plaza Hotel.

(A) Access
(B) Accessed
(C) Accessing
(D) Accessible

104 Ms. Chalmers will help with the final draft, so it is not necessary to do all the editing by -------.

(A) yours
(B) your
(C) you
(D) yourself

105 Because humidity can ------- iron, the climate in materials storage units must be controlled.

(A) damage
(B) damaging
(C) damaged
(D) damages

106 Mr. Bukowski is reviewing the training manual to see if updates -------.

(A) have need
(B) needing
(C) are needed
(D) to be needed

107 After working in France for ten years, Georgina Garcia has ------- to Madrid to plan the opening of a fancy restaurant.

(A) visited
(B) returned
(C) occurred
(D) related

108 The city council approved the bill to increase funding of its road improvement -------.

(A) statement
(B) permission
(C) ability
(D) project

109 After interviewing Mr. Finch personally, the company president ------- the committee's decision to hire him as Vice President.

(A) confirmed
(B) designed
(C) hosted
(D) created

110 Once the most recent update is installed, the tablet's platform will ------- longer support this software.

(A) not
(B) none
(C) no
(D) nowhere

111 Each sales team must ------- the result of its annual sales report by the end of the month.

(A) provide
(B) match
(C) reach
(D) earn

112 South Central School's district managers are retired executives with a ------- of expertise across a wide range of industries.

(A) fame
(B) height
(C) labor
(D) wealth

113 The first step of airport construction will be building a runway capable of ------- midsize commercial airplanes.

(A) handling
(B) handler
(C) handles
(D) handle

114 Sonja Pakov is one of the most popular musical artists in South America, ------- only the Wright Band in record sales.

(A) toward
(B) except
(C) among
(D) behind

115 Operating instructions are posted above the copy machine so that you can ------- refer to them.

(A) consequently
(B) standardly
(C) namely
(D) easily

116 The team's contributions to Narumi Skincare's marketing plan were very ------- acknowledged.

(A) favor
(B) favorably
(C) favorable
(D) favored

117 The figures we received last week ------- need to be entered into the digital database.

(A) lately
(B) evenly
(C) ever
(D) still

118 Contract holders may terminate their contract at any time, ------- notification is given in writing at least 14 days in advance.

(A) along with
(B) according to
(C) provided that
(D) regardless of

119 Choosing the best solution to elimination of computer viruses is rarely simple, ------- it is important to seek expert advice.

(A) why
(B) then
(C) nor
(D) so

120 Samuel Jenkins' original manuscript was published last year after Sylvon Publishing Company obtained his family's -------.

(A) permission
(B) suggestion
(C) comparison
(D) registration

GO ON TO THE NEXT PAGE

121 Mr. Lai's draft of Sientech Industries' new mission statement expresses the company's goals -------.

(A) precise
(B) more precise
(C) preciseness
(D) precisely

122 Yoon Station, provider of premium television content, welcomes ------- ideas for improving our services.

(A) specifics
(B) specifies
(C) specific
(D) specify

123 Jarman Food Company has attributed its recent popularity with consumers to changes in its recipes ------- its new packaging.

(A) as for
(B) even so
(C) rather than
(D) after all

124 The assembly line will continue to run unless a problem requires ------- attention.

(A) bright
(B) fluent
(C) gentle
(D) urgent

125 As the lease agreement with Charat Properties is set ------- soon, the available office space can be advertised.

(A) expired
(B) to expire
(C) will have expired
(D) expiring

126 Any furniture purchased at Green Company throughout November will be delivered ------- five business days.

(A) since
(B) between
(C) within
(D) above

127 Chung & Cho auto shop requires mechanics to contact a supervisor ------- if they notice any signs of wear on edges of belt.

(A) very few
(B) finally
(C) somewhat
(D) right away

128 ------- First Carey Bank's parking area is now open to the public, a section has been reserved only for the bank's VIP customers.

(A) While
(B) When
(C) But
(D) For

129 The contract for the Ricci Complex project will be awarded to ------- construction firm submits the most energy-efficient design.

(A) which
(B) whatever
(C) each
(D) those

130 Both Mr. Cresson's payment history and the amount ------- on his loan will be considered in his application for refinancing.

(A) interested
(B) owed
(C) joined
(D) occupied

PART 6

Directions: Read the texts that follow. A word, phrase, or sentence is missing in parts of each text. Four answer choices for each question are given below the text. Select the best answer to complete the text. Then mark the letter (A), (B), (C), or (D) on your answer sheet.

Questions 131-134 refer to the following e-mail.

To: jhewittt@mailday.co.uk
From: customerservice@powerprotection.com
Date: October 10
Subject: Product Review

Dear Ms. Hewitt:

Thank you for your recent ------- 131. We hope you are enjoying your Power Protection software. In the unlikely event that you ------- 132. any problems, please call customer service at 034-555-3746. Our technicians are ready to help 24 hours a day.

If you are happy with your product, please consider writing an online review by visiting www.powerprotection.com/yourvoice. ------- 133. They inform ------- 134. customers and help us grow our business so we can expand our line of high-quality software.

131 (A) production
(B) purchase
(C) application
(D) research

132 (A) experience
(B) experiencing
(C) should have experienced
(D) were experienced

133 (A) I just want to remind you about our monthly volunteer project.
(B) Our promotion just started when we offered discounts on all appliances.
(C) Construction will begin in about three months as scheduled.
(D) Such reviews are appreciated in several ways.

134 (A) selective
(B) required
(C) potential
(D) beneficial

From: Jane Fisherman
To: All staff
Date: May 1
Subject: New branding guidelines
Attachment: Document.pdf

------- to this e-mail is an abbreviated version of our corporate branding guidelines, including
    135.

information on a new logo, font, and color palette. These guidelines, which are now -------, have
                                                                                        136.

also been posted on our internal employee Web site.

We are still working on revising the print and electronic publicity to reflect these new standards.

-------. A complete form reflecting the changes -------.
  137.   **138.**

Please let me know if you have any problems or concerns.

135 (A) Attach
    (B) Attached
    (C) Attaching
    (D) Attaches

136 (A) out of date
    (B) in effect
    (C) beside the point
    (D) on purpose

137 (A) I'm pleased to inform you that our
       application for a grant was approved.
    (B) Please talk to your manager to join the
       program.
    (C) We hope to have the process finished by
       the end of this month.
    (D) We're going to renovate one of our
       branches for a modern appearance.

138 (A) to distribute
    (B) had distributed
    (C) was distributing
    (D) will be distributed

Questions 139-142 refer to the following information.

IMPORTANT! ------. Make sure that your new Power Tech 340 washing machine is installed on
          139.
a foundation that is strong ------- to support its weight when it is fully loaded. In order to prevent
                            140.
noise and vibration, the appliance should be leveled. This is done by ------- the height of the
                                                                        141.
small feet at the bottom corners of the machine. Be sure to attach the water-supply hoses at the

back of the machine ------- to the hot and cold water valves.
                    142.

139 (A) I believe that technology will contribute
          to improving our customers' experience.
     (B) We're famous for our speedy and
          efficient process.
     (C) I don't know exactly how many people
          will turn up.
     (D) Carefully read the following instructions
          before operating your new washing
          machine.

140 (A) enough
     (B) very
     (C) so
     (D) hard

141 (A) adjusting
     (B) examining
     (C) recording
     (D) describing

142 (A) are secured
     (B) securely
     (C) secures
     (D) security

GO ON TO THE NEXT PAGE

Questions 143-146 refer to the following article.

As flu season ------- once again, people wonder what they can do to keep from contracting the
143.

miserable virus. Getting vaccinated is the best solution, but there are many other ------- that can
144.

be taken!

Remember to wash your hands well and often. -------. If you feel sick, don't be a hero — go
145.

home and rest! ------- you don't feel too bad yet, it's often in the earliest stages of illness that you
146.

can spread your flu.

143 (A) approach
(B) approaches
(C) approached
(D) approaching

144 (A) warnings
(B) symptoms
(C) precautions
(D) communities

145 (A) They give employees up to ten days of
sick leave.
(B) The flu is spreading across borders
through the area.
(C) Keep your immune system strong with
plenty of vitamin C.
(D) Some people remain symptom-free for
several years.

146 (A) Even if
(B) As if
(C) In case of
(D) Rather than

PART 7

Directions: In this part you will read a selection of texts, such as magazine and newspaper articles, e-mails, and instant messages. Each text or set of texts is followed by several questions. Select the best answer for each question and mark the letter (A), (B), (C), or (D) on your answer sheet.

Questions 147-148 refer to the following flyer.

Seattle Movie Club

The Seattle Movie Club is proud to present our first Bollywood Festival. From September 18 through November 6, a total of eight contemporary and classic movies by Bollywood filmmakers will be shown at Coleman Theater near Lloyd Mall. The free movies, shown with Spanish and English subtitles, will begin at 7:00 P.M. each Saturday. To view the complete program, please visit our Web site at seattlemovieclub.org.

147 What is being announced?

(A) The opening of a film festival
(B) An interview with a Bollywood actor
(C) A film production
(D) A movie series

148 According to the flyer, what can be found on the Seattle Movie Club Web site?

(A) Free tickets to a new film
(B) Directions to Coleman Theater
(C) A list of events
(D) Biographies of movie directors

Air Gold

Air Gold offers special meals, free of charge on all flights lasting three hours or more. Whether you reserved your flight with Air Gold or through an authorized agency, please call our customer service hotline at 121-555-0987 at least 24 hours before your scheduled flight departure to request a special meal. Travelers with any dietary concerns or restrictions may wish to call the hotline. Our catering staff will do its utmost to accommodate your needs. For a list of special meals, sample dishes or common ingredients, visit our Web site, www.airgold.com.

149 For whom is the advertisement most likely intended?

(A) Tour guides
(B) Travel agents
(C) Airline passengers
(D) Flight attendants

150 What is the purpose of the notice?

(A) To advertise a benefit of a membership program
(B) To give information about dining options
(C) To announce the hiring of aircraft pilots
(D) To suggest some healthful eating guidelines

¡◎¡ Grand Opening Celebration!

Ashland Brothers Company

54 Thompson Plaza (Next to Kathryn's Bakery)
San Diego, CA 94789
512-555-0090

Grand Opening Specials:
30% off all desks and chairs
25% off sofa (leather only)
15% off any dining tables

Offers good from July 3 to August 3
(Free cleaning products with purchase of $30 or more: Thompson Plaza Store only)

Store hours 8:00 A.M. – 8:00 P.M.

Sign up for the Ashland Brothers Company membership — for just $25 per year, get an additional 10% off everything you buy at both our Thompson Plaza and Alina Mall store locations as well as online!

Visit our Web site at www.ashlandbrotherscompany.com.

This week only, order any bookcase online and get 40% off!

151 What type of merchandise does Ashland Brothers Company sell?

(A) Electronics
(B) Office supplies
(C) Clothing
(D) Furniture

152 What is indicated from Ashland Brothers Company?

(A) Its grand-opening specials are offered for only one week.
(B) It stays open until 10 P.M. on August 3.
(C) Its salespeople are highly trained.
(D) It has more than one location.

153 For which item will the customers get a discount only when they purchase it by online?

(A) Baked goods
(B) Cleaning products
(C) Bookcases
(D) Leather items

Questions 154–155 refer to the following text message chain.

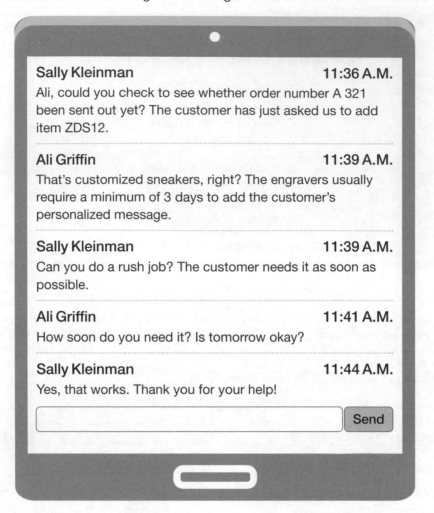

Sally Kleinman　　　　　　　　　11:36 A.M.

Ali, could you check to see whether order number A 321 been sent out yet? The customer has just asked us to add item ZDS12.

Ali Griffin　　　　　　　　　　　11:39 A.M.

That's customized sneakers, right? The engravers usually require a minimum of 3 days to add the customer's personalized message.

Sally Kleinman　　　　　　　　　11:39 A.M.

Can you do a rush job? The customer needs it as soon as possible.

Ali Griffin　　　　　　　　　　　11:41 A.M.

How soon do you need it? Is tomorrow okay?

Sally Kleinman　　　　　　　　　11:44 A.M.

Yes, that works. Thank you for your help!

Send

---

154 What does the customer want to do?

(A) Add an item to the order
(B) Exchange a product
(C) Receive a refund
(D) Use a discount code

155 At 11:44 A.M., what does Ms. Kleinman most likely mean when she writes "that works"?

(A) She plans to make a slide presentation at the meeting.
(B) She is informed that the equipment is repaired.
(C) The customer will be satisfied if the item is ready tomorrow.
(D) A shipping company will deliver the item by the end of the day.

Brilliant ideas for cutting electricity expenses.

There are some helpful suggestions for high office utility costs.

Environment: Pull up the shades and blinds for more natural light, whenever possible. Use bright wall paper to reflect more natural light.

Lighting: Replace incandescent light bulbs with florescent light bulbs, which have the same brightness and use less energy, without replacing light fixtures. Use motion sensors to reduce the usage of electricity in non-working areas where light is not constantly used, such as storage rooms or closets.

Office Equipment: Turn off printers and copiers when they are not in use. Use a power strip. It will be very convenient to turn off all office equipment with the flip of the switch. A screen saver is not an energy saver. Please turn off your monitor when you leave the office. Use an auto timer to turn off electricity when the office is not occupied.

---

156 According to the information, how can light at the workplace be maximized?

(A) By relocating light fixtures
(B) By installing motion sensors in work areas
(C) By using brighter lightbulbs
(D) By letting more daylight enter the room

157 What is NOT mentioned as a way to limit energy consumption?

(A) Replacing office equipment with more efficient ones
(B) Turning off monitors instead of using screen savers
(C) Using power strips to turn off multiple devices
(D) Installing automatic timers

GO ON TO THE NEXT PAGE

Questions 158-160 refer to the following memo.

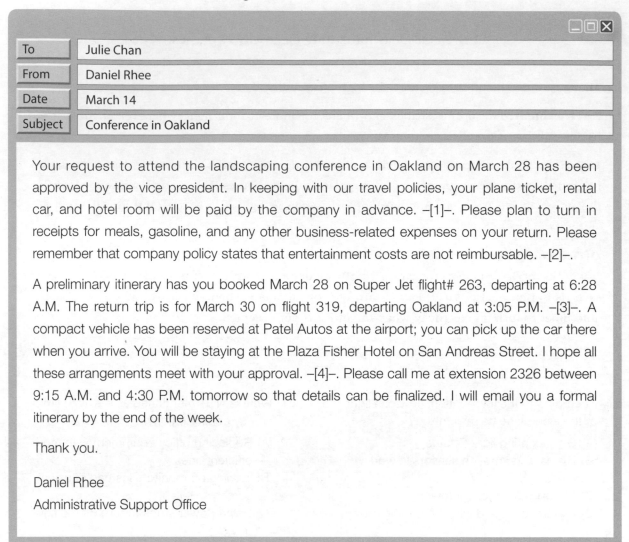

To	Julie Chan
From	Daniel Rhee
Date	March 14
Subject	Conference in Oakland

Your request to attend the landscaping conference in Oakland on March 28 has been approved by the vice president. In keeping with our travel policies, your plane ticket, rental car, and hotel room will be paid by the company in advance. –[1]–. Please plan to turn in receipts for meals, gasoline, and any other business-related expenses on your return. Please remember that company policy states that entertainment costs are not reimbursable. –[2]–.

A preliminary itinerary has you booked March 28 on Super Jet flight# 263, departing at 6:28 A.M. The return trip is for March 30 on flight 319, departing Oakland at 3:05 P.M. –[3]–. A compact vehicle has been reserved at Patel Autos at the airport; you can pick up the car there when you arrive. You will be staying at the Plaza Fisher Hotel on San Andreas Street. I hope all these arrangements meet with your approval. –[4]–. Please call me at extension 2326 between 9:15 A.M. and 4:30 P.M. tomorrow so that details can be finalized. I will email you a formal itinerary by the end of the week.

Thank you.

Daniel Rhee
Administrative Support Office

---

158 What is suggested about travel requests?

(A) They must have details about an itinerary.
(B) They must include a project proposal.
(C) They must estimate meal costs.
(D) They must be authorized by an executive.

159 What is NOT stated about Patel Autos?

(A) It accepts reservations.
(B) It is on San Andreas Street.
(C) It has a location in Oakland.
(D) It rents small cars.

160 In which of the positions marked [1], [2], [3], and [4] does the following sentence best belong?

"You will be reimbursed for any additional expenses you incur while in Oakland."

(A) [1]
(B) [2]
(C) [3]
(D) [4]

Questions 161-164 refer to the following e-mail.

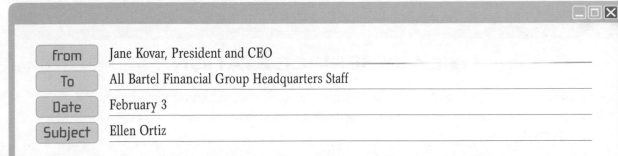

From	Jane Kovar, President and CEO
To	All Bartel Financial Group Headquarters Staff
Date	February 3
Subject	Ellen Ortiz

After careful deliberation by the Bartel board of directors, I am pleased to announce that Ellen Ortiz, our current Director of Investor Relations, will take over as European Regional Manager when Andres Hildebrand retires next month. Ms. Ortiz's promotion comes at a time of increased emphasis on international markets. Working from our Rome office, she will oversee the continued growth of Bartel in Italy and its expansion into Germany and southwestern Europe.

Those of you who have worked with her know that Ms. Ortiz is an excellent choice for the job. After graduating from Kingston University in Dublin, she worked for Ostrava Finance in Italy for a number of years before joining Bartel over 20 years ago. She is a native Italian speaker and is fluent in several other languages. During her first years at Bartel, she worked in the Brussels office before being transferred to the Paris office, and finally to the headquarters here in London. Her outstanding leadership in investor relations has helped our client base grow by over 20 percent in the last 10 years.

Finally, to commemorate Mr. Hildebrand's many accomplishments during his years with Bartel, we have planned a farewell gathering for Friday, February 28, at the Prost Café near company headquarters from 6 P.M. to 8 P.M. For more information about the event, please contact my assistant Stan Milton at extension 1259. Any questions about these staffing changes should be directed to Bill Belmore, Director of Personnel, at extension 1286.

161 What position does Mr. Hildebrand currently have?

(A) Chief Executive Officer
(B) Manager of Investor Relations
(C) Director of Personnel
(D) European Regional Manager

162 What is indicated about Ms. Ortiz?

(A) She lived in Brussels for over twenty years.
(B) She speaks several languages.
(C) She has a degree in International Business.
(D) She is leaving Bartel to work for a company in Germany.

163 What is the purpose of the event on February 28?

(A) To discuss potential replacements for Mr. Hildebrand
(B) To share investment opinions with prospective clients
(C) To announce Bartel's plans for a merger with a competitor
(D) To recognize Mr. Hildebrand's contributions to Bartel

164 In which city will the event be held most likely?

(A) Brussels
(B) Paris
(C) London
(D) Rome

GO ON TO THE NEXT PAGE

http://easyservicestation.com

EASY SERVICE STATION

Easy Service Station owns and operates a large chain of truck stops and travel centers throughout Wisconsin. Our centers are conveniently located along most major highways and are open 24 hours a day, 365 days a year.

Easy Service Station center is equipped with fueling stations, a convenience store, a full-service restaurant and other amenities to make long-distance travel more comfortable.

• Automated teller machines are available 24 hours a day.

• Check cashing and money transfer services are available Monday to Friday, from 8 A.M. to 4 P.M.

• All locations have public laundries; some have public showers.

• Each location has an indoor lounge area with cable television and wireless Internet services.

• Hot food is available in our restaurants, and coffee and baked goods can be purchased in our convenience stores.

For a full list of Easy Service Station centers, click the link below.

www.easyservicestation.com/list

165 What does the Web page describe?

(A) Roadside facilities
(B) Car dealerships
(C) Relocation assistance
(D) Discounted hotels

166 What do only some locations offer?

(A) Shower rooms
(B) A lounge area
(C) Hot meals
(D) Laundry rooms

167 What information can most likely be found by clicking the link provided?

(A) Room rates
(B) Service charges
(C) Location information
(D) Reservation details

Questions 168-171 refer to the following article.

Munich (March 22) – Munich-based Steinmeier announced plans on Tuesday to build a second processing facility. Currently, the company's sole facility is located near Frankfurt, about 480 kilometers from its Munich corporate headquarters. The new facility, which is expected to cost upwards of €30 million, is part of a corporate strategy to boost profits by expanding into overseas markets.

Executives hope the ambitious expansion to Shanghai in China will help the company to become a major competitor in the China market. Once completed, the two processing plants together will have the capacity to meet the demands of both the Chinese and European markets. –[1]–. "An added benefit is that we would be able to maintain essential production for both markets in the event that one of the facilities is temporarily shut down for maintenance work or repairs," said company president Daniel Hoffman.

Mr. Hoffman's father, Jeremy Hoffman, founded Steinmeier in 1979 after graduating from business school in Beijing. –[2]–. In its first year of business, the company managed to turn a sizeable profit, which grew by 47% the following year. Today, Steinmeier is an internationally recognized beverage brand distributed in 30 countries across Europe. Despite its enormous success, however, sales have slowed recently as market share has dropped, and a new management team under Mr. Hoffman is aggressively trying to turn the company around. –[3]–.

The full range of Steinmeier's existing beverage products should be available in 20 cities in China by the end of the summer, according to regional sales manager Amy Garrett. –[4]–. Ms. Garrett envisions launching a line of fruit-based baked goods such as cookies and cakes to complement the company's current product line. "Our hope is that we continue to grow and develop new items that our customers will love." she said.

168 Where will the new facility be located?

(A) Munich
(B) Frankfurt
(C) Shanghai
(D) Beijing

169 What is mentioned about Steinmeier?

(A) Its competitors sell less products than Steinmeier.
(B) It sells products only in Munich.
(C) Product sales have declined recently.
(D) It is planning to recruit new board members.

170 What new type of product is Steinmeier planning to develop?

(A) Desserts
(B) Cosmetics
(C) Tableware
(D) Drinks

171 In which of the positions marked [1], [2], [3], and [4] does the following sentence best belong?

"Returning to northern German, he began selling fresh-squeezed fruit juice to restaurants and supermarkets across the region."

(A) [1]
(B) [2]
(C) [3]
(D) [4]

GO ON TO THE NEXT PAGE

Questions 172-175 refer to the following online chat discussion.

Almed Abedi   _ X

Almed Abedi [4:30 P.M.]   I'd like to re-examine the way we are currently advertising our line of vitamin supplements.

Saori Iwamoto [4:31 P.M.]   Marina, since you are new to our company, let me give you some background. In order to improve sales, we started making vitamin supplements specifically designed for women.

Almed Abedi [4:32 P.M.]   We began selling these supplements a year ago, and we allocated a substantial budget to advertising in order to promote them.

Marina Jordan [4:33 P.M.]   Thanks for the detailed explanation. I think I saw the commercials on TV. I've also driven by the billboards on the side of the road. That must have helped a lot with sales.

Almed Abedi [4:34 P.M.]   That's true. I've analyzed the sales data. The results are about 20% higher than we had projected.

Saori Iwamoto [4:35 P.M.]   Because the sales are so high, I think it's time to stop paying so much to advertise it. We don't need to continue running such a big campaign anymore.

Almed Abedi [4:36 P.M.]   I agree. We can do without it. Clearly the product has responded to a need in the market. I think customers will continue to buy these supplements even if we do less marketing.

Marina Jordan [4:37 P.M.]   You're right. And I think we have to start an advertising plan for our next product.

Saori Iwamoto [4:38 P.M.]   Do you mean our newest line of vitamin supplements intended for seniors?

Marina Jordan [4:39 P.M.]   Yes. We will start selling them in about three months.

[   ] **Send**

172 What is the purpose of the discussion?

    (A) To assign specific duties

    (B) To enhance employee productivity

    (C) To write a budget proposal

    (D) To modify a promotion strategy

173 What is indicated about Ms. Jordan?

    (A) She is going to make a presentation.

    (B) She is in charge of human resources.

    (C) She has analyzed the sales data for the report.

    (D) She has just started working at the company.

174 At 4:37 P.M., what does Ms. Jordan mean when she writes, "You're right"?

    (A) She agrees it is time to develop a new product for women.

    (B) She believes the product will sell well without less advertising.

    (C) She thinks vitamins are essential for both women and children.

    (D) She suggests that they start advertising on and off line.

175 What is true about the new products?

    (A) They are specifically designed for women.

    (B) They are easy to take.

    (C) They are developed for older people.

    (D) They must be consumed with food.

Questions 176-180 refer to the following Web page information and e-mail.

 http://www.citizensfirstbank.com

CITIZENS FIRST BANK

| **ANNOUNCEMENT** | MY ACCOUNTS | FUNDS TRANSFER | EMPLOYMENT |

Introducing Special Savings Starting!

Citizens First Bank now offers a new account, Special Savings Starting. This account offers several advantages over our Choice Savings account including favorable interest rates and increased options for transferring funds.

For a limited time, we are inviting our customers to convert their Choice Savings accounts into Special Savings Starting accounts without our usual account conversion fees. In addition, customers who make the change now will enjoy a special operation fee of only $5 per month for the first 12 months. After 12 months, the rate will increase to the regular Special Savings Starting rate of $8.25 per month.

For further details or to take advantage of this offer, please speak to one of our account representatives at 800-555-0111.

To	customerservice@citizensfirstbank.com
from	jtownsend@blakeleyryecable.com
Subject	New Savings Account
Date	April 2

I recently opened a Special Savings Starting account, and it was my understanding that the balance of my Choice Savings account would be transferred into the new account automatically. However, when I log in to my online banking profile, I see that available funds listed are $0 for the Special Savings Starting account. Could you please tell me when the funds will be transferred to the new account?

Thank you for your assistance.

Jessica Townsend

176 What is the purpose of the Web page information?

(A) To request customers for a payment
(B) To advertise a new type of bank service
(C) To review online banking procedures
(D) To report on the merger of two banks

177 What is stated about the operation fee?

(A) Customers can pay it in installments.
(B) It is offered at a discounted rate initially.
(C) It is lower than the fee at other banks.
(D) Customers can negotiate its due date.

178 Why is Ms. Townsend concerned?

(A) Because her money has not yet been moved to the new account
(B) Because she has been overcharged for an operation fee
(C) Because she was unable to update her bank transaction
(D) Because her account has been accessed without her permission

179 What is most likely true about Ms. Townsend?

(A) She will close her account because of this inconvenience.
(B) Her operation fee has been increased.
(C) She will not be charged a fee for the account change.
(D) She is a new customer to Citizens First Bank.

180 In the e-mail, the word "profile" in paragraph 1, line 3, is closest in meaning to?

(A) outline
(B) equality
(C) average
(D) stability

GO ON TO THE NEXT PAGE

International Business Reconstruction Association (IBRA)

Opportunities for Information Storage

IBRA invites you to participate in a live, online seminar entitled "Strategies for Raising Corporate Funds." The seminar focuses on essential information to include in a grant proposal that will ensure your organization receives financial or other support from local and international companies.

This event will be presented by Michelle Conner, development director at the Rosario Foundation. The seminar, which will take place on July 22 from 1:30 P.M. to 3:00 P.M. GMT, will be moderated by Virginia Ross, a reporter for the television program World Business Reports. Registration is required by June 30; please visit www.ibra.org.uk/seminar0722 for information about fees and additional details.

At the time of your registration, you will be given the opportunity to submit a question for Ms. Conner. She will be able to respond to a limited number of these during the seminar. However, her answers to all relevant questions submitted by participants will be posted by August 1.

---

e-mail

From: mconner@rosariofoundation.org
To: keikomatusi@ibra.org.uk
Cc: swinkley@rosariofoundation.org
Subject: The Seminar
Sent: June 24

Dear Mr. Matusi:

I am very sorry to inform you that I am no longer able to fulfill my commitment to your organization. On the day I am scheduled to headline your event, I now, quite unexpectedly, need to travel to Barcelona on business. I have asked Smith Winkley, Associate Development Director, to present the seminar on my behalf as well as to participate in our video conference on July 31. He will be contacting you shortly by e-mail regarding these changes.

Mr. Winkley has planned and supervised fundraising campaigns for international firms for 25 years. Moreover, he is currently responsible for conducting our organization's online and in-person training sessions, so please rest assured that your seminar participants are in capable hands.

Again, my apologies for any inconvenience my cancellation causes.

Regards,

Michelle Conner

181 What is suggested about the event on July 22?

(A) It has been paid for with money from a charity organization.

(B) It is intended for international students.

(C) It will give advice about joining international corporations.

(D) It will be broadcast live by a television station.

182 What is indicated about seminar participants?

(A) They will receive professional development certificates.

(B) They should direct their questions to Ms. Ross.

(C) They must be members of the IBRA.

(D) They must sign up for the event in advance.

183 What date will Ms. Conner go on a business trip?

(A) June 24

(B) July 22

(C) July 31

(D) August 1

184 What has Ms. Conner arranged for the event?

(A) To have a financial donation sent to the IBRA

(B) To meet with Ms. Matusi in Barcelona

(C) To have her presentation video recorded

(D) To have a colleague substitute for her

185 What is suggested about the Rosario Foundation?

(A) It offers online training opportunities.

(B) It is seeking a new development director.

(C) It has been in business for 25 years.

(D) It is regularly featured on World Business Reports.

GO ON TO THE NEXT PAGE

Get your dream car at Madison Autos.

If you want a nice car but don't want to spend a lot of money, then come to Madison Autos. We are in the business of buying and selling used vehicles. Our cars may not be brand-new, but we guarantee that they are in great condition. All vehicles are serviced when they arrive on our lot, and they are sold with a one-year warranty. We offer an extended two-year warranty with a purchase over $8,000. We also do repairs and order replacement parts right here on the lot.

Prices can be negotiated, so come visit Madison Autos and find your new car! Our address is 1807 Pine Street, Twin City, MN 00987.

To	Marco Colombo <marcocolombo@madisonautos.com>
from	Sydney Payton <sidneypayton@gmail.net>
Date	March 21
Subject	A Car Purchase

Dear Mr. Colombo:

I am contacting you because one of my colleagues recommended your services. Apparently you have a reputation as a kind and patient salesperson. I am looking to purchase a vehicle because mine keeps breaking down these days. I'd like to replace it with a newer model. I was hoping that you would be able to help me find something suitable.

However, I'm on a tight budget, so I don't want to pay any more than $10,000 for a used vehicle. According to an advertisement I saw recently, your company has a few that might be suitable. I'd like to schedule a time to meet with you. Then you can tell me more about it.

Sincerely,

Sydney Payton

MADISON AUTOS

1807 Pine Street, Twin City, MN 00987

555-7465

INVOICE #: *123098*
DATE OF SALE: *March 30*

Buyer INFO.
NAME: *Sydney Payton*
ADDRESS: *8912 South Hill Dr., Twin City, MN 00989*
PHONE: *555-1423*
LICENSE NUMBER: *K500-2507-0902-00*

Car INFO.
CAR: *Prius Hybrid Z12*
REGISTRATION: *J87F09876SS*
MILEAGE: *82,000*
YEAR OF VEHICLE: *2013*
SALES PRICE: *$9,700*
WARRANTY: *Extended*
METHOD OF PAYMENT: ___√___ *check* _____ *cash* _____ *credit*

Signature of Seller: *Marco Colombo*
Signature of Buyer: *Sydney Payton*

---

186 What is mentioned about cars in Madison Autos?

(A) They receive free servicing shortly after purchase.
(B) They can be paid for through financing plans.
(C) They were previously owned.
(D) They have the most popular features.

187 What is the purpose of the e-mail?

(A) To help design a car
(B) To distribute information
(C) To describe the process
(D) To ask for consultation

188 What is suggested about Ms. Payton's current vehicle?

(A) She bought it nearly 10 years ago.
(B) It is a four-door vehicle.
(C) She wishes to sell it to her colleague.
(D) It is not in perfect working order.

189 Why is Ms. Payton given an extended warranty?

(A) Because she spent over a certain amount of money
(B) Because she is a frequent customer
(C) Because she has joined a membership program
(D) Because Madison Autos is having a special event

190 What can be inferred about Ms. Payton?

(A) She paid for her vehicle with cash.
(B) Her colleague bought a car from Mr. Colombo.
(C) She chose a car that seats two people.
(D) She bought a Sport Utility Vehicle.

GO ON TO THE NEXT PAGE

Fragment Master

If you have trouble getting rid of your old electronics, Fragment Master will come to you.

We are the region's largest recycler of electronic components. When you drop off your electronic devices, just put the materials in their proper place.

Box A: External hard devices, Miscellaneous
Box B: Monitors, Speakers, Laptop and Desktop computers
Box C: Keyboards, Accessories and Other devices

The current market for certain rare metals is strong. Therefore, for the time being, we will also be accepting small devices, including mobile phones, tablets, and hand-held video game systems through October 18.

We are here to help you. Please don't hesitate to ask for assistance at the service window.

To	dwerner@haverlyelectronics.com
From	Lgrove@fragmentmaster.org
Date	September 5
Subject	October Appointment

Dear Mr. Werner:

I'm reminding you that a Fragment Master representative, Matt Lovito, will visit Haverly Electronics on the morning of October 19. Please have your scrap electronics sorted to expedite the evaluation process. Be prepared to negotiate the price at that time.

As you are aware, prices offered are subject to daily market conditions. Let me fill you in a bit about what we are currently experiencing. Prices on reclaimed plastic have been trending downward. Similarly, because supplies of copper and silver are high now, there has been downward pressure on prices for recycled sources. You will be pleased to learn, however, that demand for titanium is unprecedented. The price has already doubled this year. A manufacturer called Baxon Ltd. in Singapore has been willing to buy all we can provide in the short term.

It continues to be a pleasure doing business with you.

Sincerely,

Lucia Grove
Fragment Master

Singapore (Nov. 1) – Baxon Ltd. today announced the initial release of its newest model laptop computer, the Moonlight X10. The new product will be the fastest and lightest laptop in its class. These high-performance qualities are made possible by the use of newly designed rare-metal capacitors. The Moonlight X10 is also one of the first mass-produced laptops containing more than 50 percent recycled material, much of it salvaged from out-modeled consumer electronics. A limited number of model Moonlight X10s will be available tomorrow at the company's flagship store in Singapore. Although international customers must wait until November 30, Baxon plans to begin shipping the device to outlets throughout Singapore by November 10.

191 What does Ms. Grove most likely do for a living?

(A) Collect antiques for sale
(B) Sell computer accessories
(C) Develop software programs
(D) Run a recycling facility

192 In the notice, the word "strong" in paragraph 4, line 1, is closest in meaning to

(A) brilliant
(B) athletic
(C) bright
(D) active

193 What is probably true about Baxon Ltd.?

(A) It runs its own recycling center.
(B) It mainly manufactures external hard devices.
(C) It is Fragment Master's biggest customers.
(D) Some components of its latest laptops are from Fragment Master.

194 What is the main purpose of the article?

(A) To explain the cost of manufacturing a product
(B) To question a change in product development
(C) To introduce a new product in electronics
(D) To report on a product malfunction

195 What can be suggested about the Moonlight X10?

(A) It has more features compared to competitors' products.
(B) It will not be sold outside of Singapore for some time.
(C) It is the lightest product ever in the market.
(D) It is made out of recycled materials only.

GO ON TO THE NEXT PAGE

From: Scott Han <shan@dyscomventures.org>
To: All staff members of Dyscom Ventures
Date: January 9
Subject: Update
Attachment: deadline schedule.pdf

Dear colleagues:

Past editions of our company newsletter have focused only on developments in the IT industry and how they affect our company. This year I'd like to start including information about our employees in every issue. I have two features in mind.

The first will be announcements of professional achievements. If you have presented a paper in a conference, won an award, or completed a degree program, for example, please email me with your name and department and a description of your accomplishments in 40 words or less.

The goals of the second feature are to recognize employees who perform volunteer service in their communities and to bring attention to opportunities for community involvement. If you are a member of a local organization that needs help, please send me some information about the frequency and type of services and activities involved, whether they are one-time events like a charity golf tournament or more frequent events like volunteering in local schools. Attached is a complete list of the deadlines and publication schedules.

Sincerely,

Scott Han
Director, Internal Relations

DYSCOM VENTURES NEWSLETTER

Material	Deadline	For publication in
photo, illustrations articles, essays	February 8	March
photo, illustrations articles, essays	May 8	June
photo, illustrations articles, essays	August 8	September
photo, illustrations articles, essays	November 8	December

Any submissions that are received after the deadline will be published in the following issue. Please contact Scott Han at shan@dyscomventures.org if you have any questions.

```
○ ○ ○                              e-mail

FROM: David Greenberg <dgreenberg@dyscomventures.org>
TO: Scott Han <shan@dyscomventures.org>
DATE: February 28
RE: Upcoming Event
ATTACHMENT: photo.jpg

Hi, Scott:

Sorry I did not get this to you earlier.

The Zuengler Library is currently accepting donations of gently used books for its annual book sale that will
be held on July 8 from 10 A.M. to 4 P.M. I will be coordinating volunteer efforts to organize the books the
day before. We tend to receive large boxes full of books, and they must be sorted into different categories so
that customers can easily find whatever type of book they looking for during the sale. It is a lot of work, so we
need your help.

I am sending you a photo of me at last year's event for the newsletter. I hope this will raise awareness of this
great event. Let me know if you need any more information.

Thanks.

David Greenberg
Research and Development
```

196 What is the purpose of the first e-mail?

(A) To encourage Dyscom employees to submit papers for a conference

(B) To announce a job opening in the research department

(C) To explain procedures for the degree program

(D) To request information about Dyscom employees

197 What is NOT mentioned about the announcements?

(A) They are a new addition to the newsletter.

(B) They must be submitted by department supervisors.

(C) They honor award recipients.

(D) They can contain as many as 40 words.

198 What is suggested about the book sale?

(A) It is held in the library of the local community center.

(B) It carries both new and used books.

(C) People donate a large number of books.

(D) The proceeds will be donated to the children's charity.

199 When will a photo of Mr. Greenberg most likely appear in the newsletter?

(A) March

(B) June

(C) July

(D) September

200 What is Mr. Greenberg planning to do on July 7?

(A) To organize materials that the Zuengler Library received

(B) To participate in a sports competition

(C) To attend a lecture by an author at the Zuengler Library

(D) To write an article about the IT industry

Stop! This is the end of the test. If you finish before time is called, you may go back to Parts 5, 6, and 7 and check your work.

等等！開始前務必確認！

- 將書桌整理成和實際測試時一樣，做好心理準備。
- 將手機關機，使用手錶計時。
- 限制時間為 120 分鐘。一定要遵守時間限制。
- 不要因為困難就跳過。盡可能依照順序解題。

Actual Test

05

 開始時間 ：

結束時間 ：

♪ 標準版-05

♪ 白噪音版-05

LISTENING TEST

In the Listening test, you will be asked to demonstrate how well you understand spoken English. The entire Listening test will last approximately 45 minutes. There are four parts, and directions are given for each part. You must mark your answers on the separate answer sheet. Do not write your answers in your test book.

PART 1

Directions: For each question in this part, you will hear four statements about a picture in your test book. When you hear the statements, you must select the one statement that best describes what you see in the picture. Then find the number of the question on your answer sheet and mark your answer. The statements will not be printed in your test book and will be spoken only one time.

Example

Sample Answer

Ⓐ ● Ⓒ Ⓓ

Statement (B), "The man is working at a desk," is the best description of the picture, so you should select answer (B) and mark it on your answer sheet.

1

2

GO ON TO THE NEXT PAGE

3

4

5

6

GO ON TO THE NEXT PAGE

PART 2

Directions: You will hear a question or statement and three responses spoken in English. They will not be printed in your test book and will be spoken only one time. Select the best response to the question or statement and mark the letter (A), (B), or (C) on your answer sheet.

7 Mark your answer on your answer sheet.

8 Mark your answer on your answer sheet.

9 Mark your answer on your answer sheet.

10 Mark your answer on your answer sheet.

11 Mark your answer on your answer sheet.

12 Mark your answer on your answer sheet.

13 Mark your answer on your answer sheet.

14 Mark your answer on your answer sheet.

15 Mark your answer on your answer sheet.

16 Mark your answer on your answer sheet.

17 Mark your answer on your answer sheet.

18 Mark your answer on your answer sheet.

19 Mark your answer on your answer sheet.

20 Mark your answer on your answer sheet.

21 Mark your answer on your answer sheet.

22 Mark your answer on your answer sheet.

23 Mark your answer on your answer sheet.

24 Mark your answer on your answer sheet.

25 Mark your answer on your answer sheet.

26 Mark your answer on your answer sheet.

27 Mark your answer on your answer sheet.

28 Mark your answer on your answer sheet.

29 Mark your answer on your answer sheet.

30 Mark your answer on your answer sheet.

31 Mark your answer on your answer sheet.

PART 3

Directions: You will hear some conversations between two or more people. You will be asked to answer three questions about what the speakers say in each conversation. Select the best response to each question and mark the letter (A), (B), (C), or (D) on your answer sheet. The conversations will not be printed in your test book and will be spoken only one time.

32 What does the woman want to discuss with the man?

(A) A remodeling project
(B) An advertising strategy
(C) An event plan
(D) A traffic problem

33 Where does the man say he is taking a client?

(A) To a manufacturing facility
(B) To a construction site
(C) To some properties
(D) To a client's office

34 What does the woman suggest?

(A) Calling a client
(B) Checking the schedule
(C) Taking public transportation
(D) Submitting a list

35 What are maintenance workers going to do by next Tuesday?

(A) Introduce the new system
(B) Install new equipment
(C) Clean the Conference room
(D) Submit the form

36 What is the woman concerned about?

(A) Testing a new device
(B) Meeting the deadline
(C) Using old equipment
(D) Rescheduling a presentation

37 What does the man suggest the woman do?

(A) Send an e-mail
(B) Try a bigger screen
(C) Go to the staff lounge
(D) Use another place

38 Why has the man come into the store?

(A) To bring back an item
(B) To get a gift
(C) To apply for a job
(D) To make a complaint

39 What does the woman ask the man to provide?

(A) Personal information
(B) Proof of purchase
(C) A gift voucher
(D) A store credit

40 What does the man let the woman know?

(A) He doesn't like the item.
(B) He is a regular customer.
(C) He came with his coworker.
(D) He lives near the store.

41 What are the speakers discussing?

(A) The completion of a project
(B) The commencement of the fiscal year
(C) The construction of a street
(D) The restoration of a bridge

42 What does the woman mean when she says, "Absolutely"?

(A) The tunnel should be renovated again.
(B) The transportation expenses will be increased.
(C) Kingston Avenue will be closed in September.
(D) There will be less traffic congestion.

43 According to the man, what will be offered in August?

(A) Discount fare
(B) New bus routes
(C) Free usage
(D) A travel card

GO ON TO THE NEXT PAGE

44 Where do the speakers most likely work?

(A) At a restaurant
(B) At a travel agency
(C) At a retail store
(D) At a hospital

45 What can be inferred about Daniel?

(A) He will handle the clothes.
(B) He is caught in traffic.
(C) He is out of town.
(D) He works as a cashier.

46 What will the man probably do next?

(A) Talk to Jasmine
(B) Restock some clothing
(C) Leave the office
(D) Put out some items

---

47 According to the woman, what will happen next month?

(A) A regional office will open.
(B) A Belgian firm will be acquired.
(C) An analysis will be conducted.
(D) A decision will be made.

48 What was the reason for the marketing director's decision?

(A) A lack of competition
(B) A certain industry regulation
(C) A shortage of hands
(D) An increase in efficiency

49 What does the man mean when he says, "I am not the right person to answer that"?

(A) He is unable to contact the CEO.
(B) He does not know the survey result.
(C) He is unable to answer the particular question.
(D) He is not in charge of the report.

50 What does Zoe ask of Isaac?

(A) If he can let her leave early
(B) If he can extend a deadline
(C) If he can give her a day off
(D) If he can buy her some new clothes

51 What does Sophia tell Zoe?

(A) She will take some time off.
(B) She can ask someone to help.
(C) She knows Rebecca.
(D) She knows Zoe's preferences.

52 By when must the work be finished?

(A) Monday
(B) Wednesday
(C) Friday
(D) Sunday

---

53 Who most likely is the woman?

(A) A charity organizer
(B) An office administrator
(C) A job candidate
(D) A research manager

54 Where does the conversation most likely take place?

(A) In a marketing office
(B) In an educational institution
(C) At a research institute
(D) At a fundraising event

55 According to the man, which group provides the most funding?

(A) Charitable organizations
(B) The government
(C) Corporations
(D) Private donors

56 What type of business do the speakers probably work for?

(A) An automobile company
(B) A financial firm
(C) An advertising agency
(D) An electronic manufacturer

57 Why does the woman say, "You're not going to believe this"?

(A) A project has made much progress.
(B) An unexpected decision has been made.
(C) An advertising campaign was very successful.
(D) The deadline will be moved forward.

58 What does the woman say about the clients?

(A) They are suffering from a lack of funds.
(B) They recently started their business.
(C) They are having difficulty exporting.
(D) They recently hired a new manager.

59 What is the topic of the conversation?

(A) A meeting plan
(B) A retirement event
(C) A sales presentation
(D) The latest car model

60 What has the woman recently done?

(A) Designed a car
(B) Updated the figures
(C) Created a chart
(D) Attended a meeting

61 What will the man do next?

(A) Contact a client
(B) Work on an estimate
(C) Revise data
(D) Attend a meeting

Department Manager Directory		
Dept.	Manager	Extension No.
Advertising	Nicole Martinez	210
Human Resources	Erica Lopez	324
Maintenance	Ethan Cabrera	420
Accounting	Lewis Moore	518

62 What is the main topic of the conversation?

(A) Plans for a seminar
(B) Adjustment of a document
(C) Ideas for a presentation
(D) Budgets for a project

63 Why does the man thank the woman?

(A) She gathered some information.
(B) She gave him a ride.
(C) She noticed some errors.
(D) She sent an e-mail.

64 Look at the graphic. In which department do the speakers most likely work?

(A) Advertising
(B) Human Resources
(C) Maintenance
(D) Accounting

Oscar Electronics

Air Purifiers Efficiency Rating

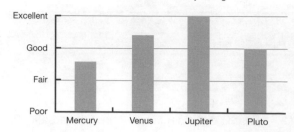

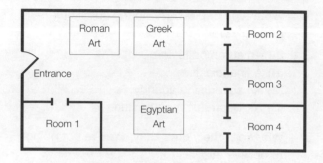

65 According to the woman, how was the sale advertised?

(A) On the Web site
(B) In the newspaper
(C) On the television
(D) On the radio

66 What does the man ask about?

(A) Where the item is displayed
(B) When a shipment will be made
(C) Whether a discount coupon is valid
(D) How a product will be used

67 Look at the graphic. Which model does the man say is the most expensive?

(A) The Mercury
(B) The Venus
(C) The Jupiter
(D) The Pluto

68 Who did the man meet yesterday?

(A) A museum director
(B) A town official
(C) A tour guide
(D) A department manager

69 How would the man like to promote the museum?

(A) In a newspaper
(B) On the television
(C) On the Web site
(D) On a street banner

70 Look at the graphic. Where will the collection of statues most likely be placed?

(A) In Room 1
(B) In Room 2
(C) In Room 3
(D) In Room 4

PART 4

Directions: You will hear some talks given by a single speaker. You will be asked to answer three questions about what the speaker says in each talk. Select the best response to each question and mark the letter (A), (B), (C), or (D) on your answer sheet. The talks will not be printed in your test book and will be spoken only one time.

71 Who most likely are the tour participants?

(A) Natural Park tourists
(B) Restaurant owners
(C) New interns
(D) Local residents

72 Where will the tour begin?

(A) At the main entrance
(B) In the manufacturing facility
(C) In the warehouse
(D) In the marketing office

73 What will participants receive at the end of the tour?

(A) An item of clothing
(B) Food samples
(C) A carrier bag
(D) A booklet

74 What was announced yesterday?

(A) A proposal has been approved.
(B) A protest is going to be held.
(C) A new business has opened.
(D) A construction project has been completed.

75 What can be understood from the report?

(A) Construction has already started.
(B) The shopping mall will be torn down.
(C) Many residents are against the project.
(D) The tax will be increased next month.

76 What did the Mayor of Finsbury mean when he said, "This development will be a boon to our city"?

(A) The tax increase will be worth it.
(B) The project will generate more income.
(C) The land should remain as open space.
(D) The construction will cost a lot of money.

77 Who most likely is the speaker?

(A) A travel expert
(B) A personnel manager
(C) A recruitment officer
(D) A department head

78 What is the talk mainly about?

(A) Employee benefits
(B) Paid vacations
(C) Business travel expenses
(D) Travel schedules

79 What is on the first page of the booklet?

(A) A hiring contract
(B) An accounting report
(C) A set of rules
(D) A dress code

80 What does the speaker imply when he says, "Look for a host of yellow-marked items throughout the store"?

(A) Expiry dates are organized by color.
(B) Shoppers must go to the service desk.
(C) The store will be renovated soon.
(D) There are many bargain items.

81 Where can shoppers get lunch?

(A) In the deli department
(B) In the vegetables and fruit section
(C) In the food and beverage department
(D) In the meat and fish section

82 What item is fifty percent off?

(A) Beef
(B) Today's fish
(C) Lunch set
(D) Orange juice

GO ON TO THE NEXT PAGE

83. Why has the speaker made the call?

(A) To arrange an interview
(B) To find out when taxes are due
(C) To share work assignment
(D) To obtain more information

84. Who most likely is the speaker?

(A) An accountant
(B) A customer service representative
(C) A secretary
(D) A store clerk

85. What does the speaker let the listener know?

(A) His taxes are completed.
(B) He lives in Liverpool.
(C) He needs her signature.
(D) He owns a coffee shop.

---

86. What does the speaker mean when she says, "we need all hands on deck"?

(A) The listeners should applaud now.
(B) The event will be held on the ship.
(C) Everyone should work together.
(D) The listeners should submit the reports.

87. How many more chairs should the employees carry?

(A) 50
(B) 100
(C) 150
(D) 300

88. According to the speaker, what task will Nathan take on?

(A) Moving the chairs
(B) Printing the programs
(C) Preparing the tables
(D) Greeting the guests

89. What is Allegra's intended use?

(A) To treat back pain
(B) To stop coughing
(C) To ease allergy symptoms
(D) To help with sleeping problems

90. What is true of the medication?

(A) It is available in two flavors.
(B) It is not for children.
(C) It only comes in capsules.
(D) It has been discontinued.

91. What does the speaker say about Allegra?

(A) It will be available soon.
(B) It causes no side effects.
(C) It is good for long-term use.
(D) It should be taken three times a day.

---

92. Who most likely are the listeners?

(A) Security guards
(B) New employees
(C) Department heads
(D) Visitors

93. What aspect of the firm does the speaker emphasize?

(A) Its strong security
(B) Its generous pay
(C) Its friendly managers
(D) Its talented workers

94. What should listeners do if they temporarily misplace their badge?

(A) Call a guard
(B) Pay a fine
(C) Use a main entrance
(D) Request a receipt

Hotel Montana – Event Bookings	
Event Date(s)	Venue
September 1-4	The Euros Room
September 2-4	The Zepiros Room
September 5&6	The Notos Room
September 6	The Boreas Room

95 What did Chloe Adams do when she was a university student?

(A) She married an entrepreneur.
(B) She studied abroad.
(C) She created a software program.
(D) She founded a company.

96 What skill does Chloe Adams teach at her seminar?

(A) Software development
(B) Strategic thinking
(C) Decision making
(D) Risk analysis

97 Look at the graphic. In which venue will Chloe Adams' seminar probably be held?

(A) The Euros Room
(B) The Zepiros Room
(C) The Notos Room
(D) The Boreas Room

98 Look at the graphic. Which bus stop will no longer be available?

(A) G1
(B) H2
(C) H4
(D) I5

99 When is the change scheduled to occur?

(A) On Tuesday
(B) On Wednesday
(C) On Thursday
(D) On Friday

100 What are employees asked to do?

(A) Hand out some forms
(B) Renew their contracts
(C) Attend a conference
(D) Give their opinions

This is the end of the Listening test. Turn to Part 5 in your test book.

GO ON TO THE NEXT PAGE

READING TEST

In the Reading test, you will read a variety of texts and answer several different types of reading comprehension questions. The entire Reading test will last 75 minutes. There are three parts, and directions are given for each part. You are encouraged to answer as many questions as possible within the time allowed.

You must mark your answers on the separate answer sheet. Do not write your answers in your test book.

PART 5

Directions: A word or phrase is missing in each of the sentences below. Four answer choices are given below each sentence. Select the best answer to complete the sentence. Then mark the letter (A), (B), (C), or (D) on your answer sheet.

101 When attaching company contracts to an e-mail, keep these documents ------- by password-protecting them.

(A) secure
(B) security
(C) securely
(D) securing

102 Reasons for the increase in computer sales throughout the nation are not ------- clear.

(A) smoothly
(B) entirely
(C) justly
(D) tightly

103 Mr. Sherman is organizing the company banquet, so please let ------- know if you are able to attend.

(A) he
(B) his
(C) him
(D) himself

104 Before laying the new carpet, make sure the surface beneath it is completely -------.

(A) flat
(B) flatly
(C) flatter
(D) flatten

105 Customer service representatives are expected to respond within two hours to callers ------- leave a voice message.

(A) who
(B) they
(C) their
(D) when

106 Oldbrook Town's annual fashion fair helps residents learn about current trends while ------- having fun.

(A) formerly
(B) ever
(C) lastly
(D) also

107 At Copper Ltd., there are ------- opportunities for professional advancement.

(A) plenty
(B) each
(C) every
(D) many

108 Herman Printing Services uses higher quality paper ------- its competitors do.

(A) what
(B) that
(C) such
(D) than

109 Because of the unfavorable weather, the painters are not finished ------- the north side of the building.

(A) with
(B) out
(C) from
(D) of

110 Patients must sign an authorization form ------- medical records can be transferred to new insurance providers.

(A) except
(B) before
(C) instead
(D) rather

111 For security reasons, visitors to the Green Bay Science and Technology Research Institute must be ------- at all times.

(A) displayed
(B) estimated
(C) conferred
(D) escorted

112 The laboratory manual details our procedures for handling materials as ------- as possible.

(A) safety
(B) safely
(C) safer
(D) safest

113 In Ms. Bukowski's -------, the shift supervisor is in charge of the restaurant.

(A) duty
(B) absence
(C) instance
(D) event

114 Call Perrybridge Office Furniture representatives ------- immediate cost estimates over the phone.

(A) to receive
(B) receiving
(C) will receive
(D) receives

115 We are ------- to discuss your remodeling needs in detail via e-mail or telephone.

(A) delighting
(B) delighted
(C) delights
(D) delight

116 The Kerton Town Council ------- receives project proposals, so applicants should expect to wait several months for a decision.

(A) quickly
(B) recently
(C) regularly
(D) similarly

117 ------- Jung's Burger opened its newest franchise, the first 100 customers were given a free soda.

(A) Now
(B) When
(C) As if
(D) After all

118 Please include the serial number of your product in any ------- with the Customer Service Department.

(A) corresponds
(B) correspondence
(C) correspondingly
(D) correspondent

119 Fisher & Phillips Insurance Company offers coverage to ------- and commercial property owners in Barcelona.

(A) habitual
(B) residential
(C) necessary
(D) settled

120 Heike Construction Company is seeking a heavy equipment ------- with at least two years of related experience.

(A) operational
(B) operating
(C) operator
(D) operate

GO ON TO THE NEXT PAGE

121 A blue label indicates a package containing extra virgin olive oil, ------- a green label indicates it contains balsamic vinegar.

(A) whereas
(B) whether
(C) both
(D) about

122 If the Vogel Marathon is canceled, ------- who prepaid the registration fee will receive a full refund.

(A) those
(B) which
(C) them
(D) whichever

123 Orangedale Publishing's Chief of Staff meets regularly with the staff to ensure that procedures ------- correctly.

(A) to be performed
(B) would have performed
(C) had been performed
(D) are being performed

124 Technicians are trying to determine exactly ------- caused the building's power failure.

(A) what
(B) that
(C) whose
(D) those

125 ------- the popularity of our new wireless speaker, production will be increased fivefold next year.

(A) As a result of
(B) On behalf of
(C) Moreover
(D) Assuming that

126 ------- having the support of local officials, the Highbrook Library renovation project experienced numerous setbacks.

(A) Conversely
(B) Otherwise
(C) Whether
(D) Despite

127 Blakeley Architects noted that the community center ------- a one-story building for maximum accessibility.

(A) that remains
(B) should remain
(C) to remain
(D) remaining

128 Nelson Groth Institute offers an ------- of professional services to meet the needs of students.

(A) array
(B) entity
(C) article
(D) item

129 ------- events this year in the second and third quarters caused profits to differ significantly from the original projection.

(A) Total
(B) Marginal
(C) Representative
(D) Unforeseen

130 Mr. Hendley ------- authority to his most trusted employees in an emergency.

(A) aligned
(B) exercised
(C) delegated
(D) nominated

PART 6

Directions: Read the texts that follow. A word, phrase, or sentence is missing in parts of each text. Four answer choices for each question are given below the text. Select the best answer to complete the text. Then mark the letter (A), (B), (C), or (D) on your answer sheet.

Questions 131-134 refer to the following notice.

At Household Superstore, we sell major appliances from top brand names. We're the only store in the area that stocks replacement parts for all of our appliances. Parts ------- by phone at 032-555-2938 or online. Registration is not ------- for online orders. However, it will make the process faster the next time you shop with us. -------. As a result, your order might arrive in several shipments. ------- will increase your shipping charges.

131. ____

132. ____

133. ____

134. ____

131 (A) should have ordered
(B) may be ordered
(C) were ordered
(D) to order

132 (A) advisable
(B) available
(C) required
(D) renewable

133 (A) To expedite delivery of your order, parts are sent directly from different suppliers.
(B) The company is currently interviewing candidates for the position.
(C) We offer all the supplies you need to prepare for any event.
(D) Please inquire at the service desk if it will be permitted on your flight.

134 (A) They
(B) Both
(C) Some
(D) This

GO ON TO THE NEXT PAGE

Questions 135-138 refer to the following e-mail.

To: Karen Karl
From: Liz Steinhauer
Subject: Special Project
Date: April 2

Good morning, Ms. Karl.

I have a list of special projects that must be completed, and I would like to assign you the job of

------- our collection of informational brochures. This will be one of your ongoing responsibilities
135.

because these pamphlets are revised periodically, and only the ------- versions are available to
136.

library patrons.

-------. Anything dated before February of this year should be replaced with the revised
137.

document, which can be printed from the library's internal Web page. Please complete this task

-------, as a number of the brochures are quite outdated.
138.

Thank you.

Liz Steinhauer
Head Librarian

135 (A) writing
(B) copying
(C) updating
(D) mailing

136 (A) initial
(B) current
(C) duplicate
(D) draft

137 (A) Thank you for becoming a member of
our library organization.
(B) Check the information displays at the
library entrance and the checkout desk.
(C) Our remodeled offices are due to open in
April as scheduled.
(D) Your support has enabled us to improve
our office products.

138 (A) promptly
(B) prompting
(C) prompted
(D) prompt

Questions 139-142 refer to the following article.

Windom Pharmacy Makes Prescription Orders Easier for Customers.

By Daniel Banaszek

Seattle (July 12) — Windom Pharmacy is about to make life easier for its tech-savvy customers. -------. Customers will be able to receive a text message ------- a prescription is ready for pickup.
                        139.   **140.**
The previous notification system required pharmacy staff to make time-consuming phone calls.

"The old system was not very -------," CEO Jessica Windom said in a press release.
                              141.

"People don't always listen to their voice mail in a timely manner. Text notifications will begin on

July 15. -------, customers who prefer phone calls still have the option," Ms. Windom noted.
        142.

139 (A) Though we are now quite busy, my staff can handle the workload.
    (B) I am writing to let you know that I have told all my friends about the service.
    (C) One of these is creating a new line of women's vitamin supplements.
    (D) The popular drugstore chain will soon offer mobile alerts for prescription orders.

140 (A) sooner
    (B) despite
    (C) when
    (D) though

141 (A) fair
    (B) efficient
    (C) profitable
    (D) clarifying

142 (A) As a result
    (B) Therefore
    (C) However
    (D) Likewise

GO ON TO THE NEXT PAGE

Questions 143-146 refer to the following e-mail.

To: All members
From: Vanessa Kwan
Date: August 21
Subject: Good News

Balmer Theater at the Durian Art Center is pleased to share good news with season subscribers.

The construction of an annex to the main building is almost finished and should be ready for the September 20 opening.

Last fall, the Durian Art Center ------- to add a studio to the theater auditorium so it can create
143.
sets for drama productions. The new ------- allows our theater to expand current events for all
144.
audiences. -------, it will be the home for classes and summer camps. -------.
145.   146.

Sincerely,

Vanessa Kwan
Art Director, Balmer Theater

143 (A) will decide
    (B) decides
    (C) decided
    (D) has decided

144 (A) report
    (B) space
    (C) donor
    (D) leadership

145 (A) In spite of this
    (B) On the contrary
    (C) Additionally
    (D) Nevertheless

146 (A) I have attached a list of events that will take place at this year's trade fair.
    (B) Located just an hour from busy downtown, we are an ideal destination for you.
    (C) Please review the open positions at our Web site and contact me for further information.
    (D) We thank you for your support and look forward to showing you our new facilities.

PART 7

Directions: In this part you will read a selection of texts, such as magazine and newspaper articles, e-mails, and instant messages. Each text or set of texts is followed by several questions. Select the best answer for each question and mark the letter (A), (B), (C), or (D) on your answer sheet.

Questions 147-148 refer to the following information.

This is to certify that

Jennifer Lloyd completed a series of three training sessions entitled
"Issues of Online News Reporting: Neutrality in Economic and Political Stories"
on May 25 at the Lamnan Professional Development Center.

Her series of sessions was rated very good by the course participants.

Mark Linksky, Training Director

Lamnan Professional Development Center

---

147 What did Ms. Lloyd do on May 25?

(A) She delivered a lecture.
(B) She underwent a training course.
(C) She appeared in a newspaper.
(D) She reported a technical problem.

148 Who most likely is Ms. Lloyd?

(A) A Web site designer
(B) A software developer
(C) A director of a development center
(D) A journalist

Questions 149-150 refer to the following warranty card.

Quentin Power Tools Inc.

WARRANTY CARD

Quentin Power Tools Inc., repairs, at no cost to our customers, any defective products, within a designated period of time. This warranty extends to the original purchaser of the product and lasts up to three weeks from the purchase date. If we are not able to repair the product, we may replace it with a comparable item.

The warranty does not cover any consumer negligence or accidental damage. It also does not cover part failure when someone other than a Quentin employee attempts to repair the product.

When sending an item for repair or replacement, you must include your name, street address and phone number for us to assist in returning shipment. It is recommended (although not required) to enclose a note explaining the problem you had using the item.

Once we receive your shipment, it normally takes 14 to 21 business days until we respond.

If you have further questions about product warranty or repair information, please call our Warranty Information Line at 1-800-555-4455.

Revised November 10

149 What information is stated on the warranty card?

(A) Names of dealers that provide replacement parts
(B) A list of tools that are covered
(C) Costs of specific types of repairs
(D) An estimation of the time needed to complete repairs

150 According to the warranty card, what must be included with a request for repair services?

(A) A copy of the warranty
(B) A photo of the product
(C) Shipping information
(D) A note explaining problems

Questions 151-153 refer to the following article.

Local Company Is Recognized

by Walter Vine

Milwaukee — In its December edition, *Adventure Wilderness Magazine* rated the Milwaukee-based Quest Out Tour Agency at number seven on its list of Top Ten Travel Companies for the upcoming year.

According to *Adventure Wilderness Magazine*, Quest Out made the list because it demonstrated a strong commitment to offering tour participants a rewarding and memorable experience. They range from canoeing, hiking, and cross-country skiing, to bird-watching, whale-watching, and dog sledding. Quest Out has developed fun-filled activities for every type of outdoor adventure.

The owner of Quest Out, Campbell Hargrove, was delighted to find out that his company had made the list. In a statement the company released yesterday, he said, "We are honored to be recognized as one of the preeminent travel companies in the country, alongside popular companies like Igloo Ice Explorer and Eco-World Travel Company, which have been in the eco-adventure business much longer than we have."

151 Why was the Quest Out Tour Agency selected by *Adventure Wilderness Magazine*?

(A) It is one of the most popular travel companies in the region.

(B) It is more committed to the environment than its competitors.

(C) It offers more outdoor activities than other travel companies.

(D) It organizes tours that are likely to be remembered for a long time.

152 What is NOT indicated about the Quest Out Tour Agency?

(A) Its trips cost a lot.

(B) It is based in Milwaukee.

(C) It takes travelers on ski trips.

(D) Its owner is Campbell Hargrove.

153 What is suggested about Eco-World Travel Company?

(A) It takes travelers to destinations outside the country.

(B) It has been in operation for quite a while.

(C) It does not offer outdoor activities.

(D) It is not as popular as the Quest Out Tour Agency.

Questions 154-155 refer to the following online chat.

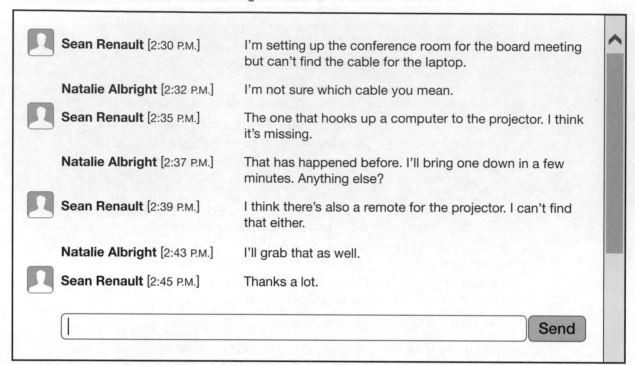

Sean Renault [2:30 P.M.]   I'm setting up the conference room for the board meeting but can't find the cable for the laptop.

Natalie Albright [2:32 P.M.]   I'm not sure which cable you mean.

Sean Renault [2:35 P.M.]   The one that hooks up a computer to the projector. I think it's missing.

Natalie Albright [2:37 P.M.]   That has happened before. I'll bring one down in a few minutes. Anything else?

Sean Renault [2:39 P.M.]   I think there's also a remote for the projector. I can't find that either.

Natalie Albright [2:43 P.M.]   I'll grab that as well.

Sean Renault [2:45 P.M.]   Thanks a lot.

Send

---

154 Why is Mr. Renault contacting Ms. Albright?

(A) To confirm the date of a board meeting
(B) To discuss a meeting agenda
(C) To ask for help with a piece of equipment
(D) To verify the event venue

155 At 2:37 P.M., what does Ms. Albright mean when she writes, "That has happened before"?

(A) She knows why the equipment is replaced.
(B) She knows which cable Mr. Renault needs.
(C) She thinks the computer is out of order.
(D) She acknowledges her mistakes.

Questions 156-157 refer to the following text message.

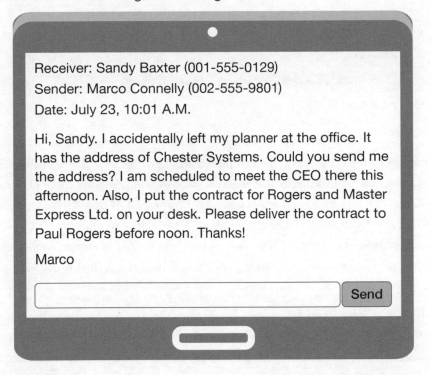

Receiver: Sandy Baxter (001-555-0129)
Sender: Marco Connelly (002-555-9801)
Date: July 23, 10:01 A.M.

Hi, Sandy. I accidentally left my planner at the office. It has the address of Chester Systems. Could you send me the address? I am scheduled to meet the CEO there this afternoon. Also, I put the contract for Rogers and Master Express Ltd. on your desk. Please deliver the contract to Paul Rogers before noon. Thanks!

Marco

Send

156 What is the main purpose of the message?

(A) To cancel a meeting
(B) To ask for information
(C) To request a new planner
(D) To schedule an appointment

157 What should Ms. Baxter do?

(A) Send a message to a client
(B) Go to the office of Chester Systems
(C) Write a contract for Mr. Rogers
(D) Give someone a document

GO ON TO THE NEXT PAGE

Questions 158-160 refer to the following memo.

To	All employees
From	Linda Meyerson, President, Meyerson Lighting Company
Subject	Office Relocation
Date	April 30

Meyerson Lighting Company has experienced phenomenal growth over the last two years, and while that is good for business, it also means that we have outgrown our original space here in the historic Creston Building. –[1]–. As discussed at the company meeting on March 29, we were in negotiation to purchase the recently renovated Barnet Building. I am happy to announce that we reached an agreement with the seller on April 14. The Barnet Building facility is almost double the size of our current location, providing additional offices, conference rooms, and much-needed manufacturing space. –[2]–.

The Barnet Building is just two kilometers away from our present location. We have contracted Kalamar & Murray Commercial Mover to assist us when we move on Thursday, May 16. –[3]–. Next week we will be providing all employees with a special packet containing information about the move, including a description of what each person will be responsible for packing and a comprehensive timeline for the week of the move. –[4]–. New office assignments and sketches of the Barnet Building that show the layout of offices, meeting rooms, and production space will also be provided. On May 13, all employees are welcome to visit the new building to become acquainted with the interior. Our goal is to resume work as soon as possible.

I look forward to seeing you all in our new facility.

158 What is suggested about the Creston Building?

(A) It was renovated to have more space.
(B) It was sold to another lighting company in April.
(C) It is where Meyerson Lighting Company first started doing business.
(D) It was originally intended to be a storage facility for Meyerson Lighting Company.

159 What is NOT mentioned as being included in the packet that employees will receive?

(A) Instruction for packing
(B) Detailed schedules
(C) A diagram of a building
(D) Directions to the new location

160 In which of the positions marked [1], [2], [3], and [4] does the following sentence best belong?

"We will now be able to increase production to meet the rapidly growing demand for our custom-designed lightings."

(A) [1]
(B) [2]
(C) [3]
(D) [4]

Questions 161-164 refer to the following e-mail.

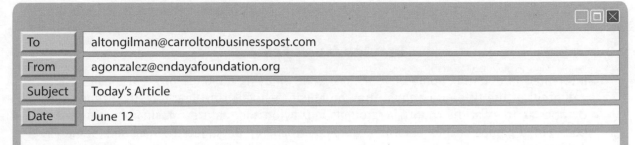

To	altongilman@carroltonbusinesspost.com
From	agonzalez@endayafoundation.org
Subject	Today's Article
Date	June 12

Dear Mr. Gilman:

Thank you for your article in today's issue of the Carrolton Business Post. Our organization is pleased that you wrote about our upcoming fundraising event in so much detail, and we loved the picture of our building that your photographer took. We're looking forward to the publicity that your articles bring. I do, however, want to clarify one point. Our speaker's name is Milo Ferris, and not "Ferriz," as written in the article.

I realize that you face deadline pressure every day, but I'm hoping that it is not too late to print a small correction notice in tomorrow's issue. We would like to avoid a situation in which another reporter might reference your article, and inaccurately list the name of Mr. Ferris. In addition, I would appreciate if you could please update the original version and email it to us once the change has been made. We would like to make the article available as part of our online media kit, which will be accessible to other news organizations.

Thank you.

Alicia Gonzalez
Ben Knight

161 What is the purpose of the e-mail?

(A) To cancel a subscription
(B) To request a correction
(C) To promote an upcoming event
(D) To recommend a new organization member

162 What is probably true about the Carrolton Business Post?

(A) It has a reader's column.
(B) It recently funded a charity event.
(C) It is published daily.
(D) It releases information on business events.

163 The word "face" in paragraph 2, line 1, is closest in meaning to

(A) confront
(B) feature
(C) oppose
(D) overlook

164 What does Ms. Gonzalez request by e-mail?

(A) A revision of the publication guideline
(B) A list of media organizations
(C) A reference letter
(D) A copy of an article

Questions 165-167 refer to the following information.

Drayton Music Festival

Interested in donating some of your time while enjoying all kinds of great music? Then volunteer at the fifteenth annual Drayton Music Festival! This year's festival runs from October 25 to 31 at the county fairgrounds in Drayton and features music from more than 50 talented groups, including local favorites Starroad Pop Band, Jazz Heroes, and Jackson's String Quartet.

Volunteers are needed to

• help with publicity — designing and posting a flyer and sending press release — starting in October.

• greet the musicians and help them locate their housing assignments from October 23 to 29. All out-of-town musicians will be hosted by area families.

• operate the ticket booth, direct guests to the parking areas during the festival, and provide general information.

In appreciation, each volunteer will receive a limited edition Drayton Music Festival T-shirt and four complimentary tickets.

If you are interested in volunteering, please contact Justin Brown at justinbrown@draytonmusicfest.org by September 17.

165 What is indicated about the event?

(A) It will take place on October 1.
(B) It features a variety of music types.
(C) It is run by a professional musician.
(D) It may be rescheduled because of rain.

166 What is suggested about some of the performers?

(A) They will be donating used instruments.
(B) They will be providing funds to the event.
(C) They will be staying at homes in Drayton.
(D) They will be receiving a major award at the event.

167 What task will NOT be done by volunteers?

(A) Selling tickets for festival performances
(B) Taking musicians to the fairground
(C) Giving audience directions to the parking area
(D) Distributing publicity materials

Questions 168-171 refer to the following text message chain.

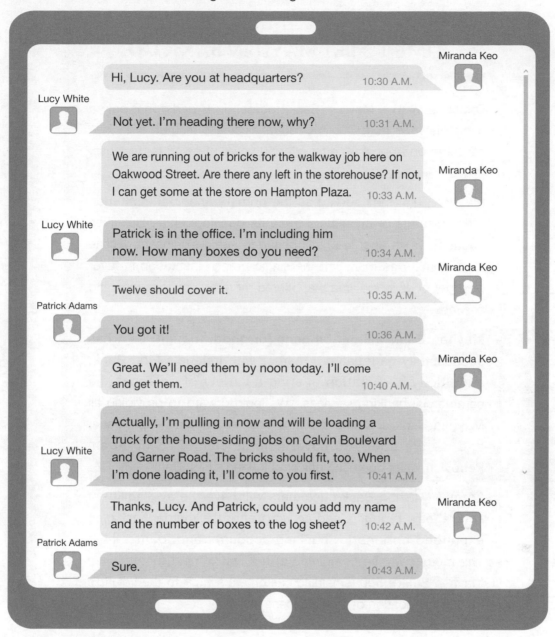

Miranda Keo
Hi, Lucy. Are you at headquarters?   10:30 A.M.

Lucy White
Not yet. I'm heading there now, why?   10:31 A.M.

Miranda Keo
We are running out of bricks for the walkway job here on Oakwood Street. Are there any left in the storehouse? If not, I can get some at the store on Hampton Plaza.   10:33 A.M.

Lucy White
Patrick is in the office. I'm including him now. How many boxes do you need?   10:34 A.M.

Miranda Keo
Twelve should cover it.   10:35 A.M.

Patrick Adams
You got it!   10:36 A.M.

Miranda Keo
Great. We'll need them by noon today. I'll come and get them.   10:40 A.M.

Lucy White
Actually, I'm pulling in now and will be loading a truck for the house-siding jobs on Calvin Boulevard and Garner Road. The bricks should fit, too. When I'm done loading it, I'll come to you first.   10:41 A.M.

Miranda Keo
Thanks, Lucy. And Patrick, could you add my name and the number of boxes to the log sheet?   10:42 A.M.

Patrick Adams
Sure.   10:43 A.M.

168 Where does Ms. Keo probably work?

(A) At an architecture firm
(B) At a delivery service
(C) At a construction company
(D) At a home improvement store

169 At 10:36 A.M., what does Mr. Adams most likely mean when he writes, "You got it"?

(A) The traffic is running smoothly.
(B) He is free to help at noon.
(C) The truck Ms. White needs is available.
(D) There is enough material for the work.

170 Where does Ms. White say she will go?

(A) To Oakwood Street
(B) To Hampton Plaza
(C) To Calvin Boulevard
(D) To Garner Road

171 What does Ms. Keo ask Mr. Adams to do?

(A) Explain the directions to Ms. White
(B) Submit a request for time off
(C) Keep an accurate record of the items
(D) Calculate how much to bill a customer

GO ON TO THE NEXT PAGE

TIME TO LET MAYHEN BANK GO

Dublin (July 1) – Mayhen Bank, located in Broadstone, only a short distance from Dublin's central business district, will close its doors on August 31 after over 50 years of being in business. –[1]–.

Mayhen Bank has served as the primary financial institution for thousands of customers since its opening. –[2]–. However, about 10 years ago, the bank began to see a significant decline in customers as many left the single-branch institution in favor of larger ones in the area that offered more branch locations and services.

Mayhen Bank will not be gone for good, though, as it has successfully negotiated a merger with Ireland's First Bank, a multicity corporation offering a variety of personal and commercial banking services. "We look forward to providing all Mayhen Bank customers with a positive banking experience, and we are happy to have them as clients," said Adam Petrovich, chief operating officer of Ireland's First Bank. –[3]–.

Former Mayhen Bank customers will have the availability of several new products and services after the merger, including expanded options for banking accounts and loans. –[4]–. The merger will be completed at the end of next month when Mayhen Bank's 500 remaining customers switch to the Ireland's First Bank location of their choice.

172 What is the purpose of the article?

(A) To announce the opening of a bank

(B) To request consumer reviews of local businesses

(C) To report on new policies affecting customers

(D) To publicize the merger between two businesses

173 Why did Mayhen Bank lose a lot of customers?

(A) Because it charged too many fees

(B) Because it has too few locations

(C) Because its employees are not well trained

(D) Because it is closed too early on weekdays

174 What is stated about Mayhen Bank?

(A) It has about 500 customers.

(B) It opened 10 years ago.

(C) Its president will resign soon.

(D) It was formerly called Ireland's First Bank

175 In which of the positions marked [1], [2], [3], and [4] does the following sentence best belong?

"Additionally, all Mayhen customers will receive a complimentary $40 gift card from Ireland's First Bank as a welcome gift as soon as their accounts are transferred."

(A) [1]

(B) [2]

(C) [3]

(D) [4]

GO ON TO THE NEXT PAGE

Questions 176-180 refer to following memo and form.

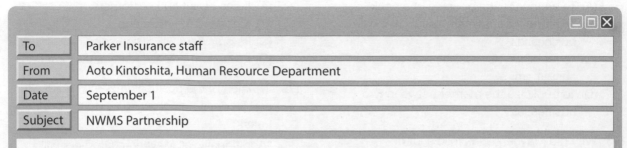

To	Parker Insurance staff
From	Aoto Kintoshita, Human Resource Department
Date	September 1
Subject	NWMS Partnership

As a part of its employee appreciation program, Parker Insurance Agency has partnered with New Way Mobile Service (NWMS) to offer employees discounted mobile phone service. Staff members who change to open either an individual or family service plan with NWMS will save 20% and 25%, respectively, off telephone charges for the first month of their subscription. Additionally, the account service charge will be waived. Subscription plans are for one year and will be automatically renewed for another year unless service is cancelled.

Employees wishing to take advantage of this offer should contact the NWMS Customer Service Department at 321-555-0123. Applications are also accepted electronically at www.nwms.com/corpsaving. To start the subscription process, employees must provide a work e-mail address and employee number. In addition, be ready to submit a valid credit card number as well as a government-issued document, such as a driver's license or passport, that carries a unique identification number.

NWMS CUSTOMER COMPLAINT FORM

Customer Details
Name: *Edward Boulanger*
Account Number: *BA834-1*
Date: *December 3*
E-mail address: *eboulanger@parkerinsurance.com*

Details of Complaint

Last October I opened a mobile phone plan account after learning about the special offer for Parker Insurance Agency employees. According to the promotional material distributed by my employer, I should not have been charged an account service charge to start the service. The NWMS representative I spoke with on the phone when I signed up also confirmed this. Nevertheless, the charge appeared on my first billing statement, dated November 30. Please remove the erroneous charge from the bill and send me an amended version. Of course, the new bill should continue to reflect a 25% discount on phone charges.

Thank you.

176 What is the memo mainly about?

(A) The addition of a benefit for employees

(B) Use of company phones for work purposes only

(C) The renewal of a mobile phone subscription

(D) Requirement for employees to register with NWMS

177 What is indicated about the account service charge?

(A) It can be paid in installments.

(B) It will be refunded if an account is cancelled.

(C) It usually costs $25.

(D) It will be complimentary.

178 What is NOT required for the NWMS application?

(A) An employee number

(B) A postal code

(C) A credit card number

(D) An e-mail address

179 What can be inferred about Mr. Boulanger?

(A) He works in Mr. Kintoshita's department.

(B) He has subscribed to the family service plan.

(C) He opened his account through the Parker Web site.

(D) He learned of NWMS' offer from one of his family members.

180 What does Mr. Boulanger request that NWMS do?

(A) Cancel his monthly plan

(B) Make changes to the revised company policy

(C) Send him a corrected billing statement

(D) Extend his discount to his friends

Questions 181-185 refer to following schedule and e-mail.

Connelly Publishing House Presents Randy Carmichael's *The Art of Daydreaming*
National Book Tour
Southwestern Region - May Public Appearances

Thursday, May 10, 6 P.M.

Jessie's Book Haven – 500 Oak Terrace, Tucson, AZ 02116

A meet-and-greet with Mr. Carmichael will take place at 5 P.M.; by invitation only.

The reading session starts at 6 P.M. and is open to the public.

Saturday, May 12, 5 P.M.

Barnes and Nomads – 218 Maynard Street, Austin, TX 78704

Book reading begins at 5 P.M., followed by the book signing at 6 P.M. Due to a scheduling conflict, Mr. Carmichael will not be able to take questions at this presentation.

Wednesday, May 16, 6 P.M.

Café Reynolds – 685 Cherry Tree Avenue, Houston, TX 19103

Limited seating. Please visit www.cafereynolds.com to register for the event.

There is a $5 advance ticket fee. Tickets sold at the door will be $8.

Monday, May 21, 6 P.M.

Jefferson Public Library – 400 Jefferson Avenue, New Orleans, LA 21202

Attendees will have the opportunity to ask questions.

Afterward, a dinner reception for all attendees will be held in the library conference center.

Additional notes:

• All dates, times, and locations are subject to change.

• Unless otherwise indicated, Mr. Carmichael will read excerpts from *The Art of Daydreaming*, sign copies, and answer questions from the audience at each appearance.

• Copies of *The Art of Daydreaming* will be available for purchase at all venues.

• On June 1, future tour dates and cities will be announced on the publisher's Web site and in local newspapers.

To request an appearance by the author, please contact Cecilia Haywood at chaywood@ connellypublishing.com.

To	Cecilia Haywood <chaywood@connellypublishing.com>
From	Jason King <jasonking@tucsonuniversity.com>
Date	May 25
Subject	Mr. Carmichael's Book Tour
Attachment	Inquiries.doc

Dear Ms. Haywood:

I want to thank Connelly Publishing for bringing Mr. Carmichael to Tucson and for inviting me to the private reception that preceded the public event. It was my honor to have an opportunity to meet one of my favorite authors in person and to exchange some words. I am planning to use *The Art of Daydreaming* in my introductory psychology class and had some questions for him. Since there was not enough time to discuss them all, he suggested I forward them to you. (See attached documents.) And I also want to speak with you about the possibility of having Mr. Carmichael visit my class to talk to my students. I try to bring in one guest lecturer each semester, and I think Mr. Carmichael is perfect. I hope to hear from you soon.

Sincerely,

Jason King

181 What is suggested about the book tour?

(A) All venues have a seating capacity of over 100.
(B) Invited guests will receive a copy of Mr. Carmichael's book.
(C) It will conclude on May 25.
(D) It is organized by Connelly Publishing.

182 What location requires an admission fee?

(A) Jessie's Book Haven
(B) Barnes and Nomads
(C) Café Reynolds
(D) Jefferson Public Library

183 What is the purpose of the e-mail?

(A) To give instructions about publishing a book
(B) To ask for assistance with making an arrangement
(C) To provide information on a psychology course
(D) To inquire about tours by other authors

184 What date did Mr. King meet Mr. Carmichael?

(A) May 10
(B) May 12
(C) May 16
(D) May 21

185 Who most likely is Mr. King?

(A) A textbook publisher
(B) A bookstore owner
(C) A university professor
(D) A newspaper correspondent

GO ON TO THE NEXT PAGE

To	All Multiflex Gym Specialists
from	Donald Warren
Date	April 22
Subject	Promotion

As you know, many Dover College students stay in town during the summer, so we will be offering the yearly 30 percent summer discount for students who enroll during the first two weeks of June. However, Multiflex Gym is also considering offering two special discounts to new and continuing members during the upcoming summer season (June 1~August 1).

We would like to hear from our staff before making a final decision about the two possible offers. The first option would be to offer a family discount. This would mean that any current member could add a household member (age 16 or older) to his or her current membership for 20 percent less than the normal membership fee.

The second possible offer would be that Gold-level members could bring a friend for free from 6 A.M. until 4 P.M. on Tuesdays and Wednesdays. These friends would have access to the entire gym, including the yoga rooms. However, the driving range for golfers would be off limits to ensure that our members do not have to wait longer than they already do for their availability.

Please reply by May 3 with the promotion that you think would be most beneficial for our members.

Thank you for your help in making this decision.

Don't Miss Out on Our Special Offers Only for Dover College Students!

Sign up between June 1 and August 1 to receive a 30% discount on your summer membership at any level and get your own personalized water bottle for free.

Bring a friend on Tuesdays and Wednesdays:
Beginning June 1, all Gold- and Platinum-level members can bring a friend for free during their fitness visits on Tuesdays and Wednesdays. Friends must sign in and show a valid ID to the receptionist to use our facilities.

Multiflex Gym

To: Kevin Diego <ksukel@bvgfitness.com>
From: Bill Pullman <avelez@bvgfitness.com>
Date: August 2
Subject: Re: Numbers

Dear Kevin:

As always, thank you for sending the report. I was thrilled to see that the numbers of Gold- and Platinum-level members have each increased by 18 percent since the start of the summer promotion.

The large number of students from Dover College who have signed up for Gold-level memberships has led us to consider that we might want to offer the student discount again when classes begin in the fall. I have also heard that the fitness facility of the college is going to be remodeled over the next school year, which means students will be looking for alternative options. Even better, our main competitor is 10 kilometers farther from the school. So, we are looking into collaborating with the college to provide shuttle buses to help students get to and from the gym. This would hopefully encourage more students to choose Multiflex Gym.

I will keep you posted.

Bill Pullman, Sales Manager
Multiflex Gym Corporate Office

---

186 What is the purpose of the memo?

(A) To announce the hiring of new instructors
(B) To remind gym members of closing days
(C) To thank employees for their service
(D) To ask employees to give feedback

187 In the memo, the word "normal" in paragraph 2, line 4, is closest in meaning to

(A) standard
(B) average
(C) natural
(D) unusual

188 What is implied about the driving range?

(A) It will be converted into yoga rooms.
(B) It has popular features.
(C) It is located in a separate building.
(D) It will be temporarily unavailable during the summer.

189 What is indicated about Multiflex Gym?

(A) It offers free snacks on Tuesdays and Wednesdays.
(B) Every family member can get a discount.
(C) Platinum-level members can get T-shirts when they join.
(D) Many students were able to bring friends during the summer.

190 What will probably happen at Dover College?

(A) The sports competition will begin in the summer.
(B) Fitness specialists will be hired.
(C) The fitness facility will be renovated.
(D) Fitness classes will be provided to the community.

GO ON TO THE NEXT PAGE

Come and Visit Carolina Apartments Open House

Carolina Apartments are having an open house this Friday and Saturday, March 1 and 2. After two years of construction, Carolina Apartments are almost complete. So people will be able to move in at the beginning of May. There are still more than 100 units available for purchase or rent. These include apartments with two, three, and four bedrooms. There are both furnished and unfurnished apartments available. All furnished apartments are only available to rent, though. The facilities at Carolina Apartments are top-notch, and the complex is located near outstanding schools and the main shopping district in London. Anyone is welcome to attend the open house. Tours of the available apartments will be given, and visitors will be shown around the entire building as well. Call 023-555-4321 for more information and to get directions to the open house.

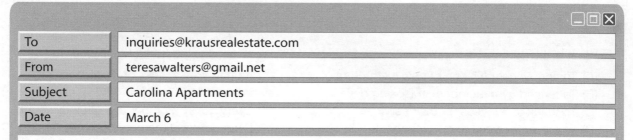

To	inquiries@krausrealestate.com
From	teresawalters@gmail.net
Subject	Carolina Apartments
Date	March 6

To whom it may concern:

I attended the open house at the Carolina Apartments last Saturday. My sons and I were impressed with what we saw, and we have agreed that we would like to live there. We are going to move to London in June, and we intend to live in the city for the next three years. After that, I will be relocated to my company's headquarters in Manchester. That's why I am not interested in buying an apartment but would instead prefer to rent one. I would like to have a three-bedroom apartment so that each of my sons can have his own room.

I'm currently in Edinburgh, but I can arrange to fly to London whenever you need me to sign a contract. So please inform me of the availability of the apartments.

P.S. I have learned that the rent on a three-bedroom unit is £1,200 a month. Is it still in place?

Sincerely,

Teresa Walters

To: teresawalters@gmail.net
From: lindakraus@krausrealestate.com
Date: March 7
Subject: Re: Carolina Apartments

Dear Ms. Walters:

Thank you for inquiring about Carolina Apartments. Like you, many people are very pleased with how the apartments look, so it's one of the most popular properties in the region. Due to that fact, there are no longer any three-bedroom units available. The last three-bedroom apartment was just sold this morning. As a result, we have only a few four-bedroom apartments still available to rent. Of course, the rent for these apartments is a bit higher. It costs £600 more a month to rent a four-bedroom unit than it does to rent a three-bedroom unit. If you are still interested, please let me know immediately, and once I receive a nonrefundable payment of £100, I can reserve one for you until you are able to fly here to sign a contract. If you are no longer interested in Carolina Apartments, I can introduce you to several other properties in the same neighborhood that I'm sure you would approve of.

Regards,

Linda Kraus
Kraus Real Estate Agency

191 According to the advertisement, what will happen at the event?

(A) Visitors will be given tours.
(B) A film will be shown to the public.
(C) Contracts will be signed.
(D) Negotiations will be conducted.

192 In the first e-mail, the word "in place" in P.S., is closest in meaning to

(A) appropriate
(B) invalid
(C) efficient
(D) good

193 What is NOT mentioned about Carolina Apartments?

(A) It is conveniently located near a school.
(B) It is currently being constructed.
(C) It is a twenty-story building.
(D) Its rent for a four-bedroom apartment is £1,800.

194 What does Ms. Kraus suggest to Ms. Walters?

(A) Paying a fee to guarantee that she gets an apartment
(B) Flying to London this coming weekend
(C) Considering buying an apartment instead of renting one
(D) Getting a smaller apartment for a lower price

195 What is implied about Ms. Walters?

(A) She visited to the Open House on March 2nd.
(B) She has already sent her rental fee to Ms. Kraus.
(C) She is moving into a three-bedroom apartment next month.
(D) She is relocating to Manchester in two years.

GO ON TO THE NEXT PAGE

Test 05

Questions 196-200 refer to the following flyer, Web page, and letter.

PLEASE SUPPORT THE STEWART DANCE COMPANY.

The Stewart Dance Company has been at the forefront of Australian Dance for 40 years. We offer great variety in repertoire and present more than 100 performances annually. To enable us to keep up the good work, your help is needed. Your financial support will allow us to maintain low ticket prices and keep dance performances accessible to everyone.

When you give to the Stewart Dance Company, we give back to you. The more you give, the more we return. For a complete list of our membership program, visit our Web site, www. stewartdancecompany.com. You can also view our performance schedule for this year.

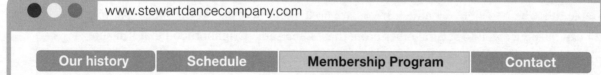

www.stewartdancecompany.com

| Our history | Schedule | **Membership Program** | Contact |

Silver $49
Benefits: Receive tickets to our weekend matinee performances once a month, and a one-year subscription to the dance magazine *Movement* (published four times a year).

Gold $99
Benefits: Receive tickets to our weekend matinee performances once a month, a 20% discount on all weekday evening performances and a one-year subscription to the dance magazine *Movement*.

Platinum $199
Benefits: Receive Gold-level benefits, specially reserved seating, tickets to opening night performances, and the opportunity to dine with renowned choreographer Tom Roman, who directed the performance for our award-winning modern dance, *Dubliners*, at the annual Stewart Dance Company banquet.

You can send your donation to Elena Gibson, fund-raising manager, Stewart Dance Company, 199 Chestnut Street, Sydney.

199 Chestnut Street, Sydney

Dear Ms. Gibson:

As always, it is pleasure that I have the opportunity to support the Stewart Dance Company this year. I have enclosed a donation in the same amount of $199 as last year.

My colleagues, Karen Myers and Justin Copperfield, who are currently working in our travel agency, showed interest in supporting the Stewart Dance Company. They will contact you in the near future and you will be receiving donations of $99 from both of them.

I will definitely attend the Stewart Dance Company's banquet this year since I had a great time in joining last year's event. I look forward to another season of fine performances.

Yours sincerely,

Amy Hollister
Hollister Travel
187 Howell St. Birmingham, Sydney

196 What is the main purpose of the flyer?
   (A) To encourage people to go to dance performances
   (B) To ask the public for donations
   (C) To announce a release of a new dance magazine
   (D) To invite people to an awards ceremony

197 In the flyer, the word "variety" in paragraph 1, line 2, is closest in meaning to
   (A) diversity
   (B) difference
   (C) entertainment
   (D) change

198 What is implied about the Stewart Dance Company?
   (A) It runs a dance performance twice every day.
   (B) It recently hired a choreographer, Tom Roman.
   (C) It hosts a banquet every year.
   (D) It will hold a performance to raise funds.

199 What benefits will Ms. Hollister receive that Ms. Myers will not?
   (A) Discounted admission prices
   (B) Free tickets to opening-night performances
   (C) A subscription to a magazine
   (D) Tickets to weekend matinee performances

200 What is NOT true about Ms. Hollister?
   (A) She is working with Ms. Myers.
   (B) She has attended the Stewart Dance Company's banquet before.
   (C) She donates more money than Mr. Copperfield.
   (D) She will receive the magazine *Movement* every month.

Stop! This is the end of the test. If you finish before time is called, you may go back to Parts 5, 6, and 7 and check your work.

Test 1

PART 1

1 (A) 2 (C) 3 (C) 4 (B) 5 (B) 6 (A)

PART 2

7 (B) 8 (C) 9 (C) 10 (C) 11 (C) 12 (C) 13 (B) 14 (A) 15 (B) 16 (B) 17 (B) 18 (C) 19 (B) 20 (C) 21 (A) 22 (B) 23 (C) 24 (A) 25 (A) 26 (B) 27 (C) 28 (B) 29 (B) 30 (C) 31 (B)

PART 3

32 (C) 33 (B) 34 (B) 35 (A) 36 (D) 37 (B) 38 (D) 39 (C) 40 (B) 41 (C) 42 (C) 43 (B) 44 (D) 45 (C) 46 (D) 47 (B) 48 (C) 49 (D) 50 (D) 51 (B) 52 (C) 53 (A) 54 (B) 55 (D) 56 (D) 57 (D) 58 (C) 59 (A) 60 (D) 61 (C) 62 (C) 63 (D) 64 (B) 65 (B) 66 (D) 67 (C) 68 (D) 69 (A) 70 (C)

PART 4

71 (B) 72 (A) 73 (B) 74 (A) 75 (C) 76 (B) 77 (B) 78 (B) 79 (C) 80 (C) 81 (B) 82 (D) 83 (C) 84 (A) 85 (A) 86 (B) 87 (D) 88 (C) 89 (B) 90 (D) 91 (C) 92 (B) 93 (C) 94 (A) 95 (C) 96 (B) 97 (B) 98 (C) 99 (A) 100 (D)

PART 5

101 (C) 102 (A) 103 (A) 104 (B) 105 (A) 106 (B) 107 (D) 108 (D) 109 (D) 110 (C) 111 (D) 112 (B) 113 (D) 114 (B) 115 (C) 116 (A) 117 (C) 118 (C) 119 (B) 120 (D) 121 (A) 122 (A) 123 (A) 124 (B) 125 (D) 126 (C) 127 (A) 128 (C) 129 (C) 130 (A)

PART 6

131 (A) 132 (C) 133 (B) 134 (D) 135 (D) 136 (A) 137 (B) 138 (A) 139 (C) 140 (D) 141 (A) 142 (D) 143 (B) 144 (B) 145 (D) 146 (C)

PART 7

147 (D) 148 (C) 149 (B) 150 (D) 151 (A) 152 (B) 153 (C) 154 (D) 155 (C) 156 (C) 157 (A) 158 (A) 159 (B) 160 (D) 161 (B) 162 (A) 163 (C) 164 (C) 165 (B) 166 (B) 167 (A) 168 (B) 169 (A) 170 (D) 171 (C) 172 (C) 173 (D) 174 (B) 175 (C) 176 (B) 177 (A) 178 (C) 179 (B) 180 (A) 181 (D) 182 (C) 183 (D) 184 (C) 185 (C) 186 (B) 187 (B) 188 (D) 189 (A) 190 (A) 191 (C) 192 (B) 193 (D) 194 (D) 195 (C) 196 (B) 197 (B) 198 (A) 199 (D) 200 (D)

Test 2

PART 1

1 (C) 2 (A) 3 (D) 4 (D) 5 (B) 6 (A)

PART 2

7 (C) 8 (A) 9 (A) 10 (C) 11 (B) 12 (B) 13 (A) 14 (A) 15 (C) 16 (A) 17 (B) 18 (A) 19 (C) 20 (C) 21 (B) 22 (B) 23 (A) 24 (A) 25 (B) 26 (A) 27 (B) 28 (A) 29 (B) 30 (A) 31 (B)

PART 3

32 (C) 33 (D) 34 (B) 35 (A) 36 (C) 37 (C) 38 (C) 39 (C) 40 (B) 41 (B) 42 (C) 43 (D) 44 (D) 45 (A) 46 (C) 47 (B) 48 (A) 49 (D) 50 (B) 51 (A) 52 (C) 53 (B) 54 (C) 55 (C) 56 (D) 57 (C) 58 (A) 59 (B) 60 (B) 61 (D) 62 (D) 63 (D) 64 (A) 65 (C) 66 (D) 67 (B) 68 (D) 69 (B) 70 (D)

PART 4

71 (C) 72 (A) 73 (D) 74 (B) 75 (B) 76 (A) 77 (D) 78 (B) 79 (A) 80 (D) 81 (B) 82 (B) 83 (D) 84 (B) 85 (D) 86 (A) 87 (C) 88 (A) 89 (D) 90 (A) 91 (B) 92 (D) 93 (B) 94 (B) 95 (D) 96 (A) 97 (B) 98 (B) 99 (D) 100 (A)

PART 5

101 (A) 102 (A) 103 (D) 104 (B) 105 (B) 106 (C) 107 (B) 108 (A) 109 (B) 110 (C) 111 (A) 112 (A) 113 (C) 114 (C) 115 (C) 116 (D) 117 (C) 118 (A) 119 (D) 120 (D) 121 (A) 122 (C) 123 (A) 124 (C) 125 (C) 126 (B) 127 (D) 128 (A) 129 (D) 130 (C)

PART 6

131 (A) 132 (D) 133 (B) 134 (C) 135 (D) 136 (A) 137 (B) 138 (B) 139 (A) 140 (B) 141 (B) 142 (A) 143 (A) 144 (C) 145 (C) 146 (D)

PART 7

147 (D) 148 (A) 149 (C) 150 (A) 151 (A) 152 (D) 153 (C) 154 (A) 155 (B) 156 (D) 157 (C) 158 (C) 159 (A) 160 (D) 161 (A) 162 (D) 163 (B) 164 (B) 165 (A) 166 (B) 167 (C) 168 (D) 169 (C) 170 (B) 171 (B) 172 (A) 173 (C) 174 (B) 175 (B) 176 (C) 177 (B) 178 (A) 179 (C) 180 (B) 181 (B) 182 (A) 183 (D) 184 (B) 185 (C) 186 (C) 187 (D) 188 (C) 189 (C) 190 (A) 191 (B) 192 (B) 193 (D) 194 (A) 195 (B) 196 (A) 197 (D) 198 (C) 199 (B) 200 (A)

Test 3

PART 1

1 (B) 2 (C) 3 (D) 4 (A) 5 (B) 6 (A)

PART 2

7 (A) 8 (B) 9 (A) 10 (C) 11 (C) 12 (A) 13 (B) 14 (C) 15 (A) 16 (C) 17 (A) 18 (A) 19 (B) 20 (C) 21 (A) 22 (C) 23 (C) 24 (A) 25 (C) 26 (A) 27 (B) 28 (C) 29 (A) 30 (A) 31 (B)

PART 3

32 (B) 33 (D) 34 (A) 35 (C) 36 (C) 37 (D) 38 (B) 39 (A) 40 (C) 41 (B) 42 (B) 43 (B) 44 (B) 45 (C) 46 (A) 47 (A) 48 (C) 49 (D) 50 (B) 51 (D) 52 (A) 53 (C) 54 (A) 55 (B) 56 (B) 57 (A) 58 (A) 59 (B) 60 (A) 61 (D) 62 (B) 63 (B) 64 (C) 65 (C) 66 (B) 67 (A) 68 (A) 69 (C) 70 (B)

PART 4

71 (A) 72 (A) 73 (A) 74 (D) 75 (C) 76 (A) 77 (B) 78 (B) 79 (C) 80 (B) 81 (D) 82 (A) 83 (A) 84 (C) 85 (D) 86 (D) 87 (B) 88 (A) 89 (B) 90 (B) 91 (A) 92 (C) 93 (B) 94 (C) 95 (D) 96 (A) 97 (A) 98 (D) 99 (B) 100 (A)

PART 5

101 (B) 102 (A) 103 (B) 104 (C) 105 (D) 106 (A) 107 (D) 108 (C) 109 (A)

110 (C) 111 (D) 112 (D) 113 (B) 114 (D) 115 (D) 116 (C) 117 (A) 118 (A)
119 (C) 120 (C) 121 (B) 122 (D) 123 (A) 124 (D) 125 (B) 126 (B) 127 (C)
128 (B) 129 (D) 130 (A)

PART 6

131 (C) 132 (A) 133 (A) 134 (D) 135 (B) 136 (B) 137 (C) 138 (D) 139 (B)
140 (A) 141 (C) 142 (D) 143 (D) 144 (D) 145 (C) 146 (A)

PART 7

147 (A) 148 (C) 149 (A) 150 (D) 151 (C) 152 (A) 153 (C) 154 (D) 155 (B)
156 (B) 157 (B) 158 (D) 159 (A) 160 (C) 161 (A) 162 (B) 163 (D) 164 (A)
165 (A) 166 (C) 167 (D) 168 (D) 169 (D) 170 (A) 171 (C) 172 (D) 173 (B)
174 (D) 175 (D) 176 (D) 177 (A) 178 (B) 179 (C) 180 (D) 181 (D) 182 (A)
183 (B) 184 (D) 185 (B) 186 (C) 187 (A) 188 (C) 189 (C) 190 (D) 191 (D)
192 (B) 193 (C) 194 (B) 195 (D) 196 (A) 197 (B) 198 (D) 199 (A) 200 (C)

Test 4

PART 1

1 (C) 2 (D) 3 (A) 4 (C) 5 (A) 6 (A)

PART 2

7 (C) 8 (C) 9 (A) 10 (C) 11 (C) 12 (B) 13 (C) 14 (B) 15 (B) 16 (B) 17 (B) 18 (A)
19 (C) 20 (A) 21 (C) 22 (C) 23 (A) 24 (B) 25 (B) 26 (A) 27 (A) 28 (C) 29 (A)
30 (B) 31 (C)

PART 3

32 (C) 33 (B) 34 (A) 35 (A) 36 (D) 37 (C) 38 (A) 39 (D) 40 (B) 41 (C) 42 (B)
43 (B) 44 (A) 45 (C) 46 (B) 47 (A) 48 (A) 49 (C) 50 (C) 51 (D) 52 (B) 53 (C)
54 (D) 55 (C) 56 (B) 57 (B) 58 (C) 59 (A) 60 (B) 61 (C) 62 (D) 63 (C) 64 (A)
65 (C) 66 (C) 67 (C) 68 (D) 69 (B) 70 (D)

PART 4

71 (C) 72 (A) 73 (B) 74 (C) 75 (A) 76 (B) 77 (A) 78 (D) 79 (B) 80 (D) 81 (C)
82 (A) 83 (D) 84 (A) 85 (A) 86 (B) 87 (C) 88 (A) 89 (C) 90 (A) 91 (B) 92 (C)
93 (A) 94 (A) 95 (D) 96 (A) 97 (B) 98 (D) 99 (A) 100 (C)

PART 5

101 (B) 102 (C) 103 (A) 104 (D) 105 (A) 106 (C) 107 (B) 108 (D) 109 (A)
110 (C) 111 (A) 112 (D) 113 (A) 114 (D) 115 (D) 116 (B) 117 (D) 118 (C)
119 (D) 120 (A) 121 (D) 122 (C) 123 (C) 124 (D) 125 (B) 126 (C) 127 (D)
128 (A) 129 (B) 130 (B)

PART 6

131 (B) 132 (A) 133 (D) 134 (C) 135 (B) 136 (B) 137 (C) 138 (D) 139 (D)
140 (A) 141 (A) 142 (B) 143 (B) 144 (C) 145 (C) 146 (A)

PART 7

147 (A) 148 (C) 149 (C) 150 (B) 151 (D) 152 (D) 153 (C) 154 (A) 155 (C)
156 (D) 157 (A) 158 (D) 159 (B) 160 (A) 161 (D) 162 (B) 163 (D) 164 (C)

165 (A) 166 (A) 167 (C) 168 (C) 169 (C) 170 (A) 171 (B) 172 (D) 173 (D)
174 (B) 175 (C) 176 (B) 177 (B) 178 (A) 179 (C) 180 (A) 181 (D) 182 (D)
183 (B) 184 (D) 185 (A) 186 (C) 187 (D) 188 (D) 189 (A) 190 (B) 191 (D)
192 (D) 193 (D) 194 (C) 195 (B) 196 (D) 197 (B) 198 (C) 199 (B) 200 (A)

Test 5

PART 1

1 (A) 2 (C) 3 (C) 4 (B) 5 (C) 6 (C)

PART 2

7 (C) 8 (A) 9 (C) 10 (B) 11 (C) 12 (C) 13 (C) 14 (A) 15 (B) 16 (A) 17 (A)
18 (B) 19 (C) 20 (C) 21 (A) 22 (C) 23 (B) 24 (C) 25 (C) 26 (A) 27 (A) 28 (B)
29 (C) 30 (B) 31 (A)

PART 3

32 (A) 33 (C) 34 (C) 35 (B) 36 (A) 37 (D) 38 (A) 39 (B) 40 (B) 41 (A) 42 (D)
43 (C) 44 (C) 45 (D) 46 (D) 47 (A) 48 (A) 49 (C) 50 (B) 51 (C) 52 (C) 53 (C)
54 (C) 55 (D) 56 (C) 57 (B) 58 (A) 59 (A) 60 (C) 61 (B) 62 (B) 63 (C) 64 (D)
65 (B) 66 (D) 67 (C) 68 (B) 69 (C) 70 (A)

PART 4

71 (B) 72 (C) 73 (A) 74 (A) 75 (C) 76 (B) 77 (D) 78 (C) 79 (C) 80 (D) 81 (A)
82 (C) 83 (D) 84 (A) 85 (C) 86 (C) 87 (C) 88 (A) 89 (C) 90 (A) 91 (B) 92 (B)
93 (A) 94 (A) 95 (D) 96 (B) 97 (C) 98 (B) 99 (B) 100 (D)

PART 5

101 (A) 102 (B) 103 (C) 104 (A) 105 (A) 106 (D) 107 (D) 108 (D) 109 (A)
110 (B) 111 (D) 112 (B) 113 (B) 114 (A) 115 (B) 116 (C) 117 (C) 118 (B)
119 (B) 120 (C) 121 (A) 122 (A) 123 (D) 124 (A) 125 (A) 126 (D) 127 (B)
128 (A) 129 (D) 130 (C)

PART 6

131 (B) 132 (C) 133 (A) 134 (D) 135 (C) 136 (B) 137 (B) 138 (A) 139 (D)
140 (C) 141 (B) 142 (C) 143 (C) 144 (B) 145 (C) 146 (D)

PART 7

147 (B) 148 (D) 149 (D) 150 (C) 151 (D) 152 (A) 153 (B) 154 (C) 155 (B)
156 (B) 157 (D) 158 (C) 159 (D) 160 (B) 161 (B) 162 (C) 163 (A) 164 (D)
165 (B) 166 (C) 167 (B) 168 (C) 169 (D) 170 (A) 171 (C) 172 (D) 173 (B)
174 (A) 175 (D) 176 (A) 177 (D) 178 (B) 179 (B) 180 (C) 181 (D) 182 (C)
183 (B) 184 (A) 185 (C) 186 (D) 187 (A) 188 (B) 189 (D) 190 (C) 191 (A)
192 (D) 193 (C) 194 (A) 195 (A) 196 (B) 197 (A) 198 (C) 199 (B) 200 (D)

EZ Talk

NEW TOEIC 多益新制黃金團隊 FINAL 終極版5回全真試題＋詳解（附QR code音檔＋防水書套）

나혼자 끝내는 신 (新) 토익 FINAL 실전 모의고사 LC ＋ RC 5회

作　　者：Jade Kim、Sun-hee Kim、NEXUS 多益研究所
譯　　者：謝宜倫、關亭薇
審　　訂：Patrick 蕭志億、Winston 黃偉軒、Yiling 以琳
企劃責編：鄭莉璇
修潤校對：鄭莉璇
封面設計：李涵硯
內頁排版：張靜怡

發 行 人：洪祺祥
副總經理：洪偉傑
副總編輯：曹仲堯
法律顧問：建大法律事務所
財務顧問：高威會計師事務所

出　　版：日月文化出版股份有限公司
製　　作：EZ叢書館
地　　址：臺北市信義路三段 151 號 8 樓
電　　話：(02) 2708-5509
傳　　真：(02) 2708-6157
網　　址：www.heliopolis.com.tw
郵撥帳號：19716071 日月文化出版股份有限公司

總 經 銷：聯合發行股份有限公司
電　　話：(02) 2917-8022
傳　　真：(02) 2915-7212

印　　刷：中原造像股份有限公司
初　　版：2019 年 8 月
初版18刷：2024 年 5 月
定　　價：699 元
I S B N：978-986-248-828-7

NEW TOEIC 多益新制黃金團隊 FINAL
終極版 5 回全真試題＋詳解 / Jade Kim,
Sun-hee Kim, NEXUS 多益研究所著；
謝宜倫，關亭薇譯 . -- 初版 . -- 臺北市：
日月文化 , 2019.08
　　面；　公分 . -- (EZ Talk)
ISBN 978-986-248-828-7 (平裝)

1. 多益測驗

805.1895　　　　　　　108011297